Also by Maura Seger

Beloved Enemy
Tapestry

Available from HarperPaperbacks

Forevermore

 MAURA SEGER

HarperPaperbacks
A Division of HarperCollinsPublishers

HarperPaperbacks *A Division of* HarperCollins*Publishers*
10 East 53rd Street, New York, N.Y. 10022

Copyright © 1994 by Maura Seger
All rights reserved. No part of this book may be used or reproduced in any manner whatsoever without written permission of the publisher, except in the case of brief quotations embodied in critical articles and reviews. For information address HarperCollins*Publishers*,
10 East 53rd Street, New York, N.Y. 10022.

Cover illustration by Jim Griffin

First printing: May 1994

Printed in the United States of America

HarperPaperbacks, HarperMonogram, and colophon are trademarks of HarperCollins*Publishers*

❖ 10 9 8 7 6 5 4 3 2 1

1

The wind blowing across the chalk downs was sharp and clear. It smelled of the great forest to the south and, farther away, of the sea. To the woman standing within the circle of stones, it was piercingly familiar.

In her dream the wind always blew, always from the same direction and with the same scent. She noticed it as she rarely did in her waking hours. But then in the dream everything seemed so much more real than in the wake-a-day world.

It was the hour between night and morning. The horizon shone blood red. Within the stone circle, nothing moved. No animal scurried, no leaf fluttered, despite the wind and the coming day. All was stillness.

The woman turned, her long skirt fluttering around her, her russet hair unbound, turning, turning, arms stretched out as though to embrace the silent, motionless space.

Her feet were bare. She could feel the soft moist earth beneath them. Her skirt billowed out around her, cloudlike. She raised her arms to the watching moon and let the dance take her.

Whirling, whirling, turning beneath the moon, calling end to night, joy to the day, feet thudding, arms lifting. The ground rippled, awakening, and the sky—the sky lit with glory. Before it, night retreated gracefully, surrendering its dark drapery. The stars winked out. Only the pale sliver of the moon remained, eternal.

The woman slumped exhausted to the ground. Her heart raced and she drew in great gulps of air to feed her starving lungs. Slowly, she raised her head and stared at the stones. They towered above her, rising ten feet and more, each shaped differently from its fellows.

Directly in front of her was the big squat one, the heel stone, as she thought of it. And next to it, the tallest one, which seemed to bend forward slightly as though in contemplation of the strange things humans did. One, two, three . . . seven . . . twelve . . . twenty-one . . . thirty. Always thirty stones, never less or more.

Not four solitary remnants, sole survivors of destruction. Not shattered fragments ground into dust. Thirty standing stones in an intact circle beneath the blazing sun, the bright helmet of the sky, and there, pale but still watchful, Mother Moon.

God help her.

Sarah awoke. She was bathed in sweat. Her heart still hammered against her ribs and she tasted sickness in her throat.

The stones were gone but their shadow remained—as

did the dream, for it was always there, hovering just out of sight, waiting to return.

She stumbled from the high four-poster bed, her legs tangled in her long night rail. A flowered china ewer and basin stood on a table near the window. Grimly, she splashed the sleep from her eyes, wishing she could wash memory away as easily.

It was cool in the room. The sweat dried quickly on her body. She stripped off the cotton night rail, folded it over the back of a chair, and washed herself. The water and the air raised goose bumps on her fair skin.

Ten minutes later, sensibly dressed in a brown serge skirt and white cotton bodice with modestly trimmed sleeves, Mistress Sarah Huxley arrived in her morning room. Sunlight poured through the leaded windows, across the oak panel walls and the deep-hued Araby carpet. Her canary, a rare and precious thing brought from the West Indies, chirruped in its wicker cage. The round pedestal table was set for two.

The elderly man looked up from his study of the *Daily Courant*. Beneath his white powdered wig, his face was narrow, seamed by age and mottled by recent exposure to the sun. He looked his sixty-four years—he would be sixty-five on Christmas Day—and more. But the eyes: the eyes put the lie to the burden of his years, for they belonged to a far younger man. No, Sarah corrected herself, a timeless one. Sir Isaac's eyes were large, slightly protuberant, and of a deep, rich hazel that shifted color with the change of light. They were also the windows to a soul she could barely contemplate, much less understand.

That he was here already, in her morning room, very much at home, still astounded her. Yet so he had arrived every day for a fortnight, ever since convincing her to help him. How exactly he had done that she still couldn't quite determine. But he had and he was here, and he had to be dealt with, the dream be damned.

"Sir Isaac," she said and put on her best smile, even managing a neat curtsey. "You are looking well this morn."

He stood, resplendent in a blue velvet frock coat, and breeches of finely woven wool. A slight flush stained his cheeks. He was, she had noticed, like a boy with women, being little accustomed to them.

Gravely, he said, "Mistress, you flatter me. But the eggs grow cold and we have much to accomplish today. I have a new theory about the geometric relationship between the inner and outer circles. Would you care to hear it?"

Sarah allowed that she would and took her place at the table. In fact, she understood little of what Sir Isaac had to say. Yet she accounted herself a woman of intelligence, unfashionable though that might be.

There was comfort in the fact that few men understood the renowned physicist and mathematician any better than she. They might claim to do so, but the truth was that Sir Isaac dwelt in a realm of thought far beyond the ordinary ken. Occasionally, he returned from there with brilliant insights into the nature of things. But otherwise he seemed as little connected to the wake-a-day world as Sarah felt herself to be.

Not, of course, that she had ever said as much to him. So far as Sir Isaac was concerned, she was a gentlewoman of good repute, from a family long resident in Avebury, with independent means and an independent nature, the latter predisposing her to venture little from her house and rarely beyond the village. She preferred her garden, her books, and her discreet good works. Solitude agreed with her.

It also allowed her to conceal from the world the fact that she was mad.

Sir Isaac seemed not to have noticed that. Indeed, he noticed little except that she could help him. Will-she, nill-she, as soon as he heard she was most knowledgeable about the strange and ancient things to be found at Avebury, he insisted that she be his guide. No excuses were acceptable, not other plans or the headache or melancholia. He would allow no exemption. In the end, it was easier to do as he wished and hope his curiosity would soon wear thin.

So far, there was no sign of that happening. Every day for a fortnight they had trundled out, in rain and in sun, in chill and in warmth, to walk the circles and the barrows. She had shown him everything she knew—or would admit to knowing—and still he was not satisfied.

Exactly how far apart were this sarsen and that? Precisely what orientation did this barrow hold to the sun? To the moon? To the constellations? And what about all that could not be seen? Or that had vanished over time? How much of it might yet be hinted at in the fragments of stone, the depressions in the earth, the markings of a vanished world visible to only the most discerning eye?

She put a kipper on her plate, pushed it to one side, and helped herself to the eggs. Sir Isaac poured tea for them both from the silver pot.

"If my calculations are correct," he said, "there should have been at least three more standing stones in the field belonging to that fellow, what's-his-name, the officious one who tried to run us off the other day."

"Tom Robinson. He is a Nonconformist, and his

faith encourages him to attack anything that smacks of paganism."

Sir Isaac clucked his tongue. He was Church of England himself, having never given any thought to being anything else. He didn't see the point.

"I thought he speculated in housing?"

"That too," Sarah said with a smile. Little escaped her eccentric friend. "He uses the stones for building or builds where they would be in the way. Our interest discomforts him. He has, so he informs me, schedules to meet, investors to be satisfied, and the like. He wants no trouble."

She spoke easily enough but the impression was deceptive. Robinson and all those like him were the stuff of nightmares. Worse yet, there was nothing she could do to stop him.

That, more than anything else, had prompted her to help Sir Isaac. Whatever his motives, he was making a precise record of Avebury. Before very long, that might be all that was left.

"Kipper?" Sarah asked and passed the plate.

They finished breakfast in silence, content with their private thoughts. When they were done, Sarah put on her bonnet, picked up her basket—for she combined their sojourns with a search for wild herbs—and joined Sir Isaac on the path in front of the house.

It was a solid structure of two stories with walls of local stone wreathed in ivy and a slate roof that sported a pair of red brick chimneys. The roof and the chimneys were relatively new, having been put on around the time of Sarah's birth twenty-seven years before. The main part of the house was older, dating back to the previous century. The kitchens at the rear were older still, being medieval. Beneath them were the remnants of an ancient keep, and in its depths, where Sarah rarely ventured, were stone arches and pillars that had belonged to a Roman bath.

On one of the pillars, some long-vanished resident had scratched a message: *Fata obstant.* The gods will otherwise.

Whether it was a reference to the eventual fate of the Romans in Britain or to some other, more obscure event, Sarah had no idea. Nor did she wish to speculate.

Beneath the baths lay still older remnants, the remains of a well guarded by a horned god, shards of pottery with strange markings, and stone mace heads with carved figurines along their rims: all of them traces of the people who had lived in Avebury before even the Romans came. The people of the circles and the barrows. Of the dream.

Enough. The bright day beckoned and, with it, Sir Isaac.

They left the house by the garden path and proceeded by a short road down the hill. From the crest, the house commanded a view of the village and miles beyond. On a clear day, it was possible to make out the great circular mounds on Windermere Hill to the northwest and, to the south, oddly shaped Silbury, surely no work of nature. There were also the barrows: round ones to the east, the largest, long and ominous, to the south.

In between was the village itself, built smack in the center of the great stone henge, and, to either side, river and streams, some rising only in the spring. It was a fertile land and a beautiful one for all its strangeness, a place where shadows danced in sunlight and the past never seemed very far removed.

A place of dreams.

No, she would not think of that. She would think of the day and the simple task Sir Isaac had set them, to measure the distance between several sarsens standing along the avenue to Kennet in the east. They had done this once already but Sir Isaac believed they had overlooked something. So be it; they would look again.

But first he wanted to stop in the village. The mail coach had come, leaving its load as usual at Mistress Goody's shop. There Sir Isaac ventured, in among the bread and shoes, the tea and cheese, tape, ribands, bacon, barrels of pickles, and reams of cloth, everything the civilized person required.

He made his way to the back under full sail and bestowed a smile on plump Mistress Goody herself, who preened in delight as she handed over his letters. He thanked her and stuffed them into his pocket after the briefest glance. It was always so, Sarah had noticed. Curiosity consumed him until he knew who had written this time; then the urgency evaporated. Yet dutifully he spent each evening answering his correspondence and each morning had a neat pile of letters to turn over to Mistress Goody.

"Again to the Royal Society, sir," the postmistress said, spying the address on top. "Whatever would they do without you?"

She meant to flatter but Sir Isaac was impervious. He shrugged his shoulders. "Find another president, I suppose. The job's simple enough for a child." He turned to Sarah. "Shall we, my dear?"

Outside on the high street, they had to wait as a wagonload of beer and ale pulled by a pair of powerful drays was maneuvered into position next to the Rose. The proprietor, John Morley, was out in front to supervise the unloading. A big, burly man, red-faced with a deliberate manner, he inclined his head in greeting to Sarah and Sir Isaac but returned quickly to his business.

Several small houses lined the road on the way out of the village. Beyond them were open fields divided by Kennet Avenue, so named for the river that ran nearby. From the village looking down the avenue, the perspective was unlike any to be found elsewhere in England, for the broad road was framed by stone upon stone, standing in solemn majesty. More than sixty of the stones still stood; in Sarah's youth there had been more.

And in the dream. . . . There a hundred and more of the stones lined the great curving avenue and between them came teeming processions of people, drums beating, voices chanting, while on all the surrounding hills, vast bonfires of ash and sacred oak burned on the sacred nights when the season turned and the world was reborn.

She had only to close her eyes and find within herself the great, dark pool of memory. But there the madness lurked. If she let herself, she would drown in it.

Better to follow Sir Isaac and do as he bid.

He set the leather sack he carried on the ground and removed his timeworn instruments, all made by himself in the days of his youth when he became proficient at such things. Besides the compass there were an astrolabe and a sextant of remarkable precision.

As he moved among the stones, Sarah kept close at his heels. Although his muttered comments meant nothing to her, she jotted them down carefully in the notebook he had given her for that purpose. She could see little significance in what he was discovering, but she said nothing. If he felt better knowing the precise angle of declination between the horizon and each of the stones, so be it.

"Perfect," Sir Isaac said and looked delighted with the thought. "Absolutely perfect. What giants they were."

"Who?" Sarah asked.

"The Druids, of course, they who moved the stones and set them here in such perfect synchronicity. Truly, they understood the relationship of air and water to earth and fire. They knew how to draw upon the vitalizing agent, the life force that transforms mere matter into life itself."

"The Druids?" Sarah repeated.

"Who else?"

Absently, her attention distracted by the warm tingling of the stone against which she leaned, Sarah murmured, "The Druids came late to this land. Avebury was old by then."

Sir Isaac lowered his sextant and squinted at her. "What's that you say?"

"Nothing. It's only a story I've heard. Shall we go on?"

He agreed but continued to look at her for a few moments as though undecided whether to question her further. Sarah was grateful that he did not. She would not have liked lying to him.

At the far end of the avenue where the land rose again stood a double circle of stones about the same size as the pair of inner circles on the great henge. There, amid the tall grass and wild thyme, they stopped to rest.

Sir Isaac took a handkerchief from his pocket and mopped his brow, for the day was growing warm.

He seemed content to doze in the sun while Sarah set off with her basket, looking for herbs. Although she grew many of the domestic kind in her garden, she had found that a few wild shoots lent strength.

She had gotten halfway down the hillside toward the river when she noticed something lying in the rushes along the water's edge. Her eyes, an unusual dark blue shot through with flecks of white, narrowed. An animal, come to drink and instead dying? No, the texture was not right. That was cloth. A bundle of rags?

Hesitantly, already half knowing what she would find, she approached. A duck, lifting off suddenly, startled her. She put a hand to her throat and moved closer, telling herself she must surely be wrong, it could not possibly be—

Sarah screamed. The sound was high and thin, almost apologetic in its weakness, for she was, above all, a woman who prided herself on self-control. There were times when she had nothing else.

The scream died quickly, for she had no breath to sustain it. All was gone in a single, terrifying rush as she realized this was no animal but a man. He lay face down, his arms thrown out as though in supplication. She could not make out his features but his clothing marked him as a Gypsy, one of the band of tinkers who came through villages like Avebury regularly. They harmed no one and no one harmed them, at least not until now.

For this was no natural death. Even without the blood still staining the rocks, she knew that. Violence hovered in the air, all the more intensely felt for being unseen.

Murder had come to peaceful, bucolic Avebury.

She was stumbling up the hill, still clutching her basket, when Sir Isaac met her. Roused from his rest by her scream, he looked for a moment so desperately concerned that she could not help but be touched.

"You had a fright. A snake, perhaps? There aren't supposed to be any about but I have always thought that—"

Sarah shook her head. Her voice was surprisingly steady as she said, "We must seek Constable Duggin at once. There has been a murder."

They hastened back to the village, arriving breathless and disheveled. At the far end of the road, away from the other buildings, was the forge. There they found Constable Duggin as expected, for he was also Avebury's smith. He heard them out in silence before nodding his bullock head and stripping off the stained leather apron draped across his massive chest.

"A tinker, you say?" he asked Sarah as he drew on his coat. Death demanded such formality, even when the deceased was only a Gypsy.

She nodded, shying away from the heat that poured off the forge. In winter, the village children all found excuses to visit Duggin, and he tolerated their presence. In summer, he worked alone.

"I did not touch him," she said, "but his clothes are of the Romany."

"They'll be gone, then," Duggin said. "Whenever there's trouble, they vanish like the wind. The parish will have to bury him."

"It will also have to find his killer," Sarah said with some asperity. She disliked the presumption that the man would have been abandoned by his friends.

Duggin raised the bushy black eyebrows set in his craggy face. "Killer? More likely he was drunk and fell down the hillside. Landing hard on the rocks would do most men."

"I smelled no drink on him," Sarah countered, "and the ground has been dry. There was no reason for anyone to slip, much less one of the Romany who know this land well."

Duggin shrugged and headed for the wide double doors standing open. "As you say, mistress. The coroner's court will decide the matter." He paused and looked back at them. "Do you want to come along?"

Sarah shook her head. The thought of going back to the river made her stomach knot. She wanted to say, Treat him gently, he was a man like you. But the words died in her throat. The Gypsy was dead. Whatever was or was not done to him now no longer mattered.

In that she was mistaken, but it took some time— and more blood—before she realized it.

2

Down the long oak-paneled corridor he walked, making his way as quickly as he could through the crowd gathered as always in front of the antechamber. A bright-cheeked grandmother, recognizing him, thrust her petition into his hands. A large-bellied baker barreled forth to do the same. The minor nobles and the would-be gentry, the hangers-on and the sycophants, bent their heads in whispered speculation about his coming.

The duke had summoned him, they said. Great plans were afoot and William Devereaux Faulkner was Marlborough's most trusted man. He had been with the duke at Blenheim and later at Ramillies, but the battlefield was not his natural setting. Warrior though he was, he trod the treacherous labyrinths of the court even more ably.

There, in particular, Marlborough counted on him to deal with the slow but stubborn Queen Anne and not incidentally with the duke's own high-tempered wife, the Lady Sarah Churchill. Difficult and touchy matters were Faulkner's specialty. He could always be counted on to act with rapier determination lightly sheathed in diplomacy.

What could have brought him here to Windsor on this sun-drenched spring day? Some new French conspiracy perhaps? Yet another quibble by the Scots on the eve of their kingdom's formal uniting with Britain? Rumblings from the German princes? Something difficult, to be sure, requiring his authority and precision. The usual assortment of emotions rippled through the crowd like a dank fog felt in the bone—envy, admiration, fear. He inspired them all, this merchant's son risen so swiftly to greatness.

A footman flung open the door at the end of the corridor to admit him. He passed through and the door closed again, shutting off the whispers and stares. He was alone in a small, scantily furnished room with a good view of the gardens just coming into bud. Opposite him was another door and beyond that the inner sanctum of the duke, where he was momentarily expected.

He tucked the petitions beneath his waistcoat—to be dutifully considered when time allowed—straightened the lapels of his velvet jerkin, and crossed the room. His large hand, tanned and calloused, rapped once.

"Come."

John Churchill, first Duke of Marlborough, was seated behind his inlaid chestnut desk. He was dressed informally in breeches and a loose linen shirt left untied at the throat. His stock was undone, and his embroidered waistcoat and jerkin lay discarded on a nearby settee. A wooden stand on one corner of the desk held his curled and powdered wig. His own hair, gray and receding in this his fifty-seventh year, was cropped close to the head, revealing the sharp angularity of his features. He glanced up, saw Faulkner, and gestured to the chair beside the desk.

"How fare you?" he asked.

"Well enough, my lord. London is quiet."

The duke nodded. "For a change."

"It won't last." This was no dire prediction but a simple statement of fact. London was never quiet for long.

"I trust your family is well?" Faulkner inquired, ever courteous. He had heard rumors that the duchess had been in high dudgeon lately, but he would not mention that.

Marlborough grimaced. "Well enough. Sarah is at odds with our daughter."

Faulkner made no comment. Difficulties within families seemed the rule rather than the exception. Certainly, he'd had his share when his merchant father learned he wanted a military career.

As it happened, the choice had been a wise one, but it could as easily have been otherwise. He had escaped death four times—three times in battle and once at the hands of an assassin. He did not begrudge the experiences; they had left him better able to appreciate life.

"How is the lovely Chantra?" the duke asked with a faint smile. He was the most regular of husbands himself, but that did not prevent him from enjoying the escapades of his younger, unmarried friends.

"She has found a gentleman more to her liking, a lawyer she thinks may be inclined to offer marriage."

Marlborough's eyebrows rose. "You don't seem especially regretful."

"It was her prerogative," Faulkner said mildly. He failed to understand why any man should feel possessive of a woman not his wife when there were so many of them and so readily available. When the need arose he would acquire another, but for the moment he was content.

"I might almost think you cold-blooded," the duke said with a hint of censure.

Faulkner stretched out his long legs more comfortably and smiled. He wore white silk breeches, finely spun hose, and plain leather shoes with single buckles. Like his waistcoat and jerkin, all his clothing was of the finest materials and well made but unfashionably simple. He wore no wig but instead kept his thick ebony hair brushed back from his face and trimmed just below the collar.

His features were strong, the prominent bones high in his lean cheeks, the jaw square, and the skin burnished. His eyes were deep set and of a shade of gray akin to pewter or, depending on his mood, silver. His mouth was generous but—as it tended to be firmly set—appeared hard. In his thirty-second year, he had all his teeth and was in excellent health, although he was subject to episodes of melancholia from time to time that he mentioned to no one, least of all the duke.

"You should think of marrying," Marlborough said, apparently in no hurry to get to the reason for his summons.

Unless that was the reason, Faulkner thought, with a sudden surge of concern. Heaven forfend.

"Sarah would be delighted to help you find someone, I'm sure."

"Thank you, my lord, but I fear I would make a

poor husband. I have little patience for the domestic pastimes that seem to so delight women."

"Not all of them," Marlborough muttered. "Some of them prefer a larger arena." He rose and went to stand by the windows, where he appeared lost in thought for a few moments. It was well known that the Duke adored his difficult wife; theirs had been a true love match. However, that had not made it especially comfortable, so far as Faulkner had been able to observe.

At length, Marlborough returned his attention to the room. He walked back to the desk and, from the tumult of papers spread out over it, extracted a single sheet. This he regarded dubiously for a moment before passing it to Faulkner.

"What do you make of this?"

Unlike the duke—and most everyone else— Faulkner read quickly. He scanned the elegantly crafted script so swiftly that his eyes appeared to flit back and forth across the page until he got to the bottom and beheld the signature. There he stopped, fixing on it for several moments before looking up.

"Why is Sir Isaac in this place . . . Avebury? It holds nothing of any importance, does it?"

"Not that I know of," the duke agreed. "Who knows what prompts him? The man's mind is a mystery. However, he is president of the Royal Society, a favorite of Her Majesty, and one of our most eminent dignitaries. I cannot ignore his complaint."

"But murders?" Faulkner said dubiously. "Surely the local authorities are equipped to deal with this?" He consulted the letter again. "Two Gypsies, he says, their bodies found a day apart but suspected of having been killed at the same time. 'A source of deep distress to a dear friend of mine about whom I have great concern,' he continues. Doesn't say who the friend is or why he should be distressed.'"

"No, he doesn't. In fact, he says damn little. But he does make it clear that he expects me to do something."

Faulkner returned the letter to the desk. He was no different from anyone else in greatly admiring Sir Isaac, but he also knew the man was something of an eccentric. What on earth could he be doing in Avebury? "Why you?" he asked.

"Because he knows me," the duke answered. "Because he perceives that I have influence."

This was an understatement. Marlborough was one of the most powerful men in England.

"I realize this is an imposition," the duke added, for he was always thoughtful of those he especially valued. "But I cannot nay-say Sir Isaac. He will be content with nothing less than direct intervention. Go you in my name. Spend a few days, enough to placate him. There is little afoot for the next fortnight or so. You will miss nothing."

"Surely he would be content with a letter," Faulkner ventured, even as he felt his fate closing around him. Leave London when it was at its best and just as all the excitement of the Scottish union was about to be felt? Rusticate a fortnight in some backwater village? Truly, this was duty above and beyond the call.

"The queen believes that Sir Isaac is the greatest man of our age," Marlborough mused. "His next complaint might be to her."

Faulkner sighed. The duke was right. Sir Isaac had been born in circumstances humbler even than his own, but he dwelt among the gods of science whom no man in this enlightened age dared deny.

"I will leave in the morning," he said, as though bound

not for the bucolic glory of the English countryside in spring but for the far shores of purgatory. To him, they might as well have been one and the same.

"It won't be so bad," the duke assured him. "A bit of a rest will do you good. You work too hard."

"Should I lessen my labors?" Faulkner asked, amused.

"No, you are too useful to me. But a spell away from the city will benefit you. Besides, you are good at detection. Look at how well you uncovered the matter of embezzlement in the military stores two years ago."

Faulkner sighed. That brief exercise in simple logic—which had brought down a greedy marquess and several high-ranking officers—still plagued him. People, the duke included, had decided he was some sort of master problem solver. It was nonsense, but there was nothing he could do about it.

"Perhaps I won't need a fortnight," he said hopefully.

"It sounds a simple matter," the duke agreed.

Indeed it did, Faulkner thought. Simple to the point of idiocy. It would undoubtedly come out that there was some confusion. Perhaps the Gypsies had killed each other or hadn't been murdered at all but died accidentally. Or perhaps the murderer—struck by the arrival of so illustrious a being as the duke's man—would lose no time confessing.

He would encourage that, Faulkner decided. At his ruthless and relentless best, he would wring the truth from Avebury and be done. Grimly, he set about it.

3

"*A visitor?*" *Sarah* asked. She fed a bit of bread to the canary, dusted the crumbs from her fingers, and watched as the small bird craned its neck for more.

"Aye, milady," Missus Damas said. "Arrived this morning. Ever so grand a gentleman up from London. Came in his coach-and-four with his man and five pieces of luggage. They stopped at the Rose. Annalise Morley told me all about it."

The housekeeper folded her hands over her starched white apron and regarded her mistress sternly.

"I suppose this means Sir Isaac won't be coming by today. Give you a bit of rest, for a change. Why don't you take a book and a bite of something down to the river? You always like that."

"Not today," Sarah said. She plucked a stray thread from the skirt of her loose-fitting sac gown and glanced out the open windows. The day was fair, with a soft breeze blowing from the south and only a few fleecy clouds to be seen. "Perhaps I'll garden."

Good Missus Damas's mouth set firmly. "Begging your pardon, mistress, but you did that yesterday and the day before. It's been almost a week since you went into the village. Are you ill, then, that you cannot stir from home?"

Sarah sighed and attempted a smile. She could not take offense at the housekeeper's interference for she had known Missus Damas all her life. Besides, she was right.

"I'm not ill," she said softly. "Must a person always be bustling about in the thick of things to be taken for well?"

"You hardly bustle," the housekeeper scoffed. "A quieter and more regular lady is not to be found. But still, t'isn't good to stay to home too much. You need to get out."

"I do get out, with Sir Isaac."

"To clamber over hill and dale counting crumbling old stones? What kind of thing is that for a young lady to be doing? You need the company of people your own age. Why only yesterday, our good curate was asking for you. I told him you were fine, but I don't think he believed me. Said he might call today, he did."

Sarah blanched. Curate Edwards was a painfully sincere young man whose enthusiasm for his faith was outweighed only by the eagerness with which he sought to share it. In time he might mellow, but for the moment a small amount of him went a great distance.

"Perhaps I will go to the river after all," she murmured. What harm could come to her there? Gypsy bodies could not keep turning up forever, please God.

The two that had been found—the second by old Missus Hemper's son, Davey—had been buried in the paupers' plot behind the church. Constable Duggin and the shire court had delivered their ruling—death by misadventure in each case. The matter was closed, at least as far as Avebury was concerned. Sarah herself was not so certain.

Unease rippled through her. She could not explain her apprehension, but it had become her constant companion since the discovery of the first body. And it had kept her close to home, fearing what might be next.

"All right," she said suddenly, "I'll go. Pack something light for me, will you? I will be back for tea."

Missus Damas nodded with the satisfaction of one who has seen her duty and done it. Before her mistress could be tempted to reconsider, the housekeeper hurried off.

Sarah went upstairs, where she exchanged the comfortable sac for something more appropriate to a day's ramble. She chose a sensible gray wool dress with a white cotton shawl tucked neatly into the bodice. Her hair she twisted into a loose knot and tucked under a starched cap. Thus ready to confront the day, she picked up her journal—for she had neglected it of late—and went back downstairs. There she found a basket of cold meats, bread, an apple, and a jug of cider waiting for her.

Just beyond the door, she whistled for Rupert. The shaggy wolfhound bounded up, tail wagging, tongue lolling. Sir Isaac was not averse to dogs but he did find Rupert's enthusiastic presence a distraction, with the result that the hound had been left at home more often of late than usual. Now he saw the chance for a long solitary excursion with his adored mistress and clearly meant to make the most of it.

Sarah ran her hand over his rough-furred head, murmured "Good dog," and set off. Rupert bounded ahead. Through long habit, they turned in the direction of the common, deserted at this hour. Beyond was the stone bridge that arched across the river. A small boy nodded to Sarah as they passed and gave her a shy smile. He carried a sack of grass over his shoulder, fodder for the cows that almost every household kept.

On the other side of the bridge lay a field of wheat already knee-high and glistening green-gold in the sun. At the far end was a dark cluster of trees. A winding road led through them, framed by ancient pollards, alder, birch, and tufts of blossomed broom.

Rupert raced on, tail wagging. Sarah followed more slowly. Off to the side of the road, well concealed from passersby, was a mossy dell. Since childhood it had been her secret place, her refuge, a source of sustenance and reassurance when the strange, darting memories of the night became too much to bear.

As the path slanted downward, the light grew softer and more distant, and sound became muted. She was entering a hidden world, nestled among sloping banks crowned by feathery willow and magnificent old thorn trees. A small stream ran along the bottom, coursing among lichen-stained rocks and between gnarled roots. There the most delicate of wildflowers grew—speckle-leafed arum with gauzy blossom balls of purple and mauve, pale orchis, enameled blue hyacinth—and large tufts of oxlip and cowslips rose like nosegays from the mossy turf.

She stepped more softly, reluctant to disturb the peace that was as a living presence throughout the dell. Rupert woofed softly, but even he was subdued. Without her calling, he came to her side and licked her hand gently.

They settled on the embankment beside the stream. The big dog stretched out with his head on his crossed forepaws, but he did not sleep. He never did in the dell, nor was he ever lured away to chase the small brown hares and industrious moorhens who lived there. Instead, he kept watch over his mistress.

Sarah breathed deeply of the perfumed air, the scent grown so familiar over the years that she could smell it even in her sleep. The dell's silken coolness caressed her gently. For a time, she sat unmoving, her thoughts stilled, her mind quiet.

Into the silence of her soul came a need. It was a small thing, a flicker of impulse really, which she could have chosen to ignore. But she knew that if she did, it would grow stronger until choice was gone and only compulsion remained.

Before that could happen, she reached into her pocket and withdrew the journal. It was a small book bound in leather and filled with white pages, some covered with her neat script, others given over to drawings, and a few still blank. She would be finished with the book soon. It would go, as had all the other like books completed over the years, into a deep wooden chest kept in the armoire in her bedroom and to which only she had the key. For several weeks, she would write and draw nothing, until the need once again became too great. Then she would take another empty book from the supply she had long since laid in and begin anew.

It was her intention that the books would never see the light of day, for if they did, the secret of her madness would surely be secret no longer. Only rarely did she even allow herself to look back through the finished volumes. Whenever she did, the mingled fascination and terror they inspired haunted her for days. She seemed destined to spend her life making the books and hiding them away, never understanding what they were or why she was chosen to be their creator.

Her eyes on the page, she began to draw with swift, sure strokes an image she did not so much see in her mind as feel in her soul. This time, to her relief, the picture seemed harmless. White cows with long, curving horns bent to drink at the stream. Beside them a child stared out of the page, a small smile lifting the corners of her mouth not unlike the smile of the boy on the bridge.

But the boy was the son of Avebury's wheelwright and the grass he carried would go to feed ordinary Jersey cows, russet-hued and short-horned, far removed from the stately white cattle that drank within her drawing. As for the girl in the drawing, she wore a rough-spun sleeveless tunic that reached to her knees. Her legs and feet were bare. Her hair was braided with flowers intertwined among the strands.

She had picked the flowers herself, Sarah thought, while following the cows to the stream. The day was warm, the sun dappling through the broad-leafed trees of summer. Not spring as it was in Sarah's world but high summer, when the earth burst forth with riotous life and the clan went into the fields singing as they worked with their stone-tipped hoes and digging sticks, the women balancing reed baskets on their heads.

The child was happy. The new teeth she was cutting had ceased to hurt. Her stomach was full and was likely to remain so, for the harvest promised to be good. Her mother had taken her along to the sanctuary only that morning and allowed her to help with the sacrifice. Soon, very soon now, when her body, too, awoke, she would begin her instruction in the secret ways. Truly, on this day nothing else remained to be asked.

Happy child, smiling out at Sarah, laughter dancing in her eyes but something more as well—an almost wistful gentleness, regretful, apologetic, as though she understood the artist's struggle and wished it could be otherwise.

Madness.

Sarah dropped the charcoal and snapped the book shut. Her hand was trembling. The child was so real. She knew every contour of her face, every strand of hair, the tilt of her head when she was curious or uncertain, the quicksilver movement of her small, lithe body berry-browned by the sun, running fearlessly, arms raised, laughing for the sheer joy of being alive, or sitting still and thoughtful by the cooking fires, or standing straight and proud before the stones, hands outstretched to beseech the bounty of the earth.

She had drawn her so many times, in so many moods, and she would undoubtedly draw her again. Moreover, she knew what lay ahead for this child, the woman she would become. The priestess.

Madness.

Rupert raised his head. He looked at her with concern. She murmured what reassurance she could but her throat was thick. She was very thirsty.

Rising, she went to the stream. On her knees she bent, cupping water in her hands, and drank. The water was cold and sweet. She splashed a little on her face and let the rest run through her fingers. Feeling better, she sat back on her haunches and looked across to the other side of the dell.

A shadow stirred in the obscurity of the trees. Her breath quickened. Rays of sunlight arched through the branches like pillars in an otherworldly cathedral. The shadow moved again, came closer, resolved itself into the shape of a man.

A very large man, to be sure, tall and broad-shouldered with black hair and burnished features, soberly dressed in dark broadcloth with a splash of white lace at his throat. His head turned, he caught sight of her, and for just a moment Sarah thought she knew him. He looked so . . .

The impression vanished as though it had never been. He was a stranger, certainly not of Avebury or anywhere else she had ever been. An interloper in her cherished privacy.

Yet as she rose with the cool water of the spring dripping from her fingers and moist earth clinging to the hem of her skirt, she could muster scant resentment. Beneath it, faint and tremulous, gladness stirred.

Far in the distance, beyond memory and dream, the sun-browned child smiled.

4

For just an instant, the air had a strange smell to it, not fertile earth and budding flowers as it should but a tingling, shimmering scent such as he had smelled only once before when on a half-forgotten battlefield a bolt of lightning had cleaved an ancient oak scant yards from where he stood. Then, too, had Faulkner smelled the air as it was at that moment, alive with ancient forces.

It was gone in the next breath, as though imagined, yet the conviction lingered along with the hairs rising on the back of his neck: Here was something unusual. In this mossy dell, all innocence and serenity, appearances were particularly deceiving.

And then there was the woman. Where had she come from? He had presumed himself alone and had just concluded that he had indeed taken a wrong turn when she rose suddenly from beside the stream, a dryad peering at him with wide, questioning eyes. A wolf stood beside her. No, a dog, large to be sure and teeth suitably bared, but only a dog for all that he had momentarily appeared otherwise.

"Good day," Faulkner said, softly, for he thought she might afright, so tentatively did she seem poised on the bank of the stream. Only a woman, he had to remind himself. Not the—something—he had thought he glimpsed in that moment when the air shimmered all around him.

"Good day." Her voice was soft and cultured, the voice of a lady, with a note of uncertainty as was only proper and expected, given the circumstances.

"I beg pardon for disturbing you," Faulkner said and sketched a slight bow. He was a naturally courteous man, and the court had made him more so. There where treachery lurked in every smile and betrayal in every word, good manners were a useful weapon.

"You did not. That is . . . I was merely surprised to see anyone else here."

"I was looking for the river." He spared a glance for the narrow creek. "I gather this isn't it."

She smiled faintly, to his great pleasure, for the smile, small as it was, transformed her features. He had thought her rather plain, but the smile made him realize how wrong he had been. Her face was oval, her skin pale, but there was great vitality within her, for all that she seemed to keep it carefully banked.

"Did you come from the village?"

He nodded. She was austerely dressed but her body, so far as he could make it out, was tall and slender. She carried herself well, back erect and head gracefully set.

A sudden, startling bolt of desire struck him without warning, and he wondered how it could be for this simply garbed, shy woman, plain but yet not plain, who stood before him with one foot peeping out beneath her skirt as though set for flight. Perhaps he needed to replace Chantra more quickly than he had thought.

"There you are, then," she said. "You turned left instead of right. The river is that way." She gestured over his shoulder in the direction he had come.

"Is it?" he asked vaguely, not caring a whit where the river had gone, not caring either for the body found there or the hue and cry it had prompted. Sir Isaac be damned.

Three sparkling stones led across the creek to the other side. He took them in quick strides before she could realize what he intended. The soil on the opposite side of the creek was softer. His boots sunk into it slightly.

She took a quick, reflexive step back but held her ground. The dog growled, white teeth gleaming, free of all illusion about this, the man they called falconer, as though he was prone to hunt with rapier-clawed birds when in fact he was content to hunt alone.

"You are the gentleman from London," she said. It was less inquiry than explanation.

"I suppose I am. Dare I ask how you know?"

"This is a small village. News travels quickly."

"Indeed, then you have me at a disadvantage. If I am the gentleman from London, who are you?"

"Sarah Huxley. And you—?"

"Faulkner. William Devereaux Faulkner." He held out his hand. Courtesy worked both ways. She offered her own. He raised it to his lips quite properly, no lingering. She was a lady, after all, and he was never one to take unfair advantage. Every other kind, to be sure, but never unfair.

The dog growled, louder still. He returned her hand and smiled ruefully. "Your protector?"

She touched the dog's head, fingers working the thick fur behind his ear. "Rupert. He means well enough."

"I'm sure he does, Mistress Huxley. I take it you live in these parts?"

"I have a house a little distance from here."

I have a house. Not "my husband and I," or "my employers," or "my parents." Merely, I have a house. No ring adorned her finger but, even more, she had a certain air of self-possession that vaguely disconcerted him. Women were supposed to belong to someone. This one seemingly did not.

"Then perhaps," he invited, "you could tell me a little something about what happened here a fortnight ago."

Her face paled. He felt a sudden piercing regret as fierce as the desire she unleashed. Yet she was no missish young thing to quail before even the mention of murder.

"What do you know of it?" she asked.

"Only what I have been told. Two Gypsies were found dead, the first by the river, the other not far away. The constable says by misadventure, but Sir Isaac hints otherwise."

Her eyes were pools of blue, wide and luminous as the sky at noon. "You are acquainted with Sir Isaac?"

"We have met. He knows my employer and wrote to him about his concern in this matter. I was sent in response."

"I see. . . . No, I do not. Who is your employer?"

"John Churchill, Duke of Marlborough."

Her reaction was most gratifying. The finely shaped lips parted and the color washed back through her translucent skin. "Sir Isaac wrote to the Duke of Marlborough about the Gypsy deaths?"

"He did."

"And you were sent?"

"I was."

"Extraordinary. I had no idea that Sir Isaac was so concerned."

"He isn't, but apparently a friend of his is, and in an effort to soothe the sensibilities of this friend, he wishes the deaths investigated. Hence my own poor presence."

"Oh, dear," she said, hands twisting in her skirt. "I never thought. . . . Truly, it is beyond belief."

"Thought what?" he asked helpfully. She was really quite lovely this close up. He had to restrain the impulse to reach out and touch the cheek, now damask-hued, the slender throat, the delicate curve of her shoulder, and—

"I very much fear I may be responsible for your being here."

"I don't see how you could be. Sir Isaac—"

"Has all sorts of friends, it seems. Would you care for tea?"

"Tea?"

"It seems the least I can do," she said and turned, skirt billowing on the fragrant breeze. Without a backward glance, she climbed the mossy bank.

He followed.

Good Missus Damas's eyes bid fair to pop from her head, so widely did she gawk at her mistress and the tall dark man she had brought home with her. Rupert loped at their heels and could not be restrained from pushing his way into the drawing room. He plopped down in front of a chair, put his head on his crossed paws, and watched attentively.

"Tea," Sarah repeated. "I know it's early, but Master . . . Sir . . ." She paused, seeking direction.

"Sir," Faulkner admitted modestly. It was a blood-stained title, earned in the gore of Blenheim. His pride in it was a personal matter.

"Sir William has come all the way from London."

"Imagine," Missus Damas murmured. "All that way." Her gaze flicked from him to her mistress and back again. "For tea."

Sarah lowered herself onto the couch. She gestured to a facing chair.

"Among other things," Faulkner said and took his seat, stepping over Rupert to get there. He spread the tails of his frock coat beneath him. His buff-hued breeches fit his muscled thighs snugly. Light glinted off his boots except where the mud beside the creek had stained them.

Missus Damas went off clucking. They were left alone, but for Rupert and the canary, who cocked its small head to one side to regard Faulkner gravely.

Silence reigned. He was content to look at her but too quickly he became aware of her discomfort, though she hid it passing well. "Have you known Sir Isaac long?" he asked, more than chitchat for he was genuinely curious, but still the question was intended to put her at ease.

Meanwhile, his mind turned over what he knew so far. This was indeed her house, no parent or husband being in evidence. The housekeeper treated her with protective affection but also with respect. The property itself bespoke solid affluence, no ostentation but the sort of comfortable country living that could still be found among those who had no aspirations to be seen at court.

Why was she unmarried? Had a husband died? Had she been disappointed in love? He wanted—needed—to know every detail of her life. Curiosity consumed him.

"A month," she said, "a little more. He came to Avebury for a rest, he said."

He? Oh, yes, Sir Isaac, the master mechanic who had set all this in motion and whom Faulkner had trouble remembering, so inconsequential had he suddenly become.

"Has he been resting?"

"No, not at all. He appears fascinated by the ruins we have here. They occupy his every waking hour. I was enlisted to help in his researches."

Dark, arching brows rose. "Help how?"

"I'm not sure," she admitted with a smile. "Mostly, I just follow along and jot down the measurements he takes."

"Was that what you were doing when you found the Gypsy?"

"Yes. What exactly did Sir Isaac say in his letter to the duke?"

Briefly, Faulkner told her. When he was done, Sarah sighed.

"I do apologize, Sir William. It is true that the murders have distressed me, but I had no idea that Sir Isaac would go to such lengths." She raised her eyes, meeting his. "Or that it would have such consequences."

"Surely you know him to be an influential man?"

"I am not so naive as to be unaware of his standing. But for the duke to send you—"

"Do I gather you feel there was no need?"

"No, not precisely. In fact—"

Whatever she had been about to say was interrupted

by the return of Missus Damas bearing a heavily laden tray. Having set it on a nearby table, she stood, hands folded primly at her waist, and regarded them. "Shall I pour, mistress?"

"That won't be necessary, thank you."

"'Tis no trouble."

"We can manage."

"The pot's heavy."

"Thank you, Mary," Sarah murmured, "but I really can handle it."

Though plainly unconvinced, the housekeeper was left with little choice. She had to content herself with a hard look at Faulkner. "As you say, mistress."

"Your servant is attentive," he observed when they were once again alone. If they were. The drawing room door had been left open. Anyone could have been standing immediately beyond.

"And curious," Sarah said. She lifted the pot gracefully to fill his cup. "We don't get many visitors from London. Sugar?"

He shook his head and took the cup from her. Missus Damas had outdone herself. There were dainty sandwiches and sweet cakes enough for half a dozen visitors. He had not eaten since the previous evening and would have preferred heartier fare but took a sandwich to be polite.

The bread was fresh, the ham well cured. He took another. "You were speaking of the need to have the murders investigated."

"Constable Duggin is an honest sort, but I believe he took the path of least resistance."

"What is that?"

"He says the Gypsies were killed by one or more of their own."

"Not an unreasonable assumption. Most murder victims are killed by people they know."

"But the Romany have been coming here for generations. Aside from the occasional missing chicken, they've never given any trouble."

"Until now."

"Yes," she agreed softly. "Until now."

Silence again, but not strained. He was a man accustomed to solitude. Indeed, he sought it out from time to time as though he needed a certain set ration and could not manage without it. One of his objections to women was that they tended to chatter, always after a man to know what he was thinking or doing.

Not Mistress Sarah Huxley, though. She merely sat, sipping her tea, and waited for him to resume. Her features were serene. He had no idea what was going through her mind. That irked—excessively—but he was damned well not going to succumb to it.

He set his cup down. "If the Gypsies weren't killed by their own, who do you think was to blame?"

"I don't know."

"You must have some idea, some thought on the matter."

"A passerby, a vagrant."

Faulkner snorted. She could not seriously imagine he would accept such a notion. "A mad killer who happens to be wandering through Avebury and selects two Gypsies for dispatch to the world beyond?"

"The alternative is someone from the village. I have known most of the people here all my life. It is inconceivable that any of them could be a killer."

He was still hungry. Talking with her, being with her, gave him an appetite. His hand reached for another sandwich. Hers did the same. Their fingers brushed.

Both drew back. Sarah pressed her lips together. Faulkner stared. There it was again, that strange sensation he'd felt by the creek, softer now but still unmistakably the same.

"Excuse me," he said, although he could not have said for what. She nodded once but did not meet his eyes. Her cheeks looked like the roses that grew in his mother's garden at high summer.

"You have known most of the people, you say. Who has come more recently?"

"Not many. The curate, a marquess and his family, one or two shopkeepers. This is a settled place."

"So I perceive. Very well, then, tell me about the ruins."

Her eyes shot up suddenly, locking with his for just an instant. Abruptly, a shutter dropped between them, but not before he felt a blast of keen intelligence that left him dumbfounded.

In his experience, women were either featherheads or adept at pretending to be. He could not remember ever being so bluntly alerted to the workings of a mind not so very much different from his own.

"Why?" she asked, exactly as he would have and just as unrelentingly.

Faulkner shrugged, having no ready answer. He was too busy mulling over the notion that this woman he unaccountably desired, this independent, self-possessed female, was also possessor of a mind that might astonishingly be a match to his own.

"Sir Isaac is here because of them," he said finally. "I am here because of Sir Isaac. So the ruins interest me. What are they?"

"Standing stones for the most part. Sir Isaac says the Druids made them."

Something was wrong there, although he couldn't identify it. Sir Isaac said? Never mind, the stones were not his true concern.

"Would you show them to me?" She was about to refuse; he could see it in her eyes and drove on relentlessly. "As well as the place by the river where you found the body. It was you who found it, wasn't it?"

"Did Sir Isaac say that?"

"No, but I can think of no other reason for you to be so distressed. Had it all happened at a distance, had you never even seen the body, you would not be so involved."

"Not even if I think one of my villagers may have done it?"

"Yours?"

"An old-fashioned notion, but all of Avebury used to belong to this manor. My family has always felt a certain responsibility for those who dwell there."

"All the more reason to help me. As well as the fact that, as you yourself pointed out, you are responsible for my being here."

She sat, hands folded. Rupert lifted his head. The canary fluttered its wings. Softly, Sarah said, "Do you play chess, Sir William?"

"From time to time. You?"

"Upon occasion." She rose, smoothing her skirt. "Very well then, I will show you the river and the stones, if you like. But I fear I can be of little help beyond that."

He stood, too, and inclined his head, the soul of graciousness now that he had won. Smiling, he offered his arm.

Warily, she took it.

5

"Here?" Faulkner asked. He bent beside the river, the breeches stretched taut over his muscled thighs, his broad shoulders flexing as he reached forward to touch the damp earth.

Sarah looked away. Her throat was dry and her senses unsteady. She could not for the life of her imagine why she was doing this. The larger part of her wanted to flee, back to her house and its walled garden, away from this man who disturbed her so greatly. Pride forbade it, that and something else stirring within her which she did not wish to examine too carefully.

"Yes," she murmured, staring down at him. The sun glinted off his dark head. He moved with the easy grace of a man accustomed to action. This was no desk-bound flunky the duke had sent.

"You say he appeared to have been struck on the head?"

"At least once."

"But you saw no weapon?"

"No, nothing. However . . . "

He turned, looking at her. "What?"

"I'm not sure, it is possible I am mistaken, but I had the impression he had been dragged here."

"There were marks on the ground?"

Sarah nodded. "I didn't think of them at the time; indeed, I thought of nothing. But now I seem to recall—" She shrugged. "I doubt it is of any help."

"If he was killed elsewhere, there could still be some trace." He stood, brushing the dirt from his hands. "Where was the second body found?"

"There," she said, pointing down the river a short distance to a clump of bushes. "It had been rolled into the water, perhaps in the hope that it would sink or the current take it away. But the clothes became tangled in some branches—"

He nodded, sparing her the details. Hands on his lean hips, he surveyed the scene. "Two men dead. One left carelessly at the edge of the water, the other unsuccessfully hidden. Was the killer interrupted or did he panic and run off?"

"At the coroner's hearing, Constable Duggin suggested the killer must have known the bodies would be found and would therefore have fled. It is true that the Gypsies who were in the area had gone."

"Was an effort made to find them?"

"Word was sent round to nearby villages. There was no sign of them. We all know the Romany can seem to disappear whenever they wish."

Faulkner nodded, but he appeared unconvinced. "Still, a better effort could have been made. One of them might have seen something." He shaded his eyes and looked up the bank of the river. "What is that up there?"

Sarah followed the direction of his gaze. High above the river, atop the overlooking hill, stone sentinels stood gray against the sky. "Just a circle. They are common hereabout."

"Part of the ruins Sir Isaac is studying?"

She nodded. "We were measuring the stones up there. He stopped to rest; I went in search of wild herbs. That's when I found the body."

"I've heard of these," Faulkner said. He began walking up the bank toward the hill. "There's a large one near Salisbury that people go to see. Stonehenge, they call it."

He was halfway up the bank and clearly had no intention of stopping. Sarah took a breath, gathered her skirts, and went after him. By the time she reached the top, Faulkner was standing in the center of the circle. He had an air of pleased surprise about him, like a child suddenly stumbled upon a fascinating toy.

"I had no idea they were so big," he said, looking round at the stones. "Or so perfectly placed. Druids, you say?"

"Sir Isaac does."

"I suppose they cast magical incantations to bring the stones here," he teased.

"More likely they brought them on barges along the river."

His smile deepened, reaching all the way to his pewter eyes. "Are you usually so prosaic, Mistress Huxley?"

No, she was usually mad, caught between the world of the dreams and the world she had so laboriously managed to make for herself. Neither place had any room for him. He was danger, a door flying open suddenly in the safety of her mind. And beyond it she could hear, smell, sense an existence so very different from her own. So very tempting.

Her hands were shaking. She hid them in her skirts and willed herself to calm. "Have you seen everything you wish?"

He did not answer but merely stood, looking at her. The sun was behind him. She could see little except the shape of his head and body silhouetted black against the sky.

"What is wrong?" he asked.

"The sun—"

"No, not that. Wrong here, with you. Are you ill?"

Her breath caught. She had been so very careful. He could not possibly know. In her best haughty voice, the one she reserved for when she most desperately needed it, she said, "I beg your pardon?"

"Perhaps it was wrong of me to ask you to do this. I underestimated what returning here would mean to you."

Relief flowed through her. He felt her discomfort clearly enough but ascribed it to the wrong cause. She regretted the Gypsies' deaths and did not want them to go unpunished, but it was not they who so easily breached her defenses.

The sun would be shining in her walled garden beside the house. The earth would be fragrant beneath her hands. If only she could get back there—

"Allow me to escort you home," Faulkner said.

She could last the few minutes it would take him to do that. Her composure could endure that long at least. "As you wish."

"That way, if you don't mind," he said and gestured

out beyond the circle along the avenue where the stones marched one upon the other. At its far end, a vast circular ditch enclosed earthworks so large that they held most of the village as well as ample pastures and orchards. In among the buildings and fields, a pair of double stone circles could clearly be seen, companions to the circle in which they presently stood.

Faulkner shook his head, amazed. "I was wrong to compare this to Stonehenge. It's far larger and more complex, isn't it?"

Sarah heard her own voice as though from a great distance. "Sir Isaac thinks so."

"The same way he thinks the Druids deserve the credit for it? What do you think, Mistress Huxley?" When she hesitated, he took her hand and with bold familiarity placed it in the crook of his arm. Smiling, he said, "Come, I'll walk you home and you can tell me all about this place. I think I'm beginning to share Sir Isaac's fascination."

The intensity of his gaze sweeping over her suggested it was more than stones and earthworks that interested him. Sarah flushed and looked away. She was trapped, unable to refuse what seemed so ordinary a request yet equally unable to comply.

The book she had been drawing in earlier in the day was still in the pocket of her skirt. She felt its weight heavy against her thigh as he led her out of the stone circle and onto the long avenue.

"A few months ago," Faulkner said, after they had walked awhile, "the London authorities deemed it necessary to dig in front of my house. Would you care to guess what they found?"

"A Roman road," Sarah answered absently. Most of her mind was on the pressing need to mislead him. What tale could she spin that would satisfy him about the stones without revealing anything untoward? What way could she find to concentrate his mind on the Gypsy killings, the better that he should solve them soon and be gone from Avebury and from her?

"How did you know that?" he asked, surprised.

"Know what?" What had she said to make him stop and look at her again with that silvered gaze that sent the strangest sensations corkscrewing through her?

"That they found a Roman road in front of my house?"

Had she said that? Sweet heaven, she would have to pay better attention. She shrugged as though it were of no account. "There are Roman roads throughout London. If you know where to look, you can hardly move for tripping over them."

"Indeed? One rarely thinks of how long people have been on this land."

"Perhaps it is best that way."

"You live here," he said, gesturing to the long sweep of stones on either side of them, "amid all this, yet you say that?"

"The past is done with. There is no reason to dwell on it." Lies, all lies, but so much safer than the truth. Sir Isaac and the other great men of their age were bent on making sense of everything. They likened the universe to the workings of a giant machine. In their reality, time did not bend back upon itself, popping up in dreams and drawings. It remained as it was supposed to be, dead as the buried Gypsies, finished and forgotten.

"The stones must represent something," Faulkner insisted. "Enormous effort went into bringing them here. There had to have been a purpose."

Indeed there had, life itself and the rhythms essential to maintain it. For the same reason a great deal else had been done, but so far he seemed to have no sense of that, seeing only the more obvious. She was grateful for such small favors but overwhelmingly anxious to get away. The ground beneath her neatly shod feet could shift at any moment, the dream and the compulsion could come upon her without warning. She needed the garden and the walls, the silence and the safety. Needed them desperately.

"I really must get back," she said, her voice tight.

He looked at her again with that same deep-seeing glance, piercing to the quick. "You are very pale."

"No, I am fine, it's just that—"

The wind gusted suddenly, pulling wisps of her hair loose. On it, sailing boldly, was the perfume of the earth, life stirring to rebirth. The scent exploded in her, making her senses reel.

Please, no, don't let this happen to her! Not here and now, with him. The madness was her darkest secret, rigidly concealed all her life. To be exposed like this, out in the bright day, before this man, was more than she could bear.

A moan slipped between her parted lips. She was filled with fear, but beneath it lay the bedrock of anger. This was a burden she had never asked for and which she could not begin to understand. Her every instinct was to reject it, to fling it out of herself and be done forever.

But the effort recoiled back upon herself with a force that stunned her. She staggered and would have fallen had not a steely arm been flung around her. Faulkner said nothing, or if he did she did not hear. He merely lifted her as easily as though she were a child and strode up the rise to the village. At the end of the avenue, he paused for a moment to get his bearings, then turned right down the lane toward the Rose.

Before he reached it, Sarah had recovered sufficiently to be alarmed. "This isn't necessary," she said urgently. "Please, sir, put me down."

"Be quiet," Faulkner said and kept walking.

Missus Goody, stepping out for a breath of air, saw them. Her mouth dropped open. "Mistress Sarah, whatever are you—"

"Good day to you," Faulkner said courteously and passed on. Sarah squirmed in his arms. She was overcome by embarrassment and by something more. The steady rhythm of his breathing, the slow beat of his heart, and the easy command with which he acted combined to steal her reason. Her own susceptibility appalled her. She was twenty-seven, for heaven's sake, not some green girl to sigh over a man. Yet green she was in many of the ways that counted most, after being kept so safe and secluded in her garden. Now safety was gone with a vengeance, there on the sun-dappled land smack in the center of the village on a day when the earth was stirring to wakefulness and she with it.

He turned in at the Rose and walked up the flagstone path. The oak door, curved at the top and studded with iron, stood open. Faulkner passed inside and, still holding Sarah, made his way to the common room.

John Morley was behind the bar. His eyes widened

when he saw them. "Sir?" he ventured, the single syllable holding a wealth of questions.

"Mistress Huxley felt faint," Faulkner said. He set her down at last on a bench near the leaded glass window, but stayed close as though he feared she might topple over. "She requires a restorative."

Still Morley did not move but stared at them, one large hand frozen in the act of inspecting tankards. He was a fussy man about his tankards, Morley was, each having to be polished just so and placed exactly. Only his daughter could arrange things to his requirements.

Why was she thinking about Morley and the damn tankards? It was Faulkner who mattered. Sarah cast a quick glance up at him through the veil of her lashes. He appeared to be enjoying himself.

"Whisky, man," he said, "and be quick about it."

"I never drink whisky," Sarah said. She judged it past time to stand up for herself, but the attempt had little effect. Morley ignored her entirely and sprang to obey Faulkner. It was undoubtedly the wiser choice, but it rankled all the same.

A small tumbler of amber liquid was placed in front of her. If her knees had possessed the least strength, she would have risen then and there and departed. But her entire body felt unaccountably weak and even—though she hated to so much as think the word—pliant. Her will seemed to be deserting her.

Yet it was not gone entirely. "Tea," she said, then added because she always did, "please."

"Kettle's cold," Morley replied. "That's the best whisky you'll find for three counties. Only the finest at the Rose, that's my motto. Your man brought your bags in, sir," he went on to Faulkner. "Will you be staying long?"

"I've no idea. Are you feeling better?" This last to Sarah and in clear dismissal of the publican.

"Yes, but I would really like to—"

A bustle at the door interrupted her. Sir Isaac hurried in. His wig was slightly askew and he peered at her with real concern. "Old Missus Hemper's son came to fetch me. Something about you being taken ill in the street. Should we summon the surgeon?"

Sarah sighed. She had no difficulty imagining the sequence of events: Missus Goody bustling off to find Missus Hemper, who as the village's resident wise woman had an instant claim on all such information; Missus Hemper dispatching her son; Sir Isaac duly alarmed and now—horrors!—suggesting good Dr. Quack be called.

Aside from the fact that it was her abiding ambition forever to avoid the ministrations of Quack and his professional kin, that would set off yet another of the frequent battles between Missus Hemper and the doctor, both locked in struggle for the right to dispense their own peculiar remedies to the population. Of the two, Sarah trusted the old woman more but she needed neither.

"I am fine, Sir Isaac," she said soothingly and prayed that he at least would believe her. Just in case he didn't, she sought a distraction. "I don't believe you've met Sir William Faulkner Devereaux. He has been sent by the Duke of Marlborough himself in response to your letter."

"Letter?" Sir Isaac repeated. He frowned at Faulkner. "Letter . . . oh, yes, my letter! Of course, to the Duke. How is Sir John these days?"

"Very well, sir," Faulkner said as he rose and inclined his head courteously.

"And the Lady Sarah?"

"Also well. Would you care to sit down?"

"Most certainly," Sir Isaac said. "I hardly expected so swift a response. You serve Sir John, do you?"

"I have that honor. He has charged me to investigate your concerns in the matter of the Gypsy deaths."

"Excellent, that's exactly what we need, an objective eye, an outsider. Someone to sort through the evidence and reach a sensible conclusion. Don't you agree, Mistress Huxley?"

Sir Isaac's unbridled enthusiasm had the effect of increasing her own apprehension, with the result that the whisky was looking more appealing by the moment. "If you say so, but I fear Sir William might be better occupied elsewhere. This is in the nature of an imposition, is it not, Sir William?"

If she could only get him to admit it, perhaps Sir Isaac would relent. But Faulkner merely smiled and shook his head. "It is never an imposition to serve the duke, mistress, or those he most admires."

Sir Isaac laughed. "Very gracious of you, my boy. But never fear, with my help and Mistress Huxley's, I am certain we can settle this matter in just a day or two. You will help, won't you, Sarah?"

"I don't quite see how—"

"She's far too modest," Sir Isaac declared. "Family's been here since before the Normans. No telling really how far back they go. You can't be linked to a place that long and not have a special affinity for it, isn't that so, mistress?"

A few drops of whisky certainly couldn't hurt her. She raised the tumbler, sipped, and instantly coughed.

"Easy," Faulkner said. "Take it slowly."

"I will not take it at all," Sarah said. Enough was

enough. She stood. "If you will excuse me, I have gardening to do." She did not quite run but reached the door before either man could say a word. Sir Isaac called after her but she pretended not to hear and hurried out into the bright day, down the lane, to the sanctuary of her garden walls and the privacy of her thoughts.

6

The sun burned. It seared the back of her neck and her bare arms. Sweat trickled down her neck beneath the light brown tunic. Her breath came in gasps but she could not stop. The chanting and the beating drums, the exhortations of the clan, were all around her, driving them on, children and adults alike, up the last desperate stretch to the top of the earthworks.

The whole clan was there, all but the oldest and youngest pulling on the ropes or pushing from behind. The rest—white-haired grandmothers and brown-legged toddlers—splashed water on the runners, handing the buckets up a long line from the stream.

Slowly, agonizingly, inch by inch, the stone came. The ropes of plaited leather wrapped around it stretched taut and threatened to snap. The wooden rollers creaked, moaning under the weight. The people sang out, exhausted voices lifting to the sky. For months they had toiled, making the axes and hardwood levers needed for cutting the stone from the chalk downs, constructing the sleds and rollers, plaiting the ropes. The entire clan was caught up in the work, all enmities forgotten in the single great need to complete the circle.

It was the last stone they were bringing, but it was also the largest, the greatest challenge yet to the strength and will of the community. Here on this autumn day as the smoke of burning stubble rose from the fields and the first crisp chill of coming winter blew from the ice country far to the north, the people toiled. The moon had risen and set ten times since they left the downs hauling the stone. They had eaten and slept beside it, prayed and dreamed.

And now . . .

Her body screamed, begging for rest. But she could see the top of the earthworks directly ahead. Only a little way more, only a short time longer . . .

The great stone edged over the rise, teetered briefly, and slowly settled upon the flat ground at the top. A ragged cheer went up. Much remained yet to be done, to pull the stone into its final position and then the rigorous work to raise it. But after the miles crossed and the effort exerted, it was time for celebration.

Her heart leaped with the joy of it all, but her body remained slumped on the damp ground. She knew she had to stand, as others were doing slowly around her, but her strength was gone. She lay gasping, her eyes closed, the scent of the earth in her nostrils.

A shadow fell across her, blotting out the sun. Coolness touched her skin. "Come," a familiar voice said. She glanced up, squinting against the light, and saw him.

He was three summers older than herself, tall for his years, with the broad shoulders and chest of a warrior. Yet he sat sometimes with the wise ones, allowed into their circle to listen to the stories they chanted, for they felt within him a part of themselves.

He had hair almost the same color as her tunic, tied at the nape of his neck with a leather thong. His beard was short, kept trimmed by his knife. His eyes were blue and surrounded already by lines, for he was a man who smiled often.

Like the other men, he wore woven breeches that ended at the knee. His calves were ribbed with muscle, as was his chest. The hand he held out to her was sinewy, the fingers blunt-tipped.

"Come," he said again. "You don't want to miss the feasting."

Above the earth, mingling with its own scent, came the aroma of meat on the spit. Many cattle had been slaughtered to make the plaited leather ropes to pull the great stone. Most of the meat would be pounded thin and dried for the winter, but the cooking fires were beginning to sputter with the dripping juices of whole joints roasting over them.

She rose, drawn up by his strength, and managed a smile of her own. Glancing back over her shoulder at the stone, she said, "I didn't think we would make it."

He looked at her intently. "Never doubt. Those who went before us began the work. Surely we can finish it."

She nodded, wanting to believe as completely as he did, but privately doubt lingered. All around her was the evidence that those who had come before had been stronger somehow, perhaps not the race of giants that was whispered but not fully part of the ordinary world either. They had brought not one stone but tens and tens more. And they had reshaped the earth herself, building vast mounds and barrows that marched across the landscape and were a constant reminder of their power.

Now the clan seemed weaker. Yet they had moved

the stone, dragging it mile after mile across the downs where it had been cut from the breast of the earth herself. Soon it would stand upright in precisely the spot the wise ones chose to please the Mother and assure the well-being of the people.

His hand was warm and strong on hers. She came only to his shoulders but the effect was not unpleasing. His gentle attention made her feel protected and cared for, even as it prompted a strange fluttering in her stomach. Thirteen summers had come and gone since her birth into the clan. The year before, her woman's time had arrived and her training begun in earnest. She'd had little chance to notice the young men until now. He was the first and, she thought, the best. Together, they found a place beside the cook fires. Her mother was there, sitting with the wise ones. She looked at them and smiled.

The summer twilight lingered long. Before it was over, the meat was roasted. Her mother rose, a long knife in her hand. Ancient words in the old tongue, words of thanks, rose to the amber-tinted sky. She cut the Mother's portion and dropped it into the flames, then cut again. Meat was taken in hand, borne on flat pieces of wood and in open clay dishes, passed round the circle until all from the noblest warrior to the smallest child was fed. So, too, were the ewers of sweet cider and beer handed from one to another, the flat breads cooked on hot stones, and bowls of mash seasoned with late summer berries.

When all were full, some of the men took up their drums again and beat a song to the chant of the old ones. A hoary grandfather, back bent but eyes still bright, rose to sing of the days when the people wandered, seeking their place upon the earth until they came to the

fair valley and the wide plain. There the wisest felt the
Mother call to them. There where sweet water was
plentiful, grass for their herds, and good soil for the
crops, where rivers teemed with fish and the worst
hunter did not come home disappointed, they built
their huts. And there, in gratitude and awe, they began
the transformation of the land that was to continue
down through the generations to that very moment.

Others took up the chant, adding their own parts, for
the knowledge of the people was shared among many
lest any death diminish it. The very cadence of the song
was a part of her soul. She had heard it her first moment
new from her mother's body, and she suspected she
would hear it even as her spirit fled to the Mother.

But there were other songs as well, and as night fell
they received their due. Songs of courage and daring, the
valor of hunter and warrior. Songs of discovery and love,
the fertility of harvester and mother. Playful laughing
songs, exciting sensual songs, as the children slept curled
beside their parents and the old ones smiled indulgently.

The night sky blazed with stars as couples slipped
away. She was tired, yet too excited to sleep. A dull
ache throbbed in her shoulders where the ropes had
bitten. He touched her there lightly, as though he felt
her pain. She turned her head, her eyes meeting his,
and felt a yearning so vast it made her tremble.

They went to the river where shadows swelled and
the ground was soft. She was frightened, eager, curious,
all at once. This was no small thing, this giving of her
body, but the time was right and the choice hers.

A bird fluttered in the tree above their heads. The
moon was rising, pouring molten silver over the
water. She took a breath to still the wild flutter of her
heart and stepped into his arms.

* * *

She stumbled and went down hard on one knee. Struggling upward, Sarah gasped. Her breath was ragged and she was shivering uncontrollably despite the warmth of the night air. Sleep would not release her. She had the terrifying sensation of being dragged back down into unconsciousness. With a wrenching act of will, she pulled away, but the effort took all her strength. She lay, hardly moving, for some timeless length until a growing sense of discomfort made her stir.

She was lying on ground damp from a late-evening shower. Through the thin silk of her night robe, she could feel the wet earth. Not far away, water flowed, gurgling over rocks.

She sat up quickly and looked around. Her heart skipped. The walls of her room had vanished. She was in the dell beside the river. The moon had risen, illuminating the scene for her disbelieving eyes.

Was she still dreaming? It had seemed so real: the stone, the ropes, the chanting, the whole desperate effort. And the boy. No, not a boy, a man, by the law of the clan and his own merit. A man worthy of the young priestess.

Terror raced through her. She had dreamt before, countless times, but she had never experienced anything so vivid, so intimate. If she had needed any further proof that she was mad, surely this was it.

Somewhere in the midst of the dream, she must have wandered from the house, come here beside the river. It was full night, the hushed time when almost nothing stirs. Slowly, she got to her feet but her legs were weak and she feared to fall again. Stretching out a hand, she encountered the smooth bark of a tree. Clinging to it, eyes squeezed shut, she prayed that this was all an illusion. When she looked again, it would be gone.

It was not. She was in the dell where she had sat the previous morning, sketching the sun-browned child. Where Faulkner had come. Sarah inhaled sharply. She must not think of him, not now when she was so vulnerable. Her breasts felt unaccountably heavy, and there was a strange tightening beneath the soft swell of her abdomen.

Her night robe was almost soaked through from the dampness. She wrapped it more tightly around herself and stumbled up the bank. The road was at the top, just as it was supposed to be, winding over the bridge and down the lane toward her house. Barefoot, she walked along, trying to think of nothing. If she could only hold on to her composure until she reached the safety of her own room, she would survive this. There had to be an explanation, a way to stop it from ever happening again. Had to.

The rough surface of the road hurt her bare feet but she hardly noticed. The night pressed in, silent, watchful. By moonlight, the contours of the earth so well known in day appeared strangely distorted. Robbed of all color save black and silver, every forest and hillock seemed drawn from another world, one until now locked safely within her dreams.

She didn't have the strength to run or she would have done so. As it was, she could only walk quickly, her eyes locked on the rise beyond which lay her house. When at last she came within sight of the high garden walls, she sobbed with relief.

So fierce was her concentration, so frantic her need, that she did not notice the sudden small patch of fire that flared red against the night.

7

Faulkner paused in the act of lighting a cheroot. An apparition came toward him. White against the shadowed night, it appeared almost to float along the road, now pausing, now moving again as though uncertainly. An unwilling ghost, a reluctant specter doomed to walk the road without purpose or surcease?

He shook his head impatiently. Such fancifulness was unlike him. It was a tendril of fog, nothing more. There was a surprisingly good bed in his room at the Rose. He should be in it, not out on the winding lane beside Mistress Huxley's house, being taunted by a mischievous mist.

But sleep had proved elusive and the night seemed to beckon. It was always so with him. Bright day had its own advantages, but in a world that grew more tumultuous with each passing season, hushed night offered rare respite. Walking abroad when no one else was about, he felt a curious possessiveness, as though the world showed him a face kept hidden from most others. Even in London and other cities he had been known to venture out, though not incautiously for he was always armed. Twice, footpads had mistaken him for prey. One he had killed. The other he merely maimed, mercilessly, for he knew how easily they abused the weak.

Here in fair Avebury he was not inclined to lower his guard. There had, after all, been two murders. But neither would he stay abed when the night called and sleep held no attraction.

Unlike the mist coming ever closer. Queer mist that could so perfectly assume the shape of a woman, coming faster now and no longer with the illusion of floating. Say, rather, it—she?—appeared to stumble and almost to fall before righting and continuing on.

She? His eyes narrowed, silver in the moonlight. Surely this was no more than beguiling fantasy? No woman would be abroad at night and certainly not arrayed in what truly did look like a filmy white mist. Unless, he thought suddenly, there was a madwoman in the neighborhood. If so, she might also be responsible for the killings.

In an instant, the cheroot died beneath his booted foot. He slipped, soundless as a cloud across the moon, behind a nearby oak. The shape came closer and did in time solidify itself. A woman for true, hurrying, her hair in disarray so that it fell across her face and with no more than a thin night robe to shield her body.

He frowned. A madwoman, perhaps. But she might also be the victim of a crime, most likely of the sort that happened behind closed doors and of which people were not supposed to speak. A sudden, piercing memory went through him: his mother bruised and weeping, the very walls of their house reverberating with his father's rage, and himself and his brother hiding in the loft, unable to do anything but grieve.

No longer. His father was in his grave, his mother in contented retirement, and he . . . suffice to say, he had no tolerance for men who hurt those weaker than themselves.

Quickly, he stepped from behind the tree and made his voice gentle. "Don't be afraid, mistress. I mean you no harm. But you appear in need of help."

She froze and made a strangled sound as though the earth had opened at her feet. The gown she wore was wet from the night air and almost transparent. Try though he did, he could not help but notice that she was exquisitely formed.

Her hair still veiled her face. He had a irresistible urge to push it aside. But before he could do so, she turned away and sought the safety of the trees on the opposite side of the road.

Discretion demanded that he not press his attentions. She was rightly terrified, by whatever had sent her out onto the road and by his sudden intrusion. Any gentleman would, at the very least, keep a decent distance between them.

But he was a merchant's son, bred in the rough-and-tumble of London's great port, come to manhood on the battlefield. He could, if pressed, play the gentleman. But here, on a moonlit lane in the shadow of the stone circles, the effort was beyond him.

"Stop," he said, still quietly, for he was a man accustomed to command. She, however, was not inclined to obedience. Desperation made her fleet.

Had he not been quicker, she might have disappeared into the surrounding wood.

His hand firm on her arm stopped her. She whirled, trying to twist free. Instinctively, he tightened his hold. There was no thought in him to hurt her, but in the heat of the moment he neglected to temper his strength. She cried out in real pain.

He was instantly contrite but the damage was done. She redoubled her efforts, striking out at him with slim, bare feet. Rather than risk her being injured further—or so he told himself—he dragged her hard against his body and held her until her strength ebbed and slowly her struggles died away.

Only then did he touch a gentle hand to her brow, brushing aside the tangled hair to reveal—

Sarah? Mistress Huxley? She of the prim garb and deceptive plainness? It could not be. This was a creature of night magic in his arms, the stuff of fantasy. Yet undeniably real, her cheeks damp with tears and anguish in her sylvan eyes.

"Please," she whispered hoarsely, "let me go."

He almost did as she asked, so great was his shock. Only the sense that if he released her he might never be able to find her again stopped him.

"What are you doing here?"

She shook her head, as though any answer was beyond her, and thrust her slender hands against the wall of his chest.

"Speak to me," he said with deliberate harshness. Her eyes were unfocused. He had the sense of her falling away from him down a path he could not go.

Without thought, he grasped her arms, peeling them from her body. She stood revealed in the moonlight, little hidden from his gaze, a dream of beauty and sensuality. The breath caught in his throat. This should not have been happening, must not. She was a gentlewoman, and even if she had not been, he would not have treated her like this. There was some explanation for her state. It was up to him to find it and help her if he could.

Not draw her close against him, tangle his hand in her amber hair, and claim her mouth with his own. Sweet mouth, he was sure, sweet woman for all that she was afraid. Fire coursed through her. The palms of his hands tingled against her skin.

The night wrapped them in shadows. The ground was soft. He could—

Angrily, he shook his head. This could not be happening to him. He was a man of reason, a product of the most rational age that had ever been. He was not, would never be, controlled by emotion. Not even here, in strange, haunting Avebury with a woman of moonlight and dreams in his arms.

Not here. Not now.

She was frightened. Something terrible had happened to her. He was a man of honor. He could not—

Not touch the petal-smooth curve of her cheek, brushing away the dampness of her tears. Not gather her into the warmth of his body, sheltering her from any danger. Not press her head close against his chest and look heavenward, willing for a moment that the world and all existence might somehow be different.

That he might lie in a silent dell with a beautiful girl and claim her, giving of himself at the same time, knowing that what they did was blessed by—

Faulkner shook himself. What was he thinking of: the dell, the girl, and his sense of it all as somehow being—Willed? Who willed? God? Not as he knew the Creator to be. Something different, then. Ancient, a voice so distant in his mind that it could barely be heard, yet lingering there still.

Protect, the voice whispered, with sudden clarity, like a sword dropped in a cave of crystal, the sound resonating in his soul.

Protect.

And so it was that for the second time in less than a day, Sir William Faulkner Devereaux raised Mistress Sarah Huxley into his arms and carried her, nestled against him, warm and womanly, the very essence of every dream he had ever most secretly possessed.

The door creaked. He shut it behind them and took the steps, two at a time. "Mary," she whispered on a breath of sound. No entreaty there, a warning instead.

He nodded and slowed his pace, going as quietly as he could. There was no reason to disturb the servants. He could care for her well enough himself.

Her room was at the end of the hall. High windows looked out over a walled garden. The floor was of slate, covered here and there by faded Araby carpets. There was a fireplace with a marble mantel and a high four-poster bed with hangings luxuriously embroidered.

The bed was unmade, the covers tossed, as though she had slept restlessly. Gently, he laid her in it. He meant—truly he did—to let her go and step back. To take his leave and return to the Rose. To never refer by word or deed to the events of that night unless she chose herself to bring them to the light of day.

Truly.

But her fingers twisted in the fine linen of his shirt

and he lost his balance, so that they slipped together to the bed. She sighed, exhausted yet content, and burrowed deeper, seeking warmth.

He sighed too, resigned as he had never been. Brave soul to accept such a fate. Even as he mocked himself, he drew her near, arms gentle, body sternly disciplined.

She stretched her limbs, moving against him. He felt the brush of her thighs and hips, the touch of her breasts. Jaw clenched, he waited as pounding waves of need pulsed through him. Resolve was his armor, honor his shield. He would not yield no matter how the fire raged, how she tempted him, how much he longed.

She turned in the curve of his body, her head on his chest. A faint smile touched her lips. Her hand still gripped his shirt, but more lightly now. Her eyelids, almost translucent, fluttered once . . . again . . . once more.

She slept.

He did not, at least not then, but girded himself for a night that might well prove endless. Yet whatever gods were laughing—and he suspected they were many—some at least proved merciful. The trip from London had been long, the rest little. He too felt the weight of sleep tugging at him until, at long last, consciousness slipped away.

8

A door creaked. Faulkner stirred reluctantly. He knew that sound, had heard it before. He was carrying Sarah into the house. She was wearing only a night robe almost transparent from the damp. He had, unaccountably, come upon her on the road. She had tried to get away from him but he would not allow it and now—

The door creaked again. He swam upward through layers of sleep, summoned by that sound. It was not quite as he remembered. It was—

Nearer. Very near. Outside in the hall.

His eyes opened. Odd, he had noticed before that the ceiling of his room was blue. He'd thought it white. He turned his head slightly, seeing the bed curtains hanging nearby. Surely the Rose did not possess such refinements.

There was a slight pressure against his arm. He looked down at amber silk spread in disarray over the pillow. Surely he had gone to bed alone?

Memory flowed back and, with it, urgency. Outside the window, the first faint light of dawn shone. It was enough. The household—Mistress Sarah Huxley's household—was astir!

The knowledge had not so much a salutary effect as an energizing one. He spared a quick glance for the woman snuggled so trustingly against him, enough to assure himself that she appeared to have survived the night intact.

Grimacing at the thought, he fairly leaped from the bed and made for the window. His foot snagged on the frame, but he got it over and perched for a moment on the eaves before realizing they could not hold his weight. Flailing just ever so slightly, he managed to reach the branches of a nearby tree and, by dint of considerable effort, swung himself down until he could drop, not without some discomfort, to the ground.

Rising, he dusted himself off with a rueful apology to his own consequence. How long had it been since he'd fled a lady's bedchamber so ignominiously? Many years and much living had robbed the experience of its enjoyment. Or perhaps it was merely because he had suffered the penalty without first savoring the delights?

Limping slightly, although he would never have admitted it, Faulkner hobbled down the lane. Behind him, the sun rose in glory, mockingly.

Early as it was, the Rose was open. John Morley was behind the counter, his daughter as well. What was her name, Annalise? A pretty thing, all golden hair and dimpled smiles. She made him think of the blancmange pastries the ladies at court were ever eating, not at all to his taste.

He waited until she went toward the kitchen and

Morley's back was turned before sneaking up the stairs. His room was at the top. He entered, closed the door, and leaned against it with a sigh of relief. Mistress Huxley's honor was preserved. Never mind that she might be less than grateful. He would deal with that later.

For the moment, he was still tired. Without bothering to pull the covers loose, he fell across the bed and, in a scant moment or two, was blissfully snoring.

The door creaked. Faulkner groaned. This was more than any man should be asked to bear. He raised his head just far enough to see a close-cropped gray head and two remorseless blue eyes.

"Sir," Crispin said, the single syllable encompassing a wealth of censure.

"I was asleep," Faulkner complained.

The valet sniffed. He entered further and shut the door behind him. "My apologies. When I heard you come in, I thought you might require some service."

"Sleep, Crispin. I require sleep." It was a vain hope. Having made the vast sacrifice of leaving London in order to accompany his master, a fact of which he had made mention not more than three dozen times during their journey, Crispin was not inclined to be tolerant.

"It is morning, sir, and if I understood correctly when we began this venture, you were anxious to conclude it as quickly as possible. If that has changed, I would appreciate being informed."

"Would you be happier elsewhere than in my employ?" Faulkner inquired, mildly to be sure, for this was a topic that had come up with some regularity in the more than ten years of their dealings together, beginning in the army where they both served, albeit in very different capacities, and continuing after

Faulkner returned to civilian life and brought his irascible manservant with him.

"I don't know, sir," Crispin replied with the air of a man turning over an interesting possibility, one he is not at all inclined to dismiss. "Although the Marquess of Shrewshire has suggested that any time I am inclined to ascertain that fact I am welcome in his household."

"He keeps a poor table."

"There is that, sir. Speaking of which, breakfast is being served."

"At this hour?" It was barely dawn. Why would anyone want to eat now?

"We are in the country, sir."

"The country," Faulkner grumbled, sinking back onto the bed, "is a convenient place for holding battles, nothing more."

"I could not agree more, sir. If you will allow me to remove your boots, I will see to it that they are polished." Punctiliously, Crispin did not comment on his master's having gone to bed still fully dressed and shod.

There was a clatter in the courtyard below, a wagonload of local farmers, by the sound of them, on their way to market. A servant girl called hello. A dog began to bark. Together, they almost managed to drown out the cock that chose that moment to crow.

"Don't bother," Faulkner said. He sat up again and swung his legs off the bed. "They'll only get dirty again."

Crispin groaned. His master's practicality always irked him. "Appearances should be maintained, even in so rustic a place as this."

"Only one appearance counts," Faulkner replied.

His thoughts drifted back to Sarah, white wraith that she had been on the midnight lane, and what could possibly have put her there. Avebury held too many mysteries for a rational man to tolerate.

He flipped open the top of the leather trunk set at the foot of the bed and removed a black scabbard. Silently, he buckled it around his lean waist.

Crispin stiffened. The sword had not been worn since their return to England, his master having never felt more than the need for a short dagger in London or elsewhere. "Sir?"

"Power counts, Crispin," Faulkner said quietly. "The appearance of it and the reality. Is that ham I smell?"

The aroma floated through the open window, reminding him that he was more hungry than tired. This place seemed to awaken all his appetites.

"I believe so, sir," Crispin murmured.

"Breakfast, then. Tell Morley we'll require our rooms a few days more, not longer."

The valet hastened off. Faulkner descended more slowly. He had much to think about, and not the least was the irony of attempting to meet magic with steel. Magic? Where had that errant thought come from? There was no magic, not here or anywhere else. Not in the stone circles or the long barrows. And not, most particularly, in Mistress Sarah Huxley.

There was only reason. The world was built on it. Nothing else could be allowed to intrude. And yet, the thought lingered, as though dancing before him along the narrow, worn steps. He put it down to an empty stomach and a fogged mind. Both would be better for the ham.

* * *

"Tea?" Annalise asked. She gestured slightly with the pot.

Faulkner nodded. He had a table to himself in the inn's common room, the other customers keeping their distance not out of any hostility but with due regard for the proprieties. That and the inadvisability of breakfasting with a man who looked as though he would be just as happy to slice through one of them as through the ham lying on his plate.

Annalise poured. Buxom blancmange, he amended, a well-endowed young woman in a frilly blouse tied at mid-cleavage, her waist nipped in and the curve of her hips visible through her bright blue skirt. Her golden hair was piled in curls atop her head, secured by a scrap of lace cap. The whole effect was a bit more sophisticated than he'd expect to find hereabouts.

Morley was behind the counter, polishing tankards. He watched them, as though resigned to the need for his daughter to serve so august a guest but determined, by God, that nothing untoward would occur.

Faulkner hid a smile. Did but Morley know it, his fair flower was as safe as a babe in arms. Sarah, now, that was another matter. He chewed the ham thoughtfully. There was the delicate matter of how to approach her when next they met. How much would she remember? How much would she admit?

He was determined to get to the bottom of whatever had happened, but side by side with that marched a reluctance to hurt her. Still, he was here to investigate the murders, and he could always claim that her extraordinary behavior suggested she might have evidence to contribute. But did it really? Or was there an entirely different reason why Mistress Sarah Huxley had been out on the road, near naked and looking as though all the demons from hell were chasing her?

There was only person he might possibly ask, and that gentleman was even then entering the common room. Sir Isaac was a natty figure in satin frock coat and breeches, carrying a silver-headed walking stick and with his wig on more or less straight for a change. He glanced around, saw Faulkner, and made a brisk line for his table.

"I thought you'd be an early riser," Sir Isaac said as Faulkner stood to welcome him. The man's age demanded such courtesy, if nothing else, but there was a certain awe about the workings of his mind, as though the frail body containing it were no more than an illusion, hiding a vast presence somewhere just beyond sight.

"I'm not, actually," Faulkner said as they sat down together. "Not by inclination."

"But by training, surely? Isn't morning the best time for battle?"

"Best wouldn't necessarily be my description. May I suggest the ham? It's excellent."

Sir Isaac raised a hand to summon Annalise. When she had come and gone, the older man said, "You've been here almost a full day. Would you care to tell me what you have discovered?"

"Not much," Faulkner replied.

It was not quite true. He had discovered a woman who both baffled and enticed him, a village that appeared to exist in both past and present simultaneously, and a part of himself he had never suspected existed. But that was not what Sir Isaac meant.

"At the moment," Faulkner said, "there is no evidence that the Gypsies were killed by anyone other than a fellow Romany. However," he added as Sir Isaac was about to speak, "there is also no evidence that the murderer was one of their own. I did speak with Constable Duggin yesterday afternoon, and he assured me that the investigation had been most thorough."

Sir Isaac snorted. "Investigation my left foot. They slammed the books so hard the dust still hasn't settled."

"Precisely. As far as I can tell, there effectively was no investigation, which suggests that the good constable may have feared where it might lead."

"Wasn't anxious to cause a rumpus in his own backyard, as it were?"

Faulkner nodded. "That raises the question of whether he suspected anyone in particular. Did he think a quiet word in the right ear would forestall further trouble? Or is he trying to keep an eye on whoever he thinks did it, hoping to discourage any further killings?"

"Or does he merely wish the whole mess would go away of its own accord?"

"It won't," Faulkner said. "The taste for blood is never easily sated."

"On the battlefield, perhaps not. But here, in this simple, wholesome place?"

"It requires more thought," Faulkner admitted, "if only to ease Mistress Huxley's concerns." He looked at Sir Isaac directly. "She is the sole reason you wrote to the duke?"

The older man sighed. "It reflects poorly on me, I know, but in the overall scheme of things, two deaths are not especially significant. Left to myself, I would have regretted them and gone on. But Sarah—" he paused, thinking for several moments. "She has been a great help to me. When I go out among the remains by myself, they are flatter, somehow, less accessible than when she is with me."

"You realize," Faulkner said softly, "that makes little sense?"

"Indeed, it makes none. But as I said yesterday, I believe she has a special affinity for this place, perhaps by virtue of her people having been here so long."

"There must be others who go back as far?"

"I doubt it. Did Sarah tell you anything about her house?"

Faulkner shook his head. "We talked about the killings and the village. She agreed, somewhat reluctantly, to show me around the ruins."

"That's interesting. The villagers say she speaks of them rarely, but they believe she can often be found among them. At any rate, in the basement of Sarah's house there is a Roman bath. The formidable Mary Damas told me of it. She claims that beneath the ruins of the bath is an even older well, dating from pre-Roman times."

"Fascinating, but what has that to do with Sarah?"

"Therein lies the tale. If Missus Damas is to be believed, the Huxley family has always lived in the same place. I stress *always.* They go back before the Normans to the days of the great Julius Caesar and even further."

"I know of no family that can trace its lineage so far."

"Nor do I, but think on it. We all had ancestors, and our ancestors had ancestors. None of us popped out of thin air. The problem is that people move around so much, names change, lines die out, particularly when they are only traced through the male. But not here, you see. Here they stayed. Here the connection remained. One has to wonder why."

"Lethargy?" Faulkner suggested. He was being only half facetious. The notion that there was anything mystical about Sarah and her connection to this place made him uneasy. He was tempted to reject it out of hand.

"Use your imagination, sir. Avebury is unique. Neither Stonehenge nor any other stone circle rivals it. People chose to expend an extraordinary amount of effort here. I wish to learn why."

Faulkner finished the last of his tea. He set the cup down. "And do you think you can?"

Sir Isaac's eyes crinkled. "Probably not, but I will enjoy the attempt."

"I wish I shared your confidence. Merely trying to solve two murders is challenge enough for me."

"Nothing is more complex than the human mind, my boy. Don't underestimate your task. However, neither should you doubt your own ability. Despite our brief acquaintance, I have noticed that—"

Sir Isaac went on but Faulkner did not hear him. He was distracted by a flash of white at the entrance to the common room, a ripple of movement, and the overwhelming realization that what he had been waiting for since first waking was suddenly within his grasp.

9

She should not have come. That much was immediately clear. Her knees were quaking and she felt an acutely unpleasant sensation in her mid-region. Had she a particle of sense, she would be home safe, doing her utmost to forget the events of the night before.

Waking in the rumpled bed, sunlight streaming through the windows, she had told herself it was all a dream. All of it. Not merely the stone and the man, the young priestess and the surging heat, troubling though that had been. Worse yet had come on the road, trying desperately to reach home only to find there, in the shadows of the oak, the last man she would have chosen to come upon. Or the first.

She would not think of that. It was a dream, nothing more. So she wanted to believe and almost managed until, turning in the bed, she spied a length of thin black

silk lying on the pillow beside her. She took it, fingers
trembling, and saw it for what it was, a ribbon unlike
any she herself had ever used, the kind a man wore to
hold his hair in a neat queue at the nape of his neck.
Faulkner wore his hair like that. Faulkner had shared
her bed. It had not been a dream.

Even then, stunned as she was, her first instinct
had been to hide. But where? Avebury was no longer
the sanctuary it had always been for her. First the
killings and now this. She had no safe place.

But she did have courage, born in ancient times
and ancient ways, honed through all the generations.
She would neither run nor hide. Avebury was hers.
He was the interloper, not she. He had to be faced,
and the sooner the better.

That conviction got her as far as the Rose, no
mean feat in itself. It even got her through the door.
But there it faltered. She stared, wide-eyed, unable to
advance or retreat, as Faulkner came toward her.

He needed to shave. The night's growth of beard
gave him the look of a brigand. No, she corrected, it
merely emphasized what had always been there.

He wore black, apparently his preferred color. His
hair hung loosely, brushing the collar of his frock coat.

She cleared her throat, thought of the priestess,
and held out her hand. "I believe this is yours."

He stared at the length of ribbon nestled in her
palm. Slowly, a faint smile lifted the corners of his
mouth. "I believe you are right."

The skin of her palm must be unduly sensitive. It
reacted even to the faint brush of his fingers as he
reclaimed the ribbon. Their eyes met, but only for an
instant. Sarah preferred to study the wall over his left
shoulder.

"Have you breakfasted?" he asked, all courtesy, as though they were acquaintances who had happened to encounter one another. Perhaps that was how he was with women. She had no way of knowing.

"I'm not hungry. I came to ask Sir Isaac if he has any plans for today."

It was a lie and they both knew it, but Faulkner had the grace to pretend he believed her. "He hasn't mentioned any, but we've been busy talking over the killings. Come and join us."

Violence and death seemed a safe enough topic, much safer certainly than desire. Sir Isaac held a chair for her. She sat, glad of the support. He regarded her benignly. "I was planning to come by later. It's time we ventured a bit farther afield, don't you think?"

"Farther?" Sarah repeated. She scarcely knew what he said, so concentrated was she on Faulkner. Had she truly lain in his arms all unknowingly? In the bright light of morning, it seemed inconceivable. Yet there was the black ribbon, tied into his hair once again, the small but incontrovertible proof of what had transpired.

"Silbury," Sir Isaac was saying. "Not natural at all, you know. Couldn't possibly be, far too uniform. But when one thinks of the work . . . take a ride out . . . measurements . . . "

"What?" Sarah asked, abruptly dragging her attention from Faulkner. "What did you say?"

"Dear girl, I thought I was clear enough. The circles, fascinating though they are, are far from the whole story. There are numerous features to the land hereabouts that bear investigating, beginning with Silbury."

"What is Silbury?" Faulkner asked.

"The hill to the southeast," Sir Isaac said. "You must have noticed it."

"It can hardly be missed. Do you have any idea who flattened off the top?"

"The same people who built it," Sir Isaac said. When he saw Faulkner's surprise, he smiled patiently. "As I have already indicated, it is far too regular in form to be a work of nature. Incredible as it sounds, I believe it to be a completely artificial construction. In short, the work of man."

"But it's immense," Faulkner pointed out. Even seen from a distance, the hill looked far too large to have been created by any people, much less those of long ago.

"We shall see," Sir Isaac said. "I propose to begin measurement today." A thought occurred to him. "The Romany camped not far from there. Perhaps you would like to accompany us to search for clues."

"It is unlikely that any would remain after all this time," Sarah said hastily.

"All the same," Faulkner replied, "it is a good suggestion. Besides, I'd like to see this Silbury at closer hand."

There was a great deal she might have said about his duty to remain in the village, to seek out the killer there. But she knew it would be futile. He would do as he wished.

Like it or not—and she told herself she most certainly did not—Faulkner was coming with them to Silbury. She took a deep breath, steeling herself, and accepted what she could not change.

* * *

"Hold that steady," Sir Isaac called. He bent to peer through the surveyor's sight. "There, that's it, one more moment." Quickly, he scribbled in his notebook. "Fine, let's move on now."

Faulkner lifted the sighting stick and paced off the distance Sir Isaac indicated before setting it down again. Sarah stood a little to the side, watching them. The sun was approaching its zenith. They had reached Silbury several hours before and had been working ever since. She marveled at Sir Isaac's fortitude, but even more so she was struck by Faulkner's patience. He seemed to have nothing whatsoever on his mind except assisting the elderly scholar.

He had spared her barely a glance. Not that she minded, not at all. She greatly preferred that he make no reference to the previous night by either word or deed. Perhaps if he did that long enough, she might eventually be able to forget what had happened.

And perhaps she would sprout wings and fly. Sighing, she kicked at the dirt with her foot. Much as she hated to admit it, she was bored. Sir Isaac and Faulkner were completely caught up in the fascination of Silbury but she had lived with it forever, knew it far more intimately than they ever would. For her it was less a mystery than a reality that, no matter how stunning, became an accepted part of life.

"Do you realize," Sir Isaac said, after he had scribbled some more, "that if my calculations are correct, this mound contains some quarter of a million cubic meters of material? Now if you figure the average size of a basket load with a weight that could be lifted by an ordinary person, that would take—" He scowled down at the numbers. "Perhaps I did something wrong."

"Why?" Faulkner asked. He put the sighting stick

aside and came over to look at the equations for himself.

"It would mean that approximately thirty-five *million* basket loads of material had to be brought to this site and carried up the sides of the mound as it grew in order to achieve the results we see today. Clearly, that's impossible."

"Not so," Sarah said quietly. Despite herself, she was drawn to the discussion. "If several hundred people from the surrounding region worked on it during the two or three months a year when crops can't be grown, they could have done it, provided they were willing to take enough time."

"It would have required a century or more," Faulkner said. "Men who began the work would never have lived to see it completed, nor their sons either."

"It was the same with the great cathedrals," Sarah replied. "Yet we accept that they exist."

"Yes, but these are primitives we're talking about," Sir Isaac insisted. "They possessed no machines and they had no grasp of science or mathematics, not to mention the extraordinary organization that would have been required. How could they possibly have achieved such marvels?"

She shrugged, not inclined to argue with him. Let him think what he would. Still, she could not quite resist a final comment. "Perhaps they were not as you believe."

Sir Isaac went off, shaking his head, to examine the mound further. Sarah assumed Faulkner would go with him. She welcomed the respite. Her head throbbed, and the cider they had brought along with them had failed to quench her thirst.

Beyond the mound was a copse of willow trees, and beyond it sparkling water ran over moss-draped stones. Avebury and its surroundings were blessed by many such streams, but she thought the sweetest of all was this spring called Swallowhead in the shadow of Silbury mound. Kneeling to drink, she did not hear the footfall until it was directly behind her.

She stiffened but did not turn. "I thought you were with Sir Isaac?"

"His measurements are done," Faulkner said. "He is happily exploring. I won't be missed."

"All the same, he is elderly. I'm not sure he should be left on his own. If he fell—" She rose, still without looking at him, and took a quick step to the side, as though to go around.

He put out a hand and stopped her. His fingers were stark brown against the paleness of her wrist. "Sir Isaac would be pained to hear you describe him so. Besides, we need to talk."

"No," she said quickly, "we don't. If you are finished with the mound, I can show you the direction to the Romany camp. There may be many useful clues still there."

"Dead fires and rabbit bones. Stop running away from me."

"I'm not."

"You are."

"Please."

The sun dazzled. It was to blame, that and the confusion he so easily aroused in her. That was why she did not draw away as his arms closed around her. Why she made no protest when his head lowered dark against the sky. Why, when his mouth touched hers, she did not resist the surge of raw pleasure he evoked.

Her lips parted, soft and yearning. The sensation was completely new to her, yet familiar. His arms tightened further, and a deep, rasping sound came from his throat.

He was so stunningly different from herself. That simple realization was, in its own way, as potent as the hot, yearning languor coursing through her. She was nothing at all like him, yet they were identical. Different? The same? It made no sense, nothing did, only the strength of his body, protective yet demanding, and the burgeoning knowledge deep within her that she wanted this man with a fierceness that banished reticence and even, for a time, made her forget all fear.

There, on the banks of the Swallowhead, in the shadow of the mound, the passion that had been growing between them from the first sprang free. Had it not been day, had not Sir Isaac been nearby, they might well have sought the fragrant, welcoming ground.

But a crow cawed above, the breeze shifted, and they heard on the ripple of air, the elderly voice calling to them. "Mistress Sarah, Sir William, come and see what I've found!"

Faulkner raised his head slowly. He took a deep, shuddering breath. "It had better be a live Druid complete with wizard's hat and magic book."

"You're thinking of Merlin," she murmured. Her lips felt astoundingly sensitive, almost as though they no longer belonged fully to her.

"I'm not thinking at all," he said and stepped back. His eyes glowed silver. "We still have to talk."

"Not here."

"Sir William!"

Swiftly, she turned in the direction of the voice. Sir

Isaac waved energetically to them from atop the mound.

"Oh, my God," Sarah murmured, "he climbed all the way up there by himself."

"And a good job he seems to have made of it," Faulkner said. He took her arm. "Let's see if we can do the same."

10

"*Antlers,*" *Sir Isaac* exclaimed. "I dug only the smallest way and there they were. It is well known that the high priests of the Druids festooned themselves with antlers for their ceremonials. They must have taken place on this very spot."

Faulkner looked at the scraps of weathered bone Sir Isaac held. They were unmistakably antlers, but he was not certain they meant anything at all. Nor did he particularly care. He had far more pressing concerns on his mind, chief among them why he, who had never regarded any woman as of more significance than a pleasing glass of claret, should suddenly be so entranced by a country maid given to wandering about almost naked in the dead of night. Clearly, leaving London had not had a good effect on him.

"This entire mound should be excavated," Sir Isaac was saying. "That's what's needed. Get a team out here, start at the top, and keep digging until we've found out exactly what's what." He looked around eagerly, eyes bright like an overly excited bird. "Perhaps it's a burial. Think of the chieftain—say, rather, the king!—who would have warranted such an effort. He could still be down there along with his full regalia: gold, weapons, the lot. I'm going to propose it to Her Majesty. Why, it could be no less than Arturius Rex himself!"

"Calm yourself," Sarah entreated. Sir Isaac's face had turned bright red. He appeared in the throes of an excitement so intense it could barely be contained. "Don't you think that if this was the tomb of Arthur, all sorts of legends would surround it? No one has ever mentioned Arthur in connection with Silbury. People merely say the old ones built it and leave it at that."

"That is puzzling," Sir Isaac admitted, relenting slightly. "No legends, you say?"

"The old ones built Silbury," Sarah insisted, "before Arthur, before the Romans, before even the Druids. No one knows how far back it goes, only that it seems to have always been here. Surely you can be content with that?"

Sir Isaac's shoulders sagged slightly. "Forgive me. I allowed myself to be carried away. It's just that I can't shake the feeling that this has been a place of great importance, perhaps in some way still is."

He gestured out over the landscape to Avebury in the near distance, the stone circles standing clearly in the noonday light and, beyond them, the serpentine stretch of Kennet Avenue leading off out of sight. "So much effort was expended over so much time by people we know nothing about." He looked at Sarah. "Doesn't that trouble you?"

"Perhaps I lack your curiosity," she murmured. His face remained flushed and his breathing, now that the energy of discovery had passed, seemed labored. Gently, she said, "I think we should return to the village."

Faulkner agreed. He assisted Sir Isaac down the mound, the descent taking far longer than the climb up as the elderly gentleman's strength seemed to have deserted him. They went carefully and were relieved when they at last reached the bottom.

Faulkner's coach waited on the road a little distance away. By the time they reached it, Sir Isaac's color had faded to a worrisome gray. Sarah got in beside him and gently took his hand in hers. Faulkner mounted the black steed he favored and road along beside them.

By the time they neared the Rose, Sir Isaac was insisting that he was fine and merely needed to rest. Sarah was unconvinced. She asked Annalise to make a soothing potash water for him, giving her precise instructions for its contents, and made him promise that he would not stir from bed for at least a day.

That done, she slipped outside and walked hastily down the lane toward her house. It would not be correct to say that she ran—precisely—only that anyone coming upon her would have seen a young woman in a great hurry. Her haste had nothing whatsoever to do with Faulkner and his stated intention to discuss the events of the previous night. Nothing whatsoever.

Or so she told herself as she hurried past the

thatched cottages with their whitewashed walls that clustered within the circle of Avebury's stones. Just beyond was the church, set back from the lane with its single crenelated tower rising above the trees. A path connected the church and parsonage to the lane. A slender black-garbed figure strolled along it. When he saw Sarah, his face lighted up and he quickened his pace.

"Mistress Huxley, how nice to come upon you! I gather from Missus Damas that you have been much occupied of late."

Sarah managed a wan smile. She did not want to hurt Curate Edwards's feelings, but neither did she feel disposed to listen to yet another lengthy exposition on the precise meaning of a specific scripture passage and how it related to their daily lives. Equally, she was not inclined to answer any questions about her own activities.

"I have just left Sir Isaac to rest," she said briskly. "We climbed Silbury this morning, and I fear it tired him. Truth be told, it did the same to me, so if you would excuse me—"

"Should I pay a call on him, do you think?" The curate's long, rather aquiline face creased with concern. "Being a stranger hereabouts, he might be in need of spiritual sustenance."

Eager though she was to part from the well-intentioned but overly eager minister, Sarah could not bring herself to turn him loose on old Sir Isaac. "I think it would be better just to let him rest. If he does feel the need, perhaps he will seek you out."

"I suppose that's possible," Edwards replied, but reluctantly, for he was a hardworking young man somewhat dismayed by the self-sufficiency of the souls entrusted to his care. That had not troubled his predecessor, Dr. Geoffrey Holbein, who never seemed particularly suited to the task fate had set him. He was retired now and living quietly in a wing of the parsonage, his mantle now resting on far more energetic shoulders.

"How is Dr. Holbein?" Sarah asked. She had not seen him in some time and did wonder how he was faring.

"In decline, I'm afraid," Edwards said somberly. "He keeps largely to himself despite my efforts to draw him out." On a brighter note, he added, "Tell me, have you met the gentleman from London who arrived yesterday?"

Met him, lain in his arms, kissed him, fled from him. "Briefly," she said.

"Is it true that he has come about the Gypsies' deaths?"

"Something was mentioned to that effect."

"Extraordinary, all the way from London. How does Constable Duggin feel about it, I wonder?"

"I have no idea, but you could ask him. Now I really must—"

"The gentleman, what is his name?"

"Sir William Devereaux."

"I thought that was what I'd heard. You do realize that he is of considerable consequence. Right hand to Marlborough, they say. He couldn't be here just about the Gypsies. It must be because of Sir Isaac."

"Possibly. Do excuse—"

"Have you any idea where Devereaux might be found? I would like to pay my respects."

"At the Rose," Sarah said without compunction. Let Faulkner manage the irrepressible curate. While he was doing so, he would not be able to come after her. "I saw him there not ten minutes ago. If you hurry—"

"Oh, yes, I must. Thank you, dear lady, but I will call, be assured. We must chat about the new roof and the organ—the organ is dreadful—and oh, yes, it occurred to me we need a sewing group for the ladies. I'm hoping you will agree to lead it. But for the moment—" He looked down the lane toward the inn, clearly torn.

"I believe Sir William said something about leaving shortly."

"Oh, dear, then I really must beg your leave. Farewell, mistress." Half tripping in his eagerness, Curate Edwards hastened off toward the village.

Sarah exhaled in relief. She would send a donation for the roof and the organ. As for the sewing circle, not all the wild horses in Christendom could drag her into such a thing.

Behind her, the sun was angling toward the west. She reached her house, passing through the gate and up the flagstone path. Muted sounds came from the kitchen: Missus Damas giving instruction to the maid, the clank of pots. She slipped past and went out back to the walled garden. There all was silence save for birdsong and the flutter of leaves in the high poplar trees that grew, a second line of defense, just within the walls.

She sat on a stone bench and looked down the neat beds interspersed with gravel paths. The garden was very old. Its location and some of the plants still growing in it suggested it had once served the medieval keep where her house now stood.

But there were other indications, older still, in the stones at the very bottom of the walls, different from those above and marked with ancient symbols that also appeared in her drawings. Even the bench where she sat rested on rough stone pedestals like miniature versions of the sentinels that formed the vast stone circles. A seeking hand could trace on their surfaces the design of antlers identical to those Sir Isaac had found upon the mound.

She closed her eyes, willing such thoughts to stop. The calmness she always sought here had deserted her. She was filled with uncertainty and, worse, growing dread. Long shadows drifted across the herb beds and the paths. Soon the sun would set. It would be night again.

Her throat tightened. She clasped her hands in her lap as a wave of panic threatened to engulf her. She did not dare sleep, not so long as there was a risk that what had happened the night before might happen again.

Since childhood, the dreams had come to her. In time, she learned to accept them. But none had been as disturbing as the dream the previous night. Never had she awakened to find herself anywhere but safe in her own bed.

Now, for whatever reason, the dreams had turned shockingly intimate. Worse, she was driven to enact them in some way she could not begin to grasp. What control she had managed to maintain was in danger of slipping entirely.

She must not sleep. Somehow, she had to find a way to stay awake, at least until she gained a better understanding of what was happening to her. There were herbs she could take infused in tea. If they failed, there were certain roots and seeds that when swallowed would hold sleep at bay.

Never in her life had she resorted to such things, but now she felt she could not avoid them. Sleep had become her enemy. The thought of oncoming night made her flinch. Sarah cast a quick look at the sky. Several hours of day yet remained. She would have to put them to the best possible use.

11

Faulkner checked on Sir Isaac before retiring. The elderly man was sitting propped up in bed, by all evidence much recovered from his exertions. He had a book on his lap and a collection of tempting dishes on the table beside him. Annalise had done her utmost and Crispin had also been by. The valet was scandalized to learn that Sir Isaac had come north by himself, without proper looking after, as Crispin put it.

"Gave me to understand a gentleman never goes anywhere unattended," Sir Isaac said. "But I'm not used to being fussed over. Tried to tell him that, but he'd have none of it. Must say, though, this soup he organized is quite tasty."

"He's a good sort. Ever since we came back to England he really hasn't had enough to do. Perhaps you can keep him busy for a while."

It was a tactful way to suggest that Sir Isaac allow

himself to be cosseted a bit. He was, after all, a national treasure.

"I don't suppose he'd like to go about measuring stones?" Sir Isaac suggested hopefully.

Faulkner thought for a moment, trying to envision the redoubtable Crispin scrambling over earthworks and around standing stones. He shook his head.

"He tends more toward arranging decent food and seeing to it that one has a clean shirt. Actually, he's quite good at that. I remember one time in France; it had been pouring rain for weeks and we were all immeasurably filthy. Most of our reserves had rotted and even the wine casks had sprung a leak. Crispin disappeared for a few hours. He returned with new wine, freshly baked bread, and an entire pig. No one ever asked him how he did it and he never offered to tell, but I can say he did immeasurable good for Marlborough and his officers that day."

Sir Isaac laughed. "A sterling performance to be sure. Very well, I will surrender myself to his ministrations for the present. Sadly, I don't seem to have the energy I used to."

"You manage remarkably well."

"Kind of you to say so, but it can be so frustrating. This place . . . what I sometimes seem to glimpse hovering round the corners of my mind but can never quite pin down. There is so much I would like to do."

"How much longer do you plan to remain?"

"I'd intended to spend only a fortnight so I've already overstayed. I do have responsibilities in London, other projects." Sir Isaac's sigh was just a bit overdone. "I fear I will be unable to complete even the most basic measurements."

"Perhaps I can help?" Faulkner suggested innocently.

"Oh, no, I wouldn't dream of it. Bad enough you got sent up here to investigate the murders. It would be far too great an imposition to ask anything more of you."

"Not at all. I will be going around the village and the surrounding area. It should be a simple matter to take a few measurements for you."

"Alas," Sir Isaac said, "they can be cumbersome to do. Often, it requires assistance." His eyes brightened. "Wait now, I've a thought. Perhaps Mistress Huxley could be engaged. She has been a tremendous help to me. There's no reason why she can't be the same for you."

"A thought indeed," Faulkner murmured. He had the distinct impression that he was being led down the garden path, but as this took him in the direction he wanted to go anyway, he made no objection.

"Splendid," Sir Isaac said. "I am much relieved. Of course, I won't be abed for long. Not more than a day or two. Do you think you can accomplish much in that time?"

Faulkner's was a hunter's smile. "You may be surprised."

He took his leave a short time later, his mood much improved, and presently sought his bed. The journey from London and the scant rest he'd had the night before had left him exhausted. Yet as he lay on the down-filled mattress, staring up at the beamed ceiling, his thoughts were of Sarah—mystery that she was—and how she fared this night. At length, sleep claimed him but sylvan eyes followed his dreams.

* * *

Moonrise and the owl cried. It fluttered in the branches just beyond Sarah's window. She sat, still fully dressed, at the table across the room from her bed. Feather soft, the bed beckoned. But she had only to envision a black ribbon coiled on the pillow to steel her resolve.

A lamp burned beside her. The herbs she had sipped had done their work. She was tired but not so much so that she had to fear sleep's overcoming her. She would remain awake through this night of the horned moon.

The book she held was one of those usually kept in the wooden chest at the back of her wardrobe. It was small, cloth-bound, and filled with sketches. The date on the last page indicated it was completed five years before.

Halfway through the book was the portrait of a man. It was a profile, but it was clear he was smiling. His hair was tied at the nape of his neck with a leather thong. He was bare-chested, dressed in breeches, with a hunting spear in one hand. He looked young, virile, and entrancing. A man seen through the eyes of love.

She had drawn him as she drew all the rest, without thinking or questioning, in the strange state that came upon her when the world faded away and there was only memory. Not hers but far older, locked into the stones and the mound, whispered on the wind, borne on the fire. Drawn him and forgotten, gone on to all the rest, but now, leafing through the book, she found him again and felt the shock of recognition. She had been in this man's arms, felt his mouth on hers.

Or was it Faulkner she remembered? There was a

resemblance, although Faulkner was larger and older, the realization perhaps of what the young hunter could become if he lived long enough. Had he? She had no memory of his fate, had neither drawn nor dreamt it. For that she was grateful.

The owl called again. She closed the book and rose, going over to the window. The moon's pale light reflected off the stately poplars beside the road. Farther off, down the winding lane, Avebury lay in shadow. The night was pleasantly warm. She felt an urge to venture out, fully conscious and aware, and try to retrace her steps of the night before. But there was risk in that. She could not forget that there might be a murderer still abroad. Faulkner might feel confident wandering the midnight lanes, but she did not.

And yet, the velvet darkness was enticing. She knew the lane by day or night as well as she knew the contours of her own face. Moreover, she hated the thought that fear would keep her trapped inside. Night had always sheltered her much like the walls of her garden. She had never been reluctant to go out in it before.

Still, she hesitated and not only because of the possibility, however remote, that a killer might also be abroad. She feared the contours of this world would prove too fragile to contain the madness that seemed to be growing in her.

Lingering there by the window, wrapped in a fringed paisley shawl that smelled of last summer's lilac, she debated what to do. Stay inside where there was at least the illusion of safety? Or dare the unknown?

The question remained unsettled when suddenly,

in the direction of the village, a light flared. It moved, bobbing and weaving, amid the trees and around the cottages. On the night wind, she thought she caught the sound of voices raised in agitation. Something was happening.

Her doubts forgotten, she hurried from the room, down the stairs, and out the front door. Beyond her gate, she paused. There were yet more lights to be seen. If this continued, soon everyone in the village would be awake. Her throat tightened. Had there been another killing?

Picking up her skirts, she ran down the lane.

12

Faulkner shot upright in the bed. He had been in the midst of a dream he was reluctant to leave, something about the mossy dell and Sarah in his arms. A laughing, happy Sarah with none of the shadows he had come to associate with her.

He would gladly have remained within the dream while it ran its promising course. But the sudden outcry in the courtyard hurtled him back into a far harsher reality.

The room was dark. He rose naked from the bed and reached for tinder and candle. When a flame was struck, he carried it over to the window and looked out.

Shapes moved below. He recognized John Morley, a lantern clutched in his hand, and beside him . . . no, it couldn't be. Not the redoubtable Crispin?

"What ails you, man?" Faulkner called from the window. The frame came up high enough for modesty's sake, and he was not about to delay long enough to dress.

"My apologies, sir, but there has been a disturbance."

"What kind of disturbance?" He had heard nothing, lost in the dell and the dream.

"Moans, sir, and the clanking of chains. It was really quite loud."

"You sleep like the dead, lad," Sir Isaac exclaimed. He too was below, hastily garbed and leaning on his cane. He looked excited and quite pleased with whatever was going on.

"I won't have it," Morley said. His face was flushed and his grip on the lantern appeared none too steady. "I'll summon a priest if I have to. Have the place exorcised. Nobody's going to do this to me, not dead or alive!"

"A priest!" This from Curate Edwards, who had just arrived from the parsonage, minus his wig and pale with excitement. Morley's threat stopped him in his tracks. "Surely not, good sir. We want no papacy in these parts."

"I'll have anything it takes to put an end to this," Morley insisted. "I pay my shire tax, I serve on juries, and I pour an honest measure. I don't deserve this."

Faulkner summoned patience. In London, he was renowned for his unshakable calm, often to the fury of his enemies. Here, it was all he could do to keep from throttling the lot.

"And what is *this*?" he demanded. "What is happening here?"

"A haunting," Sir Isaac declared. He looked delighted. "An actual, genuine haunting. I've always wanted to encounter one."

There was no going back to bed, that much was obvious to Faulkner. Resigned, he dressed, pulling on black breeches and a shirt. London might pride itself on never sleeping, but bucolic Avebury put it to shame. Truly, it was a place of ceaseless activity.

"Haunted by whom?" he asked when he had joined the growing crowd in the courtyard. The occupants of the cottages that lined the lane had turned out. Several more torches had been lit. The night was almost bright as day.

Off to one side, he saw Constable Duggin, with whom he had spoken, talking energetically with several other men. Nearby a small woman stood supported by a boy. Missus Hemper, he supposed, the wise woman Sarah had wanted to avoid. But where was the good Dr. Quack? Directly opposite his rival, perhaps, a scarecrow of a man frowning fiercely. He strode up to Curate Edwards and pointed a finger in his face as though to demand divine action.

"Monks," Morley said, mouthing the word with disgust. "Flea-bitten, incense-sniffing, fornicating monks."

"At an inn?" Faulkner asked mildly. "You'd think they'd know better."

"It wasn't always an inn, the Rose wasn't. Used to be a monastery until Henry Tudor broke with Rome. Seized it, he did, drove the monks out for their licentious ways, and took the place for himself."

"I see." Faulkner looked at the inn with new interest. It was in the Tudor style, all right, most probably Elizabethan. The outer walls were crossed by beams that stood out darkly from the whitewashed exterior. But just below the ground-floor windows was stone that looked far older.

"Have the monks always been a problem?" he asked.

Morley shook his head. The fight was going out of him. He looked tired and frustrated. "Not a peep out of them until this last fortnight. Been a horror, it has. Started out small enough, just a few moans from the graveyard back yonder. My room faces that way, so I heard it when no one else did. But then it got worse. I went to see that one, I did." He pointed at Curate Edwards.

"And I explained that exorcism is not a rite of the Church of England. However, I did offer to pray."

"Lot of good it did. How long do you think I'll have a business with this sort of thing going on?" Morley slammed a beefy fist into his palm. "I tell you, I'm getting a priest. There's one over to Dunford. He'll come."

"Wait," Edwards pleaded. "Surely, you wouldn't abandon good Anglican prayer? I'll tell you what, I'll come here. Walk around the place a bit, read scripture, pray. You can do it with me, if you like. That should fix the problem."

"It had better," Morley grumbled. He stalked off, muttering to himself. The word *priest* could be heard again, a defiance hurtled over his shoulder.

Edwards groaned. But he brightened when he spied Annalise standing off to the side, hands clenched before her and her full lips trembling. The curate straightened his shoulders, took a manful breath, and went to offer what consolation he could.

Slowly, the villagers drifted out of the courtyard. Crispin murmured his apologies and offered a hand to help Sir Isaac up the steps. Faulkner was left to himself, even the misbehaving monks having departed.

Or perhaps not all of them, for what was that white

wraith standing just there near the tree? That slender form wrapped in . . . paisley? Prosaic stuff, paisley, for all it was pretty enough. He had a hard time envisioning the specter of a monk decked out in it.

"Mistress Huxley?"

She came forward slowly, the shawl held tight around her, and stood a little way off, regarding him with veiled eyes. "A bit of a to-do."

"Surely not? I presumed this was how the good people of Avebury chose to amuse themselves of a night."

Despite herself, a smile played about the corners of her mouth precisely where he would have liked to touch his own. "Whatever can you be thinking of us?"

"Only that it seems I will have to return to London to get a good night's sleep."

She flushed; even in the moonlight he could see the bloom of color on her cheeks. He hadn't meant to remind her of the night before quite so directly. But having done it, he couldn't regret his frankness either. There had been too little candor between them.

"You weren't sleeping?" he asked.

She shook her head. "I saw the lights. I feared—"

"What?"

"Another murder."

It was a reasonable enough assumption, all things considered. "Do you believe the place is haunted?" he asked.

"I've no idea. But Morley's never impressed me as overly imaginative."

He crossed the short distance between them. She tensed but did not retreat. When he was close enough to smell the perfume of her skin, he asked, "Do you believe in ghosts, Sarah?"

The sudden downcast slant of her eyes, hiding them from him, might have been a reaction to his use of her Christian name. It was improper on such short acquaintance, and doubly so under the circumstances. But he had the fleeting thought that was not what caused her response.

What sort of ghosts wandered about Avebury? The monks rattling their chains over Henry Tudor's arrogance? Or something older, far more difficult to imagine, something rooted in the stone sentinels and the mounded earth?

Something for which Sarah—as Sir Isaac claimed—had a mysterious affinity?

"Allow me to walk you home," he said, not a request but a clear statement of intent.

She started to shake her head, recognized the futility, and shrugged instead. "Very well."

They were halfway down the lane that ran through the center of the village, cutting directly across the great stone circle, when he asked, "What happened to you last night?"

She did not answer at once but continued to walk along beside him, the shawl still wrapped tightly. "Everyone refers to you as the gentleman from London. I thought perhaps you would be too gentlemanly to mention it."

He laughed, thinking of what those who actually knew him would make of that. "You will forgive me, but when I find a beautiful woman wandering along a road late at night, it makes me curious."

"I'm sorry that I can't enlighten you," she said softly. "The truth is, I don't know what happened."

He paused, taking hold of her elbow and turning her so that she faced him. Her hair was braided down her back. A few stray wisps drifted across her brow. Her eyes were wide and luminous, shielded by heavy lashes. The mouth he had briefly tasted was full and ripe. It was incredible that he had ever thought her plain.

"Have you experienced this sort of thing before?" he asked.

"Not that I can remember."

"Do you know what sleepwalking means?"

She looked up, eyes meeting his in surprise. "Sleepwalking?"

"The victim arises from his—or her—bed and moves around as though fully awake. There are obvious dangers, a fall down a flight of stairs for instance, but it is possible for such people to actually to leave their homes and wander outside with absolutely no awareness of doing so."

He paused, resisting the impulse to draw her closer. She looked so damnably delicate, yet that was illusion. There was strength enough in her for ten men and more. "The murders may be preying on your mind. Your concern over them could explain why you would suddenly behave so strangely."

Her eyes flicked with interest. "Perhaps. At any rate, I thank you for your discretion."

"You may rely on it. By the way, despite Sir Isaac's frolicsome behavior tonight, he needs to rest for several more days. I've offered to do some measuring for him. Would you care to accompany me?"

He thought she meant to refuse, but she surprised him.

"Where to?"

"You decide." He did not let his relief show.

They had reached the bottom of the lane near the gate to her house. It was dark except for a light in the window of her room, the selfsame window he had climbed from the previous dawn. It would be dawn again soon. If he did not get some sleep, he would be no good to anyone—not the duke or Sir Isaac and certainly not to himself.

"I will think about it," Sarah said. For the briefest moment, her hand touched his. Lilac scented the air as she turned and vanished up the walk.

13

She was mad even to consider going with him. But then she was mad about so very many things, what could one more matter?

A sound—half laugh, half sob—slipped from Sarah. She put her fingers to her mouth and pressed hard to contain it. It was morning. She had made it through the night but now the day loomed ahead, full of its own challenges.

Go with Faulkner or stay hidden away behind high walls in the illusion of safety? Reason battled with desire. She crumbled a few flecks of bread between her fingers and fed them to the canary. Beyond the cage, beyond the window, the day seduced. Bright blue, brashly bold, showing itself off in all its glory.

Not a day for hiding.

"I'll be going out for a bit, Missus Damas."

The housekeeper was startled but pleased. "A walk'll do you good," she said, "but not without a bit of food to take along. Wait now." She bustled off.

Sarah waited, standing by the window. A deep well of quiet grew within her, reaching out, stilling the frantic rumblings of her thoughts. What was it that was written far below where the ancient spring still flowed? *Fata obstant.* The gods will otherwise. Perhaps they also willed the cracks that seemed to be appearing in her garden walls.

Missus Damas returned. She handed over the basket. Sarah smiled at its weight but did not protest. She went, her feet seeming to glide, down the path and through the gate. In the lane, she paused, breathing deeply of the warm spring air. A rabbit peered from beneath a bush. Sarah crossed to the other side to avoid frightening it and went on, the basket swinging from her hand.

Morley was at his tankards. He looked ill shaven, with shadows beneath his eyes. He glanced up when she entered. "Sir Isaac's not about yet."

"I should hope not," she said. "Have you seen Sir William?" It seemed so strange to give him that name when she always thought of him as Faulkner.

"Sir this and Sir that," Morley grumbled. "You'd think this was Hampton Court, the fuss people are making."

"I'm sure it will be over soon. Is he—"

The publican cocked his head. "Out by the stable. Keeps a sharp eye on those horses of his, he does. Don't know what harm he thinks could come to them here." His hand tightened around the tankard. "Fine enough place this is, always has been. Ought to satisfy any man. Cramming everyone together in one place's a filthy idea. Breeds degeneracy, it does. The cities are cesspools. You couldn't pay me to—"

"I'll just check by the stable," Sarah said hastily. She had never heard Morley carry on so and put it down to the strain of the night before. All the same, she was eager to escape.

The pub had been dark. She stood blinking in the sunlight of the stable yard. A horse's tail flashed and she heard the clatter of hooves on the cobblestones, followed by the low, soothing murmur of a man's voice.

Drawn to it, she made her way to the row of stalls in the back. The black horse was there, his ebony coat gleaming in the sunlight. Water sluiced down his powerful haunches and down the bare arms of the man bathing him.

It was warmer than she'd thought. Hot almost, as though high summer had come without warning. Perhaps that explained why Faulkner was working stripped to the waist.

Half aware that she should not be looking at him, she tried to turn away. But her body would no longer obey her mind. She stood in a circle of golden light, breathing in the aromas of the stable, and watched as horse and man enjoyed one another. The stallion whinnied again, a low sound of affection and pleasure. Faulkner laughed and rubbed his muzzle, murmuring to him kindly.

Sarah had a flashing thought of the people she had seen mistreat animals and of highborn men who would not stoop to do the simplest task. Faulkner was a gentle man—the discovery oddly did not surprise her—and his pride was of a far different sort, bred deep in the bone and sinew, in the soul itself, dependent in no way on the affectations of the world.

She had been right then to come out into the golden

day, away from the garden walls, to dare the shimmering moment when all things seemed possible.

"Good morning."

Faulkner turned, the currying brush still in his hand. She watched, fascinated, as color crept over his high-boned cheeks. "Morning. You're out early, mistress."

"As are you, Sir William." She felt curiously light-headed, as though all doubt and worry had gone the way of the vanquished moon. Perhaps it was the lack of sleep, or the splendor of the day, or the unfamiliar stirrings within herself. Whatever the cause, she was suddenly simply glad to be alive.

"Do you always groom your own horses?" she asked.

"I do this one. He's temperamental."

The stallion nuzzled Faulkner's neck. Sarah laughed. "He seems tame as a kitten," she said.

"He's showing off for you, trying to make a good impression."

"Is he indeed?"

"Outrageously." He took a halfhearted swipe at the horse, who ignored him and continued nuzzling.

"Have you had him long?" Sarah asked.

"All his life." He hesitated as though unwilling to say more but finally added, "He had difficulty birthing. I helped."

She widened her eyes in mock surprise. "A city lad like yourself?"

"And what makes you think I was city bred?"

"Only everything about you. How did you come to be midwife to a colt?"

"It's a tale," he admitted and reached for his shirt lying over a nearby barrel. Slipping the garment over his head, he tied the laces at the throat without taking his eyes from her. Sarah faced him squarely, refusing to be embarrassed. If he wished to dress in front of her, so be it. She was not some missish creature to faint at the sight of a man's bare torso. Breathe a bit more heavily, perhaps, but certainly not faint.

He tucked the shirt in and with a smile—for her fortitude?—sketched a bow. "Will you come measuring, Mistress Sarah?"

"Will you tell your tale, Sir William?"

"A bargain." He reached for the basket, then pretended dismay at its weight. "Planning a journey?"

"It's impossible to escape Missus Damas's ministrations. Indeed, it's foolish even to try."

"I'm surprised she didn't come along herself."

It was a leading remark, hinting that such chaperonage might be necessary. Sarah sensibly ignored it. "Shall we?" she said.

"On foot? We'll cover more ground if we ride."

"Where exactly do you want to go?"

"Farther out, away from whatever Sir Isaac has already covered. I'd like to get a better sense of whatever it is that's here."

She looked at him for a long moment. The debate that raged within herself was not one of words but rather of feelings, instincts, and ultimately risks.

The stallion swung his head and pawed lightly at the earth.

"I know just the place."

14

They rode out across the chalk downs in the direction from which the wind came, riding east along the path of the sun. The village faded behind them; the forests thickened, then thinned. Twisting ribbons of rivers dotted the landscape.

Sarah sat astride a high-tempered mare, strong and agile. She was another of Faulkner's horses and a match for the black stallion. Beside her, Faulkner was a silent presence, seemingly content with the beauty of the day and the rhythm of the ride. He was an easy man to be with, against all odds, undemanding in the peaceful moments but with that capacity for voracious passion slumbering just out of sight.

She had never much liked young men. Even the best of them saw her merely as a female, a vessel for passion, hopes, dreams, progeny, whatever they wished to pour into it, nothing more.

He was different. That was not merely a shocking

thought but a frightening one as well, for in difference lay peril. Yet down that winding road, over that far hill, was the destination she seemed to have been heading toward all unknowingly from the very beginning of her life.

Had the priestess felt the same when she reached out to the young hunter in the shadow of the giant stones, in the silence of the dell, in that distant past that seemed still to share space and time with the place called Avebury?

She shook her head slightly, banishing the thought. She would not think of that now. There was only the moment and the man, the sun-drenched day, and the freedom in being borne on the mare's back, riding over the high track.

They turned north. The track narrowed. Faulkner went first until they reached a clearing high on a ridge above the plain. There he drew rein. Sarah came abreast of him. Together they looked out over the downs far below.

"We've climbed higher than I thought," he said.

"It's deceptive. The path rises gradually."

He turned in the saddle, looking at her. His jerkin was tucked into his saddlebag. He wore only a white shirt open at the throat and the dark breeches he favored. His hair was caught back by the black ribbon she recognized.

"If we continue," Faulkner asked, "where will we find ourselves?"

A simple question, surely? He was a stranger in these parts, seeking direction. "There is a castle about an hour's ride from here. This track passes beside it."

"Will we disturb the residents?"

"A fox or two, perhaps, nothing more. It's an old place, much fought over. There are barrows nearby."

His eyes crinkled. "Suitable for measuring?"

"Suitable enough. Given enough time, Sir Isaac would measure every inch of these lands. But I doubt he'd come out knowing more for the effort than he does now."

"You don't trust the cold eye of science to discern truth?"

"Some truths are subtler than others. They don't yield as easily, but that doesn't make them any the less worthwhile."

Faulkner fell silent, looking out over the track. She waited, feeling the confusion in him, sympathizing with it. "This is a very old place," he said at last.

"Eternity is in the sunshine."

His eyes flashed, silver as water on rock. Softly, on a breath of sound, he nodded. "Yes, I can feel that here. It's as though if I could just look the right way, I would see them all, the people who have come before and the ones who will come after, all here together in an instant."

"You are a poet."

"No," he said, "I am a warrior. Life is conflict. There is very little room in it for poetry."

Her heart tightened. She could see him so easily, in the smoke and heat of battle, bloodied but unbowed. It was a painful image but a true one. "Then you should be at home here."

The suggestion surprised him. "Why?"

"We're on the Ridgeway."

She saw he recognized the name of the legendary route that spanned the lower part of Britain, stretching hundreds of miles from north to south. It was the route the Celts and Romans had taken, as well as the Saxons, all to glory and to death.

"Uncounted numbers of men marched along this track in their time," she said, "seeking survival, power, position, wealth, whatever they dreamt of. And now all vanished. There's only the earth and still the track, for us to follow as we choose."

A lark darted from the hedgerows beside them. The stallion started but calmed swiftly at Faulkner's touch. A cloud moved before the sun, darkening his eyes.

"I choose the castle," he said and lightly urged his mount on.

An hour later they crested the hill above Badbury and headed down the opposite side. The sky had cleared again, leaving the day to dazzle. Sarah's stomach rumbled. "I thought Missus Damas was overdoing it," she said as she dismounted, "but now I'm not so sure."

They found a flat place beside the north wall of the castle. The view below was of rolling dells and hills like inverted saucers with a scattering of tiny villages nestled between them.

"A good spot for a castle," Faulkner said, that warrior's eye again.

"It was a hill fort first, the same as Avebury."

"But never as important."

"I suppose not. Avebury had the rivers, you see, running east and west, as well as the Ridgeway going north and south. People could reach it more easily from all directions. It became a center."

He took a blanket from his saddlebag and spread it over the grass. "For what?"

"Trading and to settle the inevitable disputes over

clan boundaries and the like. It became a place for people to meet."

"You don't need stone circles and a man-made hill for that. There had to be another reason."

"Pagan religious rites? Barbaric sacrifices? Primitive mutterings and entreaties born of unenlightened minds?"

"That's not how you think of them."

"No," she admitted, "but I fear Sir Isaac does. Either that or he imagines white-robed Druid priests chanting as their victims burn."

"The Druids came late to this land."

"What did you say?"

"I—" He hesitated, suddenly, uncharacteristically, unsure. "Nothing, it doesn't matter. Is that chicken I smell?"

It was: chicken and fresh baked bread, a jug of sweet cider, and, when they were almost full, a napkin of lemon crisps to nibble on as they lay looking up at the cerulean sky.

"I had a better meal once," Faulkner said, replete. "But I can't remember where."

Sarah stirred beside him. Happiness suffused her. She wanted so much to hold on to it, to keep everything else at bay. But thoughts troubled her. What had he said? An echo of herself? Surely not. Warrior that he was, city bred, he could not possibly sense the currents eddying around Avebury. Could he?

"You were going to tell me how you came to help birth the stallion," she said.

He sighed but yielded with good grace. "My father was a merchant," he began. Sarah wiggled about, finding a comfortable position in which to listen. "Sometimes he prospered, sometimes he didn't. We lived in Cheapside close to the docks. When I was nine, we had a run of good fortune and my father bought a part interest in a stable. He managed to hold on to it through good times and bad. Eventually, it came to me."

"When did he die?"

"When I was fourteen. I was at sea at the time and hating it. When I got back, I swore I'd never go again except as a passenger. At any rate, I went by the stable, found it well run, and became friendly with the co-owner. He was a good man, formerly in the army. You could say he took me under his wing."

"He taught you about horses?"

"And a good deal else." Faulkner laughed. "I thought I'd worked hard at sea, but mucking out stalls was more than I'd bargained for. Still, the ground wasn't rocking under my feet and I no longer had my head in a bucket. Then one night my friend, Silas Fletcher was his name, was taken ill at the same time our prize mare went into labor. When the foal wouldn't come, I had to help her."

"Were you frightened?"

Faulkner looked at her sharply. It was not a question he was used to being asked.

"Terrified. But, miraculously, she calmed when she heard my voice and instinct rescued me. By the time Rascal was born, I almost felt as though I'd birthed him myself."

"Rascal? I thought he'd have a dreadfully noble name."

"He does somewhere in the breeding books, but he's always been Rascal to me."

"What happened to Silas?"

"He died. I found him cold in his bed."

Sarah pressed her lips together. He spoke with an old, hard hurt like a bruise gone deeper than healing. "I'm sorry."

"I learned afterward that he'd been in touch with the commander of his regiment on my behalf. Got him to agree to take a look at me. I was judged suitable, but I needed money to buy my way in."

"How did you get it?"

"I sold the stable. Silas had left me his share as well, so it was just enough for a commission. I kept Rascal and his mother, put her to pasture, took him with me, and set off to make a name for myself." He smiled at the thought, a touch grimly.

"It seems you've succeeded. I am informed that you are of considerable consequence."

"I am feared by most men and trusted by one."

"The duke?"

Faulkner nodded. "He's a great man. I actually mean that. I've never seen anyone so rise to the moment."

"And it contents you, to be feared?"

"It has its uses." He turned over, leaning on his elbow with his head propped in the palm of his hand, and studied her. The wind ruffled his hair.

"I don't believe I've ever been with a woman like this before."

His meaning was clear. Women there had been but only in their place, taken for passion and pleasure or simply for relaxation. Not actually talked to, honestly, on an easeful spring day of horse baths and lemon crisps.

"Perhaps you should try it more often."

He made a noncommittal sound deep in his throat and brushed a stray wisp of hair from the curve of her cheek. "There is something I don't understand."

"Only something?"

She meant to tease, to divert him from the sudden intensity of his regard. The strategy did not work.

"Why are you alone?"

Not for him the delicacy of feint and parry. He went straight for the heart. "I am not," she said quickly, for this was an old argument and an even older fear. She had her defenses ready. "There is Missus Damas and the other servants. Also, I have relatives elsewhere in Wiltshire, second cousins I believe they are. I am hardly alone just because I have chosen not to marry."

"Few women would agree with you."

She sat up, her back to him, and folded her arms around her knees. "Women marry for security or for approval. I have been fortunate to need neither."

"There is another reason for marriage."

She glanced at him over her shoulder. He too had sat up. They were so close she had only to reach out the slightest way to touch him. There was a slight tremor in her voice. "What is that?"

"Love."

His mouth was really quite beautiful, the lips perfectly shaped. She thought of how it had felt against her own.

"I would never have thought you a romantic."

"Neither would I," he replied and moved, just slightly, giving her time to draw away should she so choose.

She didn't.

15

His mouth was harder this time, less gentle. His chest beneath her seeking hands was taut with muscle. He was warm, so warm, through the fabric of his shirt. She felt the hard knot of ice deep within her, the frozen landscape of her fear, bathed suddenly in radiant sunlight.

Far in the distance, a drumbeat, the sound growing louder until it drowned out even her own breath. And higher still, floating over the hill fort and the shining river below, a reed pipe making magic.

"I have longed for you," he whispered and slipped the tunic from her shoulders. She shivered with delighted anticipation, joy blossoming in her, pleasure in the day and the man, in her own existence. They had dropped a pearl brought from the distant southern shore into the river, an offering to the Mother, before they—

Sarah's eyes opened wide. This could not be happening to her. She was Sarah of Avebury, Sarah

Huxley of the manor house and the garden, a proper gentlewoman. Sarah, who had found the dead man and whose half-formed sense of something deeply wrong in the place she knew best had brought this other man, proud and strong, to Avebury. And to her arms.

His tongue touched hers, a warm, seeking thing so alien to anything she had known and so deeply, piercingly pleasureful. Was this what it was like then? This knowing of a man at such a level as she could not have imagined? Knowing the taste and touch of him, the scent and sound? Knowing in the bone and sinew, in the beat of her heart and the indrawing of her breath? Sweet heaven, no wonder people were mad for it.

She moved, tentatively, wanting more. He obliged, giving. She tried again, daring more greatly. A tremor ran through him. He made a sound deep in his chest and closed his arms around her.

She was enveloped in granite and velvet, held safe against the world, against him, while her body sang an ancient song of recognition and welcome. How desperately she wanted him, around her, in her, drawing out the full power she possessed and filling her with life. Desperately enough to forget that she was, had always been—always would be?—quite mad.

Her arms twined round him, her legs brushed his, opening a place for him to lie there on the grass beside the hill fort, above the river, beneath the sun. Caught between heaven and earth, in this place of violence and beauty, she slipped her hands beneath his shirt and felt for the first time the freedom of his flesh.

He took his mouth from hers and touched it to the arch of her throat. She gasped, swept from plane to plane of sensation, and twisted beneath him. Her hair spilled free, pillowing her head. He said her name, harshly, as though wrenched from him, and ran his hands up beneath her skirts, along the silken skin of her thighs, touching and caressing her in ways that shattered the last slim bonds of her self-control. She stroked down his back to the hard curve of his buttocks and raised her legs, embracing him intimately.

Faulkner gasped. He reached between them to open his breeches. Another moment, a breath, and they would—

He froze. There was a roaring in his ears and beneath it a pounding, powerful and deep, like a drumbeat summoning him to ancient ritual. Above it, thin on the air, cadence of a charm, a pipe singing the siren's song.

Madness. This could be nothing else, this driven yearning to possess without conscience or honor. It was as though he had forgotten who he was, who she was, and where they stood in a world of reason and rules, as though none of that existed anymore.

Yet in some fragment of his mind, that world survived still, blurred by the great surging need within him yet enough to remind him that what he was about to do was utterly and irrevocably wrong.

And not just for the usual reasons. Honor, yes, and decency, demanded that he stop. But so did his sense of himself as a solitary, self-sufficient man aloof from entanglements. Sarah, locked in his arms, sweet, welcoming heat against him, was not a woman he could walk away from. Once taken, she would possess him forever.

A part of him would always remain here in this high place where the wind blew lightly and the earth stirred to life. He would never have that part back again. It would be lost, sacrificed to the fire within.

He hesitated, reason at war with need so ancient he could hardly give it a name. And all because of curiosity, the desire to better understand this strange, beguiling woman, seemingly so fragile yet so strong. Strong enough to decide for herself what she wanted?

"Sarah?" His voice rasped, his breath ragged. "We should not do this."

There, it was said. He had done everything reason and honor could possibly expect of him. Whatever happened now was in her hands.

As he was himself, warm, seeking hands, gentle yet irresistible. And a smile of such breathtaking knowledge that beside it doubt seemed a poor, weak thing. So it happened that in the end it was Sarah who drew him to her, her body welcoming his with only brief resistance. There on the hillside above the river, beneath the sun, as larks fluttered in the bushes and a falcon whirled overhead, they loved.

Cool air touched her thighs. Sarah sat up and looked around dazedly. She was surprised to find the world still there exactly as they had left it when they went wherever it was but in some other place far from here.

Faulkner slept. A brief glance assured her of that. She was grateful for it. More than anything, she needed time to herself to come to terms with what had happened between them.

How could she possibly have done such a thing? How could a properly reared gentlewoman give herself to a man not her husband in a wanton display of lust that violated every rule she had ever been taught?

And not regret a moment of it?

She stood, a little experimentally, for she half expected her legs not to support her. But they held and she was able to move away, down the slope toward the river.

There she knelt, and cupping water in her hands, bathed her heated face. Her clothes were in disarray, the bodice of her gown opened and pushed aside. She splashed water on her neck and breasts, shivering in the sudden coolness. With a quick check over her shoulder to be sure Faulkner was not stirring, she dampened her petticoat and dabbed between her legs. There was a little blood, not much. Had she been a bride, her chastity might have been in doubt. As it was, there was no doubt at all.

Unchaste, whore, fallen woman: all those terms could be applied to her now and more. So where was the horror, the self-hatred, the terror that should have accompanied them? On this blithe, blue-sky day, it was curiously absent.

Perhaps later, she thought, and started back up the hill. Faulkner was waking. She sat beside him, steeling herself to bear whatever he might say. His eyes opened, pewter-sheened. They focused on her. He took a breath.

"Sarah, I'm sorry."

Not bad, really, not remotely as terrible as it could have been. A tiny fraction of relief crept into her soul.

"I'm not," she said and went to fetch the horses.

16

They rode back along the Ridgeway in silence. Sarah seemed to neither want nor expect conversation, and Faulkner was glad of it. He was utterly at a loss as to what to say to her. How in the name of heaven did he apologize for despoiling a gently born virgin? For virgin she had been, he had no doubt of that. Yet as passionate and willing a woman as any man could ever hope for. Strange combination, strange woman. Strange day, when the world seemed turned upside down and every certainty he had ever possessed no longer counted for anything.

Rascal caught his tension and shied beneath him. Faulkner settled the horse with a touch. They were nearing the village. He shot a quick glance at Sarah beside him. She appeared completely serene, not a hair out of place, as though the extraordinary encounter by the hill fort had never occurred. Only the deep, abiding peace of his body and the resonance of shattering pleasure assured him that it had.

Her brows, delicate as a bird's wing, drew together. At last, some hint of concern. But she was looking not at him or even off into space. Instead, her gaze was focused on—

"Who's that?" Faulkner asked.

"Davey Hemper, Missus Hemper's son. He has himself well rigged out."

The boy did appear more elaborately dressed than Faulkner remembered seeing him before. He had on a new hat and jerkin, a pure white shirt, well-tailored breeches, and boots that would not have put Crispin to shame.

"He must have come by a bit of coin," Sarah said thoughtfully.

"Good for him. Look, we really have to—"

She ignored him and urged the mare forward. Faulkner muttered under his breath. She really was the most infuriating woman, to fuss over a boy's new clothes rather than acknowledge what had taken place between them.

Not that country lads came by moneyed jobs very often, did they? He could only guess that most work in the country was probably done for barter. Where then had Davey Hemper gotten the coin to outfit himself so well?

Despite the events of the day, Faulkner had not forgotten the mission that had sent him north. Guilt heaped on guilt as he considered that while pleasuring himself with Sarah he had done precious little to solve the killings.

That would have to change, and immediately. He had never in his life shirked a duty, and he wasn't about to begin now. But neither could he simply take his leave of her and go on about his business as though nothing had happened.

Sarah solved that problem for him. As they reached the Rose, she dismounted and said, "Kindly tell Sir Isaac I will call on him later to see how he fares."

Before Faulkner could do more than incline his head, she continued on her way. He was left to stare after her in bewilderment and, truth be told, growing anger. By the time he had unsaddled Rascal and the mare and made them comfortable, his temper was boiling. He stomped into the common room, ordered an ale, and sat down in the first chair that presented itself.

How dare she behave in such a manner? Had she no sensibilities at all to go off and leave him with nary a word or gesture to recognize what they had shared?

Fine, let her do as she would. He would have his ale and then seek out Constable Duggin and Davey Hemper. The boy might have some explaining to do. That young curate, Edwards, he'd talk with him as well. And while he was at it, he'd question that plump woman who ran the shop. Before he was done, he was going to know everything there was to know about Avebury and its inhabitants. If there was a murderer among them, he would not go undiscovered. Sarah be damned.

Annalise approached, eyeing him cautiously. He realized the picture he must present, scowling as he was, and mustered a faint smile. She set the tankard down and scurried away.

He sighed, putting her from his mind. The ale was cool and crisp but he had no intention of lingering over it. The tankard was half empty and he was rising, leaving it unfinished, when a sudden clamor in the courtyard announced the arrival of the Bath coach.

In a great spray of dust and jangle of harnesses, the

coach rolled to a stop. Morley bustled out to greet the passengers. Faulkner followed. He stood, leaning insouciantly against the doorpost with his arms crossed over his chest, and watched the excitement.

They were a mixed lot: several commercial travelers, a weary-looking woman with a small child, and two elaborately dressed young men who were making a great show of waving handkerchiefs in front of their noses and complaining loudly of the discomfort.

"Damned vile, traveling this way," the shorter of the two said. "Can't think why I let you talk me into it."

"The novelty, old sport," his companion replied. "Give you a yarn to tell at the club on a slow evening."

"No such thing, Buffer, but we're here and I suppose that's what counts. Do forgive me, though, if I resist the impulse to kiss the ground."

Buffer—what the hell kind of name was that?— sighed elaborately and gestured to Morley. "Ale, my good man, and plenty of it. My throat's as parched as the Araby sands."

The publican scowled. In the midst of ushering the commercial travelers inside, he said, "They'll be ale for the pair of you when I've coin in my hand. Not before."

The color flared in Buffer's horselike face. "Are you mad? How dare you speak to me like that?"

"I'll dare plenty with what I'm already owed by you lot. Now off with you and don't come back unless it's to settle your account."

The affronted young man took a step forward, his fists clenched and mayhem in his eyes. Faulkner observed him narrowly. He had seen his sort before. Angry, pride wounded, but unable to remedy the situation in the only way that counted—namely, by paying his bill—the young gentleman was violence prone.

Fortunately, his friend was cut from more sensible cloth, if not by much. "What do you care what he thinks?" he said, tugging at Buffer's sleeve. "Come on."

"Nobody speaks to me like that, much less a dirt common publican. I'll—"

"I'm telling you it doesn't matter. Let's go." He pulled again urgently at his friend's arm. Reluctantly, Buffer yielded. He allowed himself to be led away but not without a hate-filled scowl directed back at Morley.

The publican's answer was to spit decisively on the spot where the two young gentlemen had been standing. That done, he bustled after his customers, leaving Faulkner to ponder what he had just seen.

But not so deeply that he failed to notice Annalise, peering around the side of the building, her hands clasped before her and a look of utmost deprivation stamped on her pretty face.

Faulkner cleared his throat. He was more convinced than ever that he had absolutely no understanding of women. But at least Annalise was a known quantity utterly unlike maddening, mysterious Sarah.

"Excuse me," Faulkner said, very politely, for he did not wish to startle her. "Would you happen to know who those two young men are?"

Despite his best efforts, Annalise jumped as though he had struck her. He half expected her to flee, but she gathered her wits about her with an obvious effort. Her voice low and mournful, she stared after them as she said, "That was Viscount Justin Hoddinworth. He is the son of the Marquess and Marchioness of Hoddinworth. I am not acquainted with the other gentleman."

"The taller one—Buffer?—is Hoddinworth?"

Annalise nodded, still with that look of desperate longing, rather like a puppy after a new shoe, Faulkner thought unkindly. "He is residing nearby with his parents."

"I see." Sarah had mentioned something about a marquess being in the neighborhood. "Have they been here long?"

"A few months. They are down from London."

Understanding dawned. No members of the nobility would willingly exile themselves from the capital at such a time if they could by any means remain. The Hoddinworths, it seemed, lacked those means. He would have to add young Hoddinworth—Buffer, of all things—to his list of people to be questioned.

Cheered by the prospect and determined to keep himself busy, he was not yet disposed to let her go. "Have you seen Sir Isaac today?"

"Oh, yes, sir, he was down for breakfast and took a bit of a stroll. Then your gentleman suggested he have a rest."

"Good for Crispin. Tell him I'll be back in a while." Almost as an afterthought, he added, "And tell him also that Mistress Huxley will be calling on Sir Isaac later."

Annalise bobbed her head. She waited an instant longer, until it became clear he did not intend to detain her further. Released, she fled back in the direction of the inn.

Faulkner stood out in the lane, hands thrust deep in his pockets, and looked around. He had to start somewhere. Duggin's blacksmith shop was shuttered. The constable appeared to be away, probably in the fields he also kept. It was spring, he reminded himself. Quite a few of the villagers would be busy at their planting. But not all of them. The shop was still open. He caught the flutter of an ample skirt near the door and stifled a sigh. The things he did for queen and country. And for the duke.

Missus Goody was delighted to see him. Indeed, so boundless was her joy—and her person—that she threatened to burst a seam. The moment he mentioned the Gypsy killings, she was off and running.

"Bad lot, they are," she said. "Always said they shouldn't be allowed around decent people, I did."

"You had trouble with the Romany, then?"

"Well, no, not in so many words, but they could never be trusted, could they? Always had to watch your back when they were about."

"Were you surprised when the killings happened?"

"Not on your life. That sort's always going at each other about something, aren't they? A goat, a horse"— she looked at him sidelong—"a woman: anything's likely to set them off."

"Yet they gave no trouble?"

"Not so as you can tell," she admitted. "But the potential was there, you see. So when we found the bodies—well, no one was surprised. Why would they be?"

"Mistress Huxley was."

The shop mistress nodded somberly. "Ah, well, there is that. Terrible taken back she was, but then she found the first one and that'd be bound not to sit a body well. Still and all, if you don't mind my saying, I think she raised a bit too much of a fuss. They were only Roms, after all."

"I gather Mistress Huxley didn't think that mattered."

"That's the sort she is, decent as the day is long. A perfect gentlewoman. You can't fault that kind, now can you, even if they don't quite seem to understand the ways of the world."

Faulkner mulled that over, trying to reconcile it with the woman he had gotten to know so very well on the hill fort. Decent, he didn't dispute. Sarah Huxley might be an enigma, but he had an instinctive faith in her character. Perfect gentlewoman was another matter. He suspected she herself might protest such a designation. That left the matter of how well she understood the ways of the world in which she seemed only precariously perched. Yet there was wisdom in her, bone deep and soul strong. Wisdom to know when the Romany had been wronged and when justice needed to be done, for their sake and for Avebury's.

"Tell me," he instructed, "what do people hereabouts think of my being sent? Be honest now, I truly want to know."

Mistress Goody appeared flustered. Merely being the focus of his interest was potent enough. To be asked to comment on so delicate a matter threw her into confusion. She took refuge in flattery.

"Sir Isaac is a great man, sir, as I'm sure you are yourself."

"That's very kind of you, but it doesn't quite address the question. Do people resent my being here, asking about the killings, perhaps stirring up matters that might be otherwise left buried?"

"Matters, sir?" She looked genuinely confused.

He shrugged as though it should be obvious. "There are bound to be certain resentments, rivalries, old grudges, that sort of thing in a place like this, aren't there?"

"No more so than anywhere, I'd think."

"Surely you aren't suggesting that everyone in Avebury gets along perfectly?"

This was too good a bit of bait to be resisted, as he had hoped. She cast a cautious glance toward the door to be sure they were not overheard. "Well, now, I wouldn't say that exactly. Master Morley, for instance, has a tart tongue and not much in the way of patience. He and the old curate had words a time or two."

"What about the young one?" Faulkner asked, thinking of how eagerly Edwards had gone to comfort fair Annalise.

"I've only heard him say he talks too much, is all. He's a good enough sort. Tried to patch things up between Dr. Quack and Missus Hemper, he did."

"Is that really the doctor's name, Quack?"

Missus Goody grinned. "Bit of truth there, if you want to know. Still, you'd have thought he'd change it, going into the medical profession and all." She leaned forward confidentially. "Likes his port, Quack does. Not that I blame him. Most folks hereabouts still go to the old woman first."

"What about the Hoddinworths? Have they caused problems?"

The shop mistress wrinkled her face disdainfully. "That lot? Nothing but, coming here lording it over the rest of us, expecting free this and free that just because they're gentry. If you ask me, they ought to be run out. We don't need their sort, we don't.

"Not," she added hastily, "that I've anything against the gentry, sir. It's just that—"

Faulkner raised a hand, cutting her off. "I quite understand, Missus Goody. You've been very helpful." Was that a flash of azure blue on the other side of the lane? Sarah had been wearing a dress of that color. Had she returned to see Sir Isaac?

But when he looked again, there was no sign of her.

Missus Goody was going on and he felt condemned to listen. His thoughts wandered.

What was Sarah doing? Thinking of him and what they had shared? Regretting it, for all her brave words to the contrary? The possibility stabbed through him. He could not bear to imagine her hurt or sad. Her feelings were suddenly, shockingly, more important than his own.

"So I said to the curate, I did, You can't expect people to—"

"Forgive me, Missus Goody. I fear I have taken far too much of your time."

"What? Oh, no, not at all, sir. I'm mighty pleased to be of help. Now as I was saying—"

She rambled. He half listened. But his thoughts were of Sarah and of what she was doing. There were dozens of possibilities: resting, well advised, all things considered; bathing, an image he would be wise not to dwell on just then; gardening; feeding her canary; sitting at her window looking out, perhaps even thinking of him.

Another moment and he would be addled as a lovestruck boy. He could not, would not, let this happen to him. She was a woman, nothing more, taken, enjoyed, put aside while he went on, as men had done since time immemorial, part of the natural order.

And yet, the vision of her—resting, bathing, pondering—would not release him. He could imagine her a dozen, hundred, thousand ways. However, none happened to come remotely near the truth, failing as they did to involve either a teapot or the struggle not to hurl it at a certain offending head.

17

"My dear," the Marchioness of Hoddinworth said, "I'm delighted to actually find you in. If your housekeeper is to be believed, that is rarely the case."

And would have been again, Sarah thought, if Mary Damas hadn't happened to step out for a few moments. Returning to the house, Sarah had actually been glad to pass unobserved. Until she was so foolish as to answer a knock at the door and find herself face to face with Avebury's answer to high society.

To be fair, the marchioness was not an unattractive woman. She had the sleek, cared-for look of the pampered rich, a group to which she had genuinely belonged and which she wanted desperately to rejoin. Until that happy day, she had to make do with surroundings she would normally have considered far beneath her.

"I trust the house is comfortable?" Sarah asked. She kept a tight hold on the teapot lest it find itself winging in the direction of her guest. Less than a half hour in the marchioness's company had been enough to set her badly jangled nerves even more on edge.

Just when she most needed solitude, she was forced to endure a woman she would have gone far out of her way to avoid. Worse yet, Elizabeth Hoddinworth was a sophisticate, wise in the ways of the world. There was a possibility, however remote, that she might suspect Sarah had been out for more than a pleasant ride on a spring day.

"The house is . . . adequate," the marchioness said, the delicate pause making clear that it was anything but. There was actually a remote family connection between the Huxleys and the Hoddinworths. Sarah had lost track of the details, but it was sufficient to oblige her to make a property she owned outside the village available to them with no discussion of so tawdry a matter as rent. So be it. She would rack it up to Christian charity and hope their fortunes would soon be restored. But did she also have to endure the marchioness's razor-eyed stare and a smile that resembled nothing so much as a tigress dangerously past her mealtime?

"About the best that can be said for country life," Elizabeth continued, "is that it is exceedingly restful."

Sarah found it anything but, she refrained from comment. Sooner or later, her guest would get around to the reason for her visit. If at all possible, she would agree to it. Anything to send Elizabeth on her way as quickly as she could.

"I want an introduction to Devereaux."

A splash of hot tea struck Sarah's hand. She didn't notice. "What did you say?"

"You heard me. He is here and you have met him.

Now I wish to do the same. To be precise, I want all of us, Justin, myself, and Lord Harley to make his acquaintance."

Lord Harley was the marquess, Elizabeth's husband of almost thirty years, yet never referred to by her with other than the utmost formality tinged with a dollop of disdain. They did not get along. In London, they had been able to avoid each other almost entirely. The enforced intimacy of Avebury was telling quickly.

"I see," Sarah murmured. In fact she did not, but Elizabeth wasted no time enlightening her.

"You don't have the slightest notion who he is, do you?"

"He is the duke's man, Marlborough—"

"Good God, do you think that's all? Certainly, Devereaux has the duke's trust, but that's only the beginning. He's the brightest man in London, they say, and certainly the most ruthless. No one dreams of crossing him. His wealth is legendary, his power enormous; there is no telling where he will end."

Wherever he chose, Sarah suspected, but she resisted saying so. Elizabeth sighed, summoning patience, and continued.

"I realize this is all quite beyond your ken, but try to understand. Devereaux is immensely important. He can order marvels with a single word. Should he so choose, we could be restored in an instant: wealth, position, everything."

"Sounds a bit godlike, don't you think?"

"Mock if you must, but it's true all the same. Having Devereaux here is an extraordinary bit of luck. I absolutely must make the most of it."

"What makes you think I can help?" Sarah asked cautiously.

"You have met him."

"So has John Morley. You might as well ask him to do the honors." It was a cruel suggestion and she regretted it as soon as it was made. But her patience was wearing thin. She felt dangerously exposed, unexpectedly weak, and suddenly very frightened. All this talk of Faulkner had that effect on her.

"Don't be absurd. You are a gentlewoman, not without position yourself, or what passes for it here. He would accede to a request from you."

"Would he?"

"For God's sake, Sarah, what's the matter with you? You know perfectly well he would. You aren't entirely without appeal, for all that you go to great lengths to conceal it."

If there was one thing she absolutely was not going to discuss, it was whatever appeal she might hold for the illustrious Sir William Faulkner Devereaux.

"I fear you may be riding for disappointment. Even presuming that I can manage an introduction, how inclined would he be to help you?"

"Not very," Elizabeth admitted. Her shoulders sagged slightly, but she straightened them at once. "Still, it is worth the effort. And," she added more vigorously, "it is not as though we would require a great deal of help. Merely a word of his in the right ear would be more than sufficient."

"You appear to have enormous faith in his ability."

"In his power, dear," Elizabeth corrected. "In the final analysis, that is all that matters."

I am feared by most men, Faulkner had said, and seemingly it was true. Yet he had also revealed the boy he had been, however unknowingly, proud, aloof, hurting, determined to find a place for himself. A boy who could defy the father who sent him to sea, chart his own course, and still ache inside for the friend who, dying, had helped set him on his way.

And he could bathe a horse in the morning sun, lie replete on a hillside, bring her to greater joy than she had ever believed possible.

And ask her about love.

A complex man, to be sure, but also a dangerous one.

Sarah set the teapot down. She looked out, past Elizabeth, past the fragile white curtains blowing gently at the windows, past the garden to the high walls and, in her mind's eye, to the rolling hills and deep shadowed glens of the only world she had ever known.

Softly, she said, "I will do what I can."

The day, begun with the handing over of a basket, wound down in the same way.

"I put a crock of marrow in," Missus Damas explained. "Spread thin on bread, it will set Sir Isaac up just fine."

"I'm sure it will," Sarah said, hefting the basket. It was almost but not quite as heavy as the morning's. She left it on the floor by the door as she took her shawl from a peg and tied her bonnet in place. That done, she ventured out, going swiftly down the path before she could think better of it.

Elizabeth had departed amid promises of swift action. The lane was empty, everyone else being sensibly at their supper. The sky remained clear, and already the days were noticeably longer. More than a few of Avebury's citizens would be back in the fields come evening. With any luck, no one would have the time or energy to notice her whereabouts.

The Rose was empty. The day's coach had departed, the travelers dispersed. With the planting to see to, the villagers had no time to linger. It was a slow stretch for Morley but he was making the most of it, polishing his tankards with even greater than usual care.

"Good evening," Sarah said as she entered.

He looked up, grunted, and cocked his head toward the side door. "If it's Sir Isaac you're after, he's taking a bit of air, although why a man his age would want to risk his lungs like that I can't tell you."

It was on the tip of her tongue to ask if Faulkner was with him, but she stopped herself. Ignoring the flutter in her stomach, she stepped outside. Sir Isaac was there, standing by a small iron gate that separated the premises from the old graveyard in the back. He was alone.

On a surge of mingled relief and regret, she went to join him.

"Sir Isaac?"

He turned, saw her, and smiled. "There you are, Mistress Huxley." His smile faded slightly. "Are you well?"

Surely her secret was safe from the elderly scholar who was reputed to live a monk's life. Or was it?

"Perfectly," she said. "I've brought you some of Missus Damas' best. She says it will set you up splendidly."

"Very kind of her, I'm sure, and of you. How did the measuring go?"

"The measuring?" Sweet Lord, she'd forgotten all about it. "There were some problems, actually. I fear we got nothing of use."

He looked surprised but only for an instant. His

smile returned, gentle and patient. "That's quite all right, my dear. I'm sure if you try again you'll do better, Faulkner as well."

If they did much better than they had, there would be nothing found of them. But she wasn't about to mention that.

"Have you had an opportunity to assess your findings?" she asked as they walked together back toward the Rose.

"Not very much, I'm afraid. It is all very complex. However, I am more convinced than ever that Avebury and its surroundings were deliberately constructed for religious purposes. Beyond that, further investigation is needed."

"Religious purposes?"

Sir Isaac nodded. "The trick is to free your mind of preconceived notions. We are dealing with an age long before the faintest glimmer of Christianity, or indeed of our Judaic antecedents. People saw themselves in a very direct relationship with the forces of creation."

"I suppose they would have had to, living so intimately with nature."

"Precisely. It is my belief that Avebury is a sort of cathedral, albeit on a massive scale undreamt of even in our own time. If I am correct, it must have been the religious center for this entire part of Britain. Beside it Stonehenge, for example, looks quite puny."

"Fascinating," Sarah murmured as they stepped back inside the inn. She was surprised by how far he had come from his white-robed Druids and chanting primitives. Indeed, he was straying remarkably close to truth.

To test how close, she asked, "Is the haunting related?"

"The haunting? Oh, you mean here at the Rose. Heavens, I don't think so. If Morley's right, it's the monks."

"Do you think that's possible?"

"Long-dead monks seeking vengeance for old Henry Tudor's crimes?" Sir Isaac shrugged. "Who knows? I suppose what matters is that Morley believes it. I gather it's wearing on him."

"He doesn't look well," Sarah agreed.

"Perhaps I ought to let him have a bit of Missus Damas's best."

A shape moved in the shadows near the door. She was aware of it an instant too late to have any chance to prepare herself.

"Let who have what?" Faulkner asked.

18

Sarah gasped. Faulkner was standing right inside the door as though he had risen straight up through the floor. His sudden appearance left her floundering.

Fortunately, Sir Isaac was at no such loss. "Morley," he said pleasantly. "We were just saying that our host doesn't look well."

"You're a bit flushed yourself, Mistress Huxley," Faulkner said. With a bite to his words, he added, "Not feverish, are you?"

"Oh, dear," Sir Isaac said. "I do hope not. Didn't you say you felt perfectly well?"

"And so I do," Sarah interjected hastily. She shot Faulkner what she hoped was a quelling look but it only glanced off him. "Sir William is exaggerating."

Had she truly thought Elizabeth's smile tigerish? Faulkner's was far more threatening. And while she was pondering it, why was he so angry? Not disdainful or contemptuous or anything similar such as a properly reared fallen woman ought to expect, but simple, cold anger rolling off him in waves that threatened to swamp her.

She took a quick step back, steeled herself, and handed the basket to Sir Isaac. "I must be going." Whatever she had promised Elizabeth would have to wait. This was no time to ask Faulkner for anything.

"So quickly?" Faulkner fairly purred. "And just when I thought we might get better acquainted."

That did it. A dark flush swept over her cheeks. She opened her mouth, intending a devastating riposte, but absolutely nothing came out.

Sir Isaac, blissfully unaware—or was he?—stepped into the chasm. "An excellent idea. Might I suggest supper? Morley's kidney pie is quite good. I'd be delighted to join you but I really must rest. Ah, there's a free table." Actually, they were all free but why quibble. "Good Morley, you've two for supper. Is that fresh baked bread I smell?"

"It's always fresh here," Morley grumbled as he came out from behind the bar. He eyed them dubiously but with interest. Any customer was better than none. "Supper, is it?"

"Go on," Sir Isaac urged. "You can mull it all over: the Gypsies, the ruins, everything. I'll be fascinated to hear whatever you come up with." Basket in tow, he trotted toward the stairs. "Don't forget to try the cobbler. It's marvelous."

"No cobbler tonight," Morley said. "Bread pudding."

"Oh, well, if there's no cobbler," Sarah began.

"Annalise," her father bellowed, "start the cobbler! Sit down, the pair of you. Ale for you, Sir William? And what will you have, mistress? A nice sherry?"

"I hate sherry," Sarah said. If she was stuck having supper with Faulkner and no way out that wouldn't have the whole village awash with gossip before cockcrow, she was damn well going to drink what she pleased. "Stout."

Morley's eyebrows met his hairline but he didn't argue. He bustled off while Faulkner, who appeared mightily amused, pulled a chair out for her. "Stout?"

"It's a perfectly decent drink."

He made a noncommittal sound and sat down. They eyed each other across the expanse of rough-hewn pine. "So," Faulkner said, breaking the silence. "You drink stout, dislike bread pudding, and keep your promises regarding old men you intend to visit. I feel as though I'm getting to know you better every moment."

"Stop it," Sarah demanded. "Perhaps you play these games at court, but I won't. I don't know why you're so angry but—"

"You don't? You have no idea?"

"No, I don't. How could I possibly? You're an enigma to me. The great Sir William Faulkner Devereaux before whom armies tremble and courtiers bow down. How am I supposed to know what you're thinking even for a moment?"

"I see," he said slowly. Leaning back in his chair, he folded his arms over his broad chest and regarded her from shuttered eyes. "Whereas you, the unworldly country maiden—excuse me, a poor choice of word: the unworldly country *gentlewoman*—is entirely straightforward, uncomplicated, clear as a summer day. Have I got that right?"

"Are you sure you aren't a lawyer?"

"How so?"

"You argue like one, using words for weapons."

"As a matter of fact I have been accepted at the bar, but that's neither here nor there. The point is"— he leaned across the table, close enough to touch her—"I am also a human being. I do possess some semblance of feeling. You may wish to ignore what happened this morning but I cannot. Indeed," he added ominously, "I will not."

She was saved from reply by Morley's return bearing their tankards. He set them down with a solid thump, informed them the rest of supper would follow, and disappeared into the back. Sarah took a quick sip of her stout. She drank it rarely but liked the rich, slightly nutty flavor. For good measure, she took another sip.

"I don't understand you," she said. "Aren't men supposed to regard such things lightly and be glad when there is no entanglement?"

"Where did you get that idea?"

"From the very air we breathe. It is how our society functions, isn't it?"

"Only up to a point. This morning—"

"What point? Where do you decide that you have or have not some responsibility to the female involved? However do you distinguish?"

She was pushing him hard and knew it, but some contrary impulse of her nature would not let her stop. Still, when she saw the color creep over his burnished cheeks she wished she had exercised more caution.

"It's very simple," Faulkner said, knife-edged. "If I'm paying, the responsibility ends there. If the lady is willing and experienced, it is essentially the same. But," he continued, glaring at her, "if she is a virgin and far beyond her depth, then I must be excused for feeling a certain obligation when matters get entirely out of hand."

"Is that what happened?" Sarah asked, more gently. She had not expected him to be so concerned. Indeed, it amazed her to find him like this. Yet perhaps it should not have. There were aspects of him she was only beginning to discover.

"Yes," he replied. His voice was gruff. "I have never lost control like that in all my life. You must realize, what I did was unforgivable."

"Don't you mean what *we* did? That shocks you, doesn't it? You can't accept the idea that I wanted this to happen as much as you did. If there was fault, and I question that, we both share in it."

He shook his head, as though he could not grasp what she was saying. "I realize you have lived an unusual life, cut off from much of what passes for normal. But all the same—" It must have been the look on her face that stopped him. "What is it?" he asked.

"Only that you are right," she said dryly. "My life has been, shall we say, unusual. But it is my life, and I am more or less content with it." That was a lie. Whatever balance she had managed to find in the midst of madness was fast eroding. But she would not admit it, not to him, not now. He was burdened enough by his own concerns.

Morley returned. They kept silent while he deposited the food in front of them, asked if there was anything else they wanted, and went on his way. It was very quiet in the common room. The door stood open, admitting fragrant evening air and the fading light. Nothing stirred along the lane.

Sarah's stomach growled. She laughed and cut into the kidney pie. There were advantages to madness, after all. If she stopped trying to fight it, surely a futile effort anyway, she could accept anything that came along. Even Faulkner.

"Eat your supper," she said gently. "Sir Isaac was right, it's quite good."

His look was of pure male exasperation, and beneath that, running deeper, genuine bewilderment. "You cannot dismiss this so easily," he insisted.

She put down her fork and looked at him. "When this is over, however it ends, you will go back to London?"

"Yes, of course."

"I will stay here." There it was said, out and in the open. She would stay in Avebury; he would go. Beyond that, there could be nothing else.

"It isn't so simple—"

"Yes," she said firmly, "it really is." As indeed it had to be, for to leave Avebury, she would first have to conquer the madness that seemed far closer to conquering her instead.

Steam rose from the bread. She broke off a piece and offered it to him. His fingers brushed hers. A warm curl of pleasure unfolded deep within her. Hard on it came regret that there could be no future for them. But it was a foolish wish and she beat it down, determined to hold firm to what for her passed as reality.

Faulkner took the bread. He looked no happier than he had before. She sought for something that might ease his mood, comfort him somehow, for his sadness was far harder to bear than her own.

"Surely you will not need to take much longer here?" she began, but no, that was wrong. She was rewarded by a scowl that would have sent a brave man scurrying. As she had nowhere to go, Sarah stood her ground. Or rather sat it, there at Morley's table with the kidney pie before her and the soft light fading beyond the door.

It was a perfect spring evening in the country, save for the tension roiling between them.

And for the sudden scream that ripped the silence and sent the blackbirds in hasty flight toward the darkening sky.

19

"*Dead not a* quarter hour," Dr. Quack said. He straightened up from the body, which was still boldly clad in the new white shirt and frock coat, the well-tailored breeches and the shining boots.

Davey Hemper, or what had been Davey, lay on his side in an alley between the inn and the church. His throat had been cut. The stones of the graveyard wall were cold against Sarah's back. She put a hand to her mouth to keep from crying out. Pain twisted inside her, for Davey, for Avebury, for the hideous violations that had come among them.

"It wasn't the Gypsies," she said.

Curate Edwards looked up from his horrified contemplation of the body. He was pale and shaking in his first encounter with violent death. Whatever he had eaten recently was threatening to return. "Gypsies?" he repeated numbly.

"The Romany are gone," Faulkner said. "They can't

be blamed for this one, and if they can't, they probably weren't responsible for the first two either."

The young minister's eyes widened. "You mean—"

"The killer is one of your own, curate. You might as well reconcile yourself to that."

"It can't be," Edwards protested. "These are good people here. They—"

"Same sort of blow to the head in the back that the others had," the doctor said. "That probably stunned him long enough to finish the job."

Faulkner swept the ground with his eyes. "No sign of a weapon. Any idea what it could have been?"

Quack shrugged. He wiped his bloodied hands on a square of cloth. "A knife, for sure, but not too large a blade. The kind a man might carry for skinning small game or whittling wood, even notching a hole in a horse's leather. You could find such knives anywhere you cared to look."

Faulkner nodded. "No footprints; the ground is dry." He bent down beside Davey and touched him gently. "What were you doing back here, boy?" he murmured. "On your way elsewhere or did you come to meet someone?"

"He can't tell you," Quack said.

Faulkner straightened but continued looking at the body. "You'd be surprised what the dead can do. We'll take him to your surgery. I want every piece of clothing he's wearing examined. Curate, find Constable Duggin and tell him to meet us there. Also tell him I want men he can trust—presuming there are any—to close off this entire area until it can be thoroughly searched."

He turned slightly and looked toward the inn.

"Miss Morley will have to be questioned, but that can wait a bit." Annalise had found the body and a terrible racket she'd set up, not that she could be blamed. Her father had whisked the shuddering, sobbing girl back inside. Neither had been seen since, although Sarah thought she'd glimpsed Morley peering from a window of the inn.

Faulkner touched her shoulder. "Will you go to his mother?"

She nodded, dread filling her but with no thought of refusal. This was her duty as mistress of Avebury, to share the worst times as well as the best, to give whatever comfort she could.

The small thatched cottage that Missus Hemper inhabited was dark. No light shone from the two windows on either side of the front door. Sarah knocked. When she got no answer, she eased the door open and stepped inside.

"Missus Hemper?"

There was no reply. Not until her eyes adjusted to the dimness did she make out the figure huddled on a stool beside the cold fire.

"Missus Hemper?"

The figure moved slightly. A reed-thin voice spoke. "It's you, then."

The old woman was wrapped in a shawl, her arms drawn around herself as though to ward off a dread chill. Sarah took a deep breath, steeling herself. She knelt beside the stool.

"I'm so sorry . . . Davey . . ."

"The gray mare took him, didn't she? It's the time of year, you know. Cruel spring, we used to call it, when lambs died and the first green shoots wilted in the fields."

To another, the ramblings might have seemed no more than the disjointed anguish of a elderly woman.

But Sarah understood only too well. When Avebury was young, the gray mare was already the harbinger of death.

"We will find who did it," she promised, her hands clasping Missus Hemper's. "I swear we will. But you must help us. If he said anything, the slightest hint of what he was involved in, we must know."

"He said nothing," the old woman replied, bitter for the lost child who had not trusted her enough to confide what might have saved him. "Pleased with himself, he was, strutting like a peacock. But wouldn't say a word about where he'd come by the coin even when I begged him to tell me. I knew they'd be nothing good ahead."

A sob broke from her.

"Said he was going to London. Going to see the world and make a place for himself. What place has he now? A pile of dirt in the churchyard when he had his whole life before him."

She put her head in her hands and wept, not loudly but with the deep, endless despair of a woman who has seen the ultimate violation of nature, her child dead before her.

Sarah held her for a long time, cradling the old woman against her. There was nothing else she could say or do. Some pain was truly too deep for any hope of healing.

In time, Missus Goody came, brought by the news, and Missus Damas as well. One after another, the women of the village assembled there in the small cottage, the shock and horror of Davey's murder filling them as well. But there were things to be done, tea to be made, the fire built up, Missus Hemper urged to bed. And words to be spoken, of Davey's bright smile and the favors he'd done each of them as a small boy, pulling weeds or toting bundles. Nothing much about later, for he'd been a hard lad, but that didn't matter now.

"Angels sing him to his rest," Missus Damas murmured and wiped the tears from her eyes, true tears, honestly shed, for the grief that had come upon them. She touched a hand to Sarah's shoulder. In the hush of the cottage, her voice held the ring of steel. "Something must be done, mistress."

The teapot stilled in the hand about to pour from it. A piece of tinder waited to be dropped upon the fire. All eyes—eyes of the women of Avebury—turned to Sarah.

"Yes," she said quietly, looking round at each of them. "There must be justice." Slowly, one by one, they nodded. Justice there would be. They would, all of them together, see to it.

Faulkner knew what had to be done. In his investigation two years ago of embezzlement from the military stores, the most useful clues had come from the body of a light colonel killed in a riding accident. Papers in the man's pockets and sewn into the lining of his coat had been key to solving the crime. All the same, he did not look forward to going through Davey Hemper's garments.

"Can't imagine what you're expecting to find," Constable Duggin said. He had come swiftly upon hearing the news and stood now to one side of the surgery. After a hard look at the body, he kept his eyes averted.

"Neither can I," Faulkner agreed. "But you never can tell. Good fabric this. The tailoring's not bad either."

Duggin peered more closely, at the garments, not the body. "They *are* well made," he said with some surprise. "How did the likes of Hemper come by them?"

"Exactly what I would like to determine. Did he have a job?"

"He helped his old mother and did day work for the farmers when he could get it."

"Such as now?"

"Maybe," Duggin said with a note of doubt. "It's planting time, there's plenty of work. Still, it doesn't pay all that well."

Faulkner went over to the table where Davey lay, still and pale. He lifted each of his hands. "His nails are clean and unbroken."

Duggin spared a glance, looked away again. "They wouldn't be if he'd been doing field work."

"Then it was something else. Any ideas?"

"There's gambling now and again, cockfighting over toward Dunford, that sort of thing. Maybe he got involved in something like that."

"And someone killed him for it?"

"It could be," the constable insisted.

"How does that explain the Gypsies?"

"Doesn't have to. Separate matters altogether."

Faulkner laughed, a harsh, cruel sound. "Is that the line, then? The Roms were murdered by a fellow Gypsy who has since vanished, while poor Davey here met his end because of cockfighting in Dunford? That's quite a stretch."

"You've still no reason to think it was anyone from hereabouts," Duggin insisted. He had the defensive air of a man clinging to a position he knows he cannot protect but hates to yield.

"Give it up," Quack said. "Davey's tied to the Gypsies

somehow. They all died here, and it's here you've got to look for the murderer."

"What about the passengers off the Bath coach?" Duggin asked. "One of them could have done it."

"For God's sake!" Quack erupted. "They were all long gone before this happened. Open your eyes, man, and while you're at it, take an honest look at what's lying here. Davey Hemper was one of your own, born and bred in Avebury. Whatever you thought of him—and I didn't think much—he's got a right to have his killer found."

Duggin sighed, his broad shoulders drooping. Unhappiness was stamped clear on his ruddy features. "This is all out of my ken. I've no idea how to ferret out a murderer."

"Which is why we've got Sir William, isn't that so, milord? He'll put it together."

"Your confidence delights me," Faulkner muttered.

Quack grimaced and reached into a cupboard. He withdrew a bottle and offered it around. Faulkner shook his head but Duggin was moved to take a swig. It made him cough violently, which Quack thought amusing. He took a long pull, wiped the back of his hand across his mouth, and looked to Faulkner. "What now?"

"The clothes, inch by inch and seam by seam, if necessary. I want to know where they were made and by whom."

"Neither of us could tell you that," Duggin said. "We don't know anything about it."

"Who does?"

"One of the women, I suppose. Who—"

"Mistress Huxley?" Quack suggested but doubtfully, Sarah not being well known for her dedication to fashion.

"Morley's daughter, more likely. She's always turning up in some frippery."

"She has to be questioned anyway," Faulkner said. He lifted the pile of garments. "I might as well throw these in too."

"Good luck to you," Quack said and had another swallow. He passed the bottle back to Duggin, who hesitated but took it all the same.

Faulkner left, carrying the clothes with him. Outside, it was almost full dark. He walked along the lane, glad of the moon to show his way. There was a light now in Missus Hemper's cottage. The evening was warm enough for the door to have been left open. He caught a glimpse of several women standing there, watching him, and wondered if Sarah was among them.

"Absolutely not," Morley said. He straightened to his full height, throwing off for the moment the guise of a beaten man, and shook his head firmly. "I'll not have her disturbed."

"It's important that I speak with your daughter," Faulkner said. His tone was gentle, even with a touch of kindness. Morley was bound to resist, any father would do the same. But Faulkner would not yield. Annalise would have to speak, and tonight, before memory had the chance to dim.

"She is sleeping," Morley insisted.

"I doubt that. This was a great shock to her. It will help her to talk."

"How would you know what will help her?" Morley flared. "She's been sobbing and shuddering ever since she came upon him. I fear for her health."

"Then let her speak. I have only a few questions, and it will be done. She can begin to put this all behind her."

The publican shot him a sharp look. "You think so?"

"She is young and undoubtedly resilient. But if she doesn't speak with me tonight, she will have to tomorrow. If not then, the next day. Eventually, she could be summoned before the coroner's jury."

"Not that!" Morley exclaimed. "She could never bear to tell it before so many."

"Then she speaks now and answers all my questions, fully and truthfully. Or she appears before the jury. You decide."

Pressed into that corner, Morley still hesitated. But there was no way out for him and they both knew it. At length, he agreed but with a condition. "I'll go upstairs and fetch her. You'll ask your questions down here with me present."

Faulkner had expected nothing else. He nodded. Morley vanished up the stairs. Barely had he gone than Crispin appeared. "Sir Isaac sent me, milord," the valet said. "He is weary but wishes to know if it's true about the boy."

"It is. Morley's daughter found him, but I'll be surprised if she can cast any light on what happened."

"Odd, don't you think, three murders in a village this size all within the month?"

"Exceedingly odd," Faulkner said.

"But then it's an odd place, full of strange goings-on."

"The haunting, you mean, Morley's monks?"

"That and more, the circles everywhere you look, the mounds and barrows. Yesterday I saw an owl by daylight. That shouldn't be, should it?"

"Not that I've ever known. Still and all, it's only a village. Tell Sir Isaac not to worry, we will get to the bottom of whatever is happening."

"I certainly hope so, sir," Crispin said. "London has its drawbacks, but I find it a good deal more peaceful, all things considered."

He departed, leaving Faulkner to his own contemplation. He was just beginning to think that Morley did not intend to return when there was a rustle on the steps. The publican came first, trailed by his daughter. Annalise was fully dressed but her hair was disordered, as though she could not quite manage to put it up as usual.

Eyes downcast, hands clasped at her waist, she took the seat her father indicated.

"As you can see," Morley began, "she's not herself. Weary, she is, and still in shock. I hope you'll be quick."

"My very thought," Faulkner assured him. He gave the girl what he hoped was a reassuring smile. "Now, Miss Morley, if you would just be good enough to tell me exactly what you saw when you came out into the alley."

Her reply was so muted he could not hear it.

"A little louder, if you please. I realize this is a strain, but it is necessary."

"A body," she whispered. "I saw him, Davey Hemper."

"Did you see anyone else?"

"No, only him."

"Was he moving?"

She cast a quick glance at her father. "No, he wasn't. At first I thought he was asleep, but it seemed a strange place for anyone to take a rest. I looked closer and that was when—" Her voice broke. She shuddered violently.

"Easy, now," Morley said. He put a hand on her shoulder. "I told you she wasn't up to this."

"You realized he was dead," Faulkner continued. The girl had been through a bad experience, but she couldn't be a complete ninny. She had to know her evidence was essential. "You saw no weapon, a knife, for instance?"

She shook her head. "Nothing, only him. Please, sir, that's all I can tell you—"

"Just one more thing." Faulkner laid the frock coat he carried on the table. "Have you seen this before?"

Annalise stared at it. Her brow furrowed. "I don't . . . wait, that's his, isn't it? Davey's? I saw him in it for the first time this morning and then again—" She stopped and put a hand to her lips, trying to stop their trembling.

"When you saw it this morning, did you say anything to him about it?"

"Why, no, I didn't. He was on the other side of the lane, you see. I only caught a glimpse."

"Kindly look more closely at it now. He acquired it only recently, perhaps yesterday. There can't be too many places around here to purchase such a garment."

Annalise's manner eased somewhat, although she remained very tense. Despite the trauma of the day, the coat caught her attention. It was a gaudy thing of a style that had been fashionable a few seasons before and was only now reaching the country. The outer fabric was velvet with a satin lining and gilded buttons down the front.

"You shouldn't be bothering her with this," Morley objected.

"It's all right," Annalise said softly. "Sir William is right, there aren't many places Davey could have gotten this. In fact, I can think of only one, Madame Charlotte's over at Dunford."

"And who is Madame Charlotte?" Faulkner asked.

"A very fine seamstress formerly of Paris, France, in which capacity she performed sewing for the Bourbons themselves."

"Indeed?" He made a valiant effort to hide his skepticism. "Until she decided to come to—where?— Dunford?"

"That's right. She set up shop and has done very well. I have a few things of hers myself. My guess is she made this."

"Thank you," Faulkner said and meant it. He had a bona fide clue that, followed properly, might even help him discover where the boy had gotten his money.

"That's all, then," Morley said as though it were his decision. He helped his daughter up and steered her firmly back toward the steps. "I trust you won't be needing anything more, milord."

Faulkner gave him no such assurance but he did let him go. It was growing late. He still wanted to examine the clothing further and consider carefully what else should be done.

And, oh, yes, there was one another thing. The small matter of Mistress Huxley and his unwillingness to let her spend this night alone.

20

Sarah sat at her dressing table near the window. She held a silver brush. Her hair hung loosely down her back but she was not brushing it. Instead, she stared out the window absently.

The exhaustion in her ran bone deep. She had not slept at all the night before, and the day had been tumultuous. Had it truly begun on the hill fort with Faulkner, rejoicing in the ultimate power of life, only to end with a sad death?

Missus Hemper had fallen into an uneasy sleep before Sarah left. Some of the other women stayed, but she desperately needed to rest. Tomorrow would bring a whole new host of problems to be dealt with, chief among them the search for the killer.

Wearily, she put the brush down and stood. It was very quiet in the room. She could hear the soft plop of wax running down the candle beside the bed. Her eyes burned and there was a deep ache inside her, yet still she shied from sleep. Fear of the dream haunted her more than ever. She had to stay here, firmly anchored in this reality, not slip away to that other.

Yet another night without dreams and the madness would be closer than ever.

Uncertain, she pulled the covers back but only sat on the bed. The house sighed around her. It had always been her comfort and her sanctuary, but now her soul stretched against it, pushing at the boundaries, straining outward.

What was Faulkner doing? He was no more likely to be asleep than she, but at least he had work to occupy him. Accustomed as he was to being in command, he had taken over the investigation at once. Unlike the Gypsy deaths, this one had a fresh trail to follow and the real chance of a solution. She almost envied him the ability to act while she sat, drained of strength, her mind a jumble.

A sigh escaped her. She swung her legs up onto the bed and sat back against the pillows. Sleep beckoned almost irresistibly. But it was a shadowed, ever-shifting landscape where she feared to misstep.

Her eyelids were weighted. She caught them closing and jerked upright, her heart beating wildly. There was a movement near the window.

"What—?"

"Hush," a deep voice said. "It's me."

As though that somehow made it all right. She stared, dumbfounded, as Faulkner eased himself over the windowsill, straightened, and dusted his hands off. "You're still awake," he observed.

"Of course I'm still awake. What are you doing here?"

It really was Faulkner, not some phantom of her

imaginings. He wore the same white shirt and dark breeches he'd had on earlier, his dark frock coat donned in deference to the cooling evening. His hair was drawn back as usual, freeing his chiseled features, and his eyes shone with a light that warmed her everywhere.

He advanced toward the bed and stood looking down at her, his brow slightly creased. "You're very tired."

"Don't change the subject. You can't just climb in my window as though—"

"Should I have gone round and rung the bell?"

"Good lord, no, you'd wake the servants."

"My point." Grinning, he sat down on the edge of the bed and began pulling his boots off. "I thought we'd at least try to be discreet."

A tremor of anticipation surged through her, only to falter against the wall of fatigue that surrounded her. "Faulkner—"

"Hush," he said again. "We're both exhausted. I only want to hold you."

"But—"

"No buts. Seriously, Sarah, there is a murderer loose here in Avebury. You can't expect me to let you be alone at night while that's the case."

She couldn't? That was a novel thought for one who had been independent most of her life, yet a tempting one. To be cared for, protected, looked after in a way she had never been. Truly, that was as seductive as anything they had yet shared.

"This house has strong doors," she pointed out, but only absently, for it was very hard to think of much else as he stood again and removed his frock coat. His shirt followed. Clad only in his breeches, he got into the bed beside her and drew her into his arms.

Softly, against her ear, he said, "What if you wander?"

She stiffened but only for a moment. He was right, of course, this man who in some ways seemed to know her better than she knew herself. If the dream came upon her again and moved her as it had before, she might find herself anywhere. And so, just possibly, might the killer.

"Is that how you think of it?" she murmured against his chest. "That I merely wandered?"

"It's as good an explanation as any, isn't it?"

She made a soft sound, half laugh, half sob. "Better than most—or at least kinder."

"I am not kind," he insisted and carefully tucked the covers around her, holding her safe as the night deepened and sleep crept over them both.

He had to find a better way. This business of climbing out of a lady's boudoir before dawn held only limited appeal. Besides, there were people in London who would pay a great deal to know he had done such a thing.

Faulkner took a firmer grip on a branch, swung his foot down to another, and let go, preparing to shift his hold. He missed, his balance gave way, and he fell, crashing through layers of branches to land ignominiously on his behind at the bottom of the tree.

Sarah leaned out the window, alarmed. "Are you hurt?"

He stood up sheepishly, and grimaced. "Only my pride. I'll be back in an hour. We're going to Dunford."

"Dunford? What for?"

"I'll tell you on the way. Be ready."

She darted back inside. He flecked the dust from his breeches and turned toward the lane but got no further than a pace or two when, from the corner of his eye, he caught the startled stare of Missus Damas standing with her broom at the back door. She gazed at him in astonishment. "Milord?"

Faulkner smiled and sketched a bow. He went on his way, his mood improved. Loyalty to her mistress would keep the housekeeper silent, at least so far as the village went. But he didn't doubt she would have a few words for Sarah.

As Sarah herself seemed to give no thought at all to the implications of their liaison, he was glad of anyone who might encourage her to do so. As long, that was, as she did not withdraw from him.

That quite simply he could not bear. He shook his head, astounded by the thought. Never in his life had he so needed a woman or so cared about her feelings. Truly, he had found more in Avebury than he had bargained for.

But he had not found the murderer, and Davey Hemper was dead as a result. Grimly, he turned his thoughts to the task ahead.

Crispin laid out fresh clothes for him while Faulkner bathed and shaved. He had just finished dressing when Sir Isaac stuck his head in to ask if there was anything he could do. Faulkner was inclined to say no but thought better of it. He finished tying his stock, slipped his frock coat on, and said, "How are you at spying, Sir Isaac?"

The old man looked bemused. "Do you know, I've no idea."

"I'd like you to find out. Drift about the village, if you will. Drop in wherever you reasonably can: the shop, the church, downstairs. See what you can pick up."

"As relates to the killings?"

"Not necessarily. I simply want to know what people are saying about each other. Is anyone particularly angry at anyone else, has there been a recent falling-out, is anyone looked at with suspicion or disfavor? That sort of thing."

Sir Isaac nodded. "Rather like a meeting of the Royal Society. If I can manage that I can certainly do this. I'll report back this evening." He went off briskly, eager to get at it.

"Should I do the same, sir?" Crispin asked.

Faulkner shook his head. "I want you to ride to Bath. If the usual schedule is followed, yesterday's coach driver should be laying over today. Find him, pour a few ales down his throat, and inquire what he thinks of the good folk of Avebury. He's an outsider who passes through regularly. He may have insights we haven't picked up on."

Crispin nodded. He seemed pleased with the commission. "Very good, sir, and you will be—"

"In Dunford making the acquaintance of a certain Madame Charlotte, late of Paris, France."

"Sir?" It wasn't quite censorious but it came close.

Faulkner laughed. "She's a seamstress, Crispin, nothing more. And besides, I'm taking a chaperone along."

Crispin's expression was resigned. He'd had years of dealing with Faulkner's foibles. Nothing surprised him anymore. However, he was not above getting a bit of his own back. "As you say, sir. Kindly give my regards to Mistress Huxley."

"How did you—?"

But Crispin was gone and Faulkner was left to ponder the futility of any man's trying to keep secrets from his valet.

21

Davey Hemper had been more successful in keeping secrets from his seamstress. Madame Charlotte was a plump, florid woman clinging to the remnants of youthful prettiness, and Faulkner's sudden appearance in her establishment left her quite overcome. Sarah had to speak a bit sharply to her before she calmed enough to answer his questions.

"Well, yes, these were sold here," she said, looking at the garments Davey Hemper had worn. Word of the murder had already reached her. She stared at the clothes with horrified fascination as they lay spread out on the counter but made no attempt to touch them.

"You're sure?" Faulkner asked.

"Absolutely. He was in just day before yesterday to buy them."

"Were you surprised that he made such a purchase?" Sarah asked.

Madame Charlotte nodded vigorously. "Very

surprised. I made him show me his money before I would serve him."

"And he had enough?"

"Enough and more. He had a sack of coins. The ones he showed me were sovereigns."

"Did you ask him how he came by such wealth?" Faulkner inquired. He leaned against the counter, his legs crossed, looking for all the world as though he had nothing more pressing on his mind than what he might have for dinner. Sarah wasn't fooled. She recognized the slumberous, almost bored attitude as a mask hiding a ruthless drive for truth.

"I teased him about it a bit," Madame Charlotte allowed. "Asked him if he'd a good run of the horses."

"Had he?" Faulkner asked.

"I don't think so. You know how people are when they have something they'd like to say but can't? That's how he seemed. As though he was bursting to let it out but determined not to."

"And you've no idea what this something could have been?" Sarah asked.

Madame Charlotte shook her head. "No, I don't—wait." She thought for a moment. "Right at the end as he was leaving, he did ask me if I might be interested in taking on someone in the shop. He said he knew a young lady who was keen on fashion and who he thought would suit me well."

Faulkner and Sarah exchanged a glance. "Did he give you her name?" he asked.

"He didn't. I remember thinking it a bit odd, he'd seemed so taken up by himself, getting his fancy clothes. It surprised me that he had anyone else on his mind at all."

"What did you tell him?" Sarah asked.

"That I might consider taking someone on if she had genuine talent and would work cheap."

"What was his response?"

"He said he'd have the young lady get in touch with me."

"Has she?"

"Not so far."

"If she does," Faulkner said, "you will notify me at once."

Madame Charlotte's head bobbed up and down in agreement. Clearly, it would not occur to her to do anything else.

They left the shop shortly afterward and walked a short way down Dunford's main street. The village was slightly larger than Avebury and without any trace of ancient ruins. It was far more what Faulkner expected when he thought of rural England, on those rare occasions he did think of it, back when London and the court were the world, those fast-receding days before Avebury and its mysteries absorbed him so completely.

"What do you think?" he asked as they reached the stable where they had left Rascal and the mare Sarah was riding.

"It may mean nothing," she said, "but from Davey's description, the young lady he was talking about is likely to be Annalise Morley."

"Does she want to leave home?"

"I don't know," Sarah said thoughtfully. "Annalise's mother died several years ago after a long illness. She's been the mainstay of the family, taking care of a younger brother and sister, helping her father in the inn. Perhaps she's tired enough of it all to want to get off on her own."

"And perhaps she has a more immediate reason. You're aware that she has a tendresse for young Hoddinworth?"

Sarah's eyes widened. "How do you know that?"

"Simple, I saw them." He looked pardonably self-satisfied. "Oh, not doing anything, she was merely watching him with a certain puppylike expression that told the tale."

"What a dreadful way to put it. Besides, Hoddinworth doesn't know she's alive."

"Or pretends not to. More to the point, if there is something between them and if they were trying to keep it a secret, he wouldn't be able to pay off Davey Hemper. He has no money."

"He may have no money," Sarah corrected. "The Hoddinworths' funds are, as the saying goes, exhausted. Bad investments and an even worse run at cards are the reason. However, Justin was always better at the tables than his parents, more inclined to win. He may have resources they don't know about."

"All right, what about Edwards?"

"Our curate? You can't be serious. It's true he seems drawn to Annalise, but I hardly think—"

"Has he a decent living here?"

"Reasonable as these things go." She hesitated before adding, "His family is wealthy. I'm sure they give him a generous stipend."

"So he could afford to pay off Davey, if necessary. The question is, could he also kill? If I had to guess, I'd bet on Hoddinworth."

"I think this is the time to tell you that the Hoddinworths are my second cousins."

"Really? How convenient."

"The marchioness came to see me. She seems to think

that merely meeting you will be to their advantage."
Her skepticism could not have been more clear, but he
seized on the notion at once.

"What a splendid idea. Why don't you invite us all
to supper?"

"Because I would rather have my nails drawn one
by one than sit through such an encounter."

"You astonish me, Sarah. How could you be so
neglectful of your relations." He bent closer, his
breath brushing the curve of her cheek. "Or of me?"

There in the quiet of the stable, the air heavy with
the scents of leather and straw, she shivered. He was
too close by far, all around her, in her, shattering her
reserve and drawing her out in ways she could not
resist.

She turned her head slightly and met his eyes.
"You are a dangerous man."

Faulkner grinned. "Is that what Missus Damas
says?"

Sarah's cheeks flamed. He was forever catching
her off balance. "Did you get caught on purpose?"

"Not at all. I'm the soul of discretion."

"So is she, it seems. She assures me our secret is
safe."

"What else does she say?"

"I wouldn't dream of telling you."

He looked immensely pleased. "I knew I could
count on her."

The mare nickered. Sarah broke away and went to
her. She leaned her head against the sleek flanks and
wished, for just a moment, that the whole complex,
contrary world would go away. Then she straightened,
took a deep breath, and lifted herself back into the
saddle.

* * *

"Crown of lamb," Missus Damas said, "for the main course, preceded by a nice bisque and some poached salmon. I'll make my compote of turnips and potatoes for the side, and we'll round out with a nice tart and cheese for the gentlemen. It will all be splendid."

"It will all be a great deal of trouble," Sarah countered.

"Nonsense. I've always said you should do more entertaining. There just hasn't been any reason. But now"—the housekeeper sighed with delight—"the Marquess and Marchioness of Hoddinworth, Viscount Hoddinworth, and—most marvelously of all—Sir William Faulkner Devereaux all under the same roof, and me to cook for them! I can hardly believe it."

"A rare joy, to be sure," Sarah muttered. She stared out the drawing room windows. It had begun to rain, a cold, discouraging pall that splattered against the flagstones outside and made spring seem a mirage.

They were wakeing Davey Hemper at his mother's house. She had to go. It seemed absurd to be planning a supper party, much less one she was loath to give, under such sad circumstances.

"Just do your best," she said as she stood. "I realize I've given you very little notice." It was as close as she could come to saying that she wanted no fuss, but Missus Damas refused to take the hint.

"Don't worry for a moment." She cast her mistress a knowing look. "It will all be splendid," she repeated. "And why wouldn't it be, for isn't everything here the equal and more of anything to be found in London? It would take a blind man not to know that, or a fool."

"We are very far from London," Sarah said softly. "And we always will be."

Missus Damas was frowning mightily as Sarah went out into the hall and put her cloak on. It had been warm when they rode to Dunford, but now there was a real chill in the air. She was glad of the cloak as she set off down the lane toward Missus Hemper's cottage.

There was a crowd gathered. The men stood when she entered; the women nodded their greetings. She spoke gently to Missus Hemper and took a seat next to her, holding her gnarled hands in her own.

The evening passed slowly.

22

Sarah turned over in bed. She was wrapped in warmth. The cares of the long day had vanished. She floated in bliss, completely relaxed, completely safe.

Her eyes opened. She stared directly at Faulkner's bare chest, the skin drawn taut over powerful muscles lightly dusted with dark hair. He was there again, in her bed, in the night, protecting her against all dangers.

Except, of course, for those he brought with him.

She stirred tentatively, afraid to wake him, afraid not to. He made a low sound but did not move. Emboldened, she sat up slightly and looked at him. Asleep, he looked younger and far less—what was the word exactly?—domineering, aggressive, insufferable? Superb? No, not less superb, only more approachable.

Very, very approachable.

But not by her. Absolutely not. What had happened on the hill fort was one thing entirely. What happened in her own bed was entirely another. Wasn't it?

There were no excuses here. Ancient Avebury did not whisper around her now. In fact, it seemed oddly still. She had a sense of being unusually anchored in her own time and place. In her own decisions.

Well, now, what would a proper gentlewoman do, waking to find a man not her husband in her bed? Screaming was such a nuisance. Besides, all things considered, it was flatly ridiculous. She could simply go back to sleep. She could get up and go elsewhere. She could—

Touch her lips ever so lightly to his, just the merest brush as gentle as a breeze that would not even stir the fluff of a dandelion from its perch.

And she could, out of simple curiosity, gaze down the length of his body visible above the sheet, marveling at how extraordinarily different he was from her and wondering at the forces that had made him so. There was a thin white scar on his left shoulder and another, broader, with the edges still puckered, on the right side of his ribs. Her throat ached. She touched her mouth to the arch of his throat, feeling there the pulse of his life's blood.

And still he slept.

Kind of him, she thought, for all that he claimed not to be a kind man. She glanced toward the window. The light had a soft gray texture, creeping up to take the night by surprise. It would be some time yet before the house stirred.

They would bury Davey Hemper today. And they would set themselves to find the killer who had violated the peace of Avebury. It would be a hard time, full of trial. But first there was this hour, wrapped in silence, fraught with possibilities.

The bed creaked slightly beneath her. She held her

breath, waiting, then let it go when still he did not stir. Her hand trailed down his chest experimentally. He was so very warm while she felt all a-shiver.

With utmost care, hardly breathing, she lifted the sheet. A long sigh escaped her. Truly, she must have been worn out last night not to notice that he had, this time, removed his breeches. Indeed, now that she thought to notice, they were tossed over the back of her dressing-table chair.

Ah, well, the man had a right to be comfortable, didn't he? Although by the looks of it, comfort was fast fleeing. Could that really happen while he was still asleep? Amazing. Nature was full of absolutely astounding marvels, rather beautiful too, as she grew more used to the sight of it, so filled with life and vigor, so—

Ummph!

The world revolved around her. One moment, she was sitting up, contemplating the mystery of man and nature. The next moment, she was flat on her back, the man firm between her legs and nature more than evident.

"You're awake," she said, unnecessarily.

His smile glinted white. "So are you."

She should say something—about decency, responsibility, propriety—something. But all she could think of was the feel of his skin all along the length of hers. They had not been so close before, not like this, with only the thin cotton of her night rail to separate them. The sensation engulfed her. She could hardly breathe.

Undoubtedly, he realized that and meant to help. That must be why he lifted her slightly and removed the night rail with deftness she could not help but admire, even born as it obviously was of long experience.

There was so little time. Day crept upon them and with it the whole busy, tumultuous world. He would find the killer; he would leave. She would stay. There was only this tiny morsel of eternity to share together.

Her hips moved, urgent and welcoming. He gave a low groan and bent his head, dark against her breasts, suckling her. Pleasure coiled through her, poised on the knife edge of pain. She cried out, clinging to him, and let the moment sweep her where it would.

"Heavenly Father, receive into your care the soul of David Francis Hemper. Give to his mother solace in the bearing of her burdens, to his neighbors consolation before the immensitude of thy will, and to each of us light to see the path of righteousness and courage to follow it in our daily journey according to thy will. This we ask most urgently in thy name. Amen."

The curate lifted his head. He looked weary but resolute. Missus Hemper wept, supported by the village women on either side of her. Tears slipped soundlessly down her withered cheeks.

The ache in Sarah's chest was as a vise, pressing the hope from her, leaving only sorrow and seething far below it in a dark and deadly place, rage. She lifted her head, welcoming the rain against her cheeks.

A throat was cleared. From beside Edwards, a bent old man gathered his strength. Dr. Geoffrey Holbein, their retired curate, had come from his bed to be present at the graveside. He was content to let his young successor conduct the service, but now he had something to say.

They waited. In his prime, longer ago than most could remember, Holbein had not been especially attentive to his duties. He was a good-enough soul, but the scholarly life drew him more than the spiritual. That had suited the villagers fine. They'd wanted no one looking too carefully at the state of their souls.

Yet now they gazed past young Edwards to this old voice in their midst and wondered what he had to tell them.

"There is evil here," Holbein said, flatly and without equivocation. His voice was surprisingly firm for a man of his age. "It's an insidious thing that has come among us slowly. Time was we thought more of the welfare of our souls than the comfort of our bodies. We were not afraid to consider eternity and our place in it. A man could turn aside from worldly goods and find his richness in the love of God. But no longer."

He stared down at the open grave wherein lay the simple oak box. "Now we think only of what we have rather than what we are. A man is judged by his possessions. Nothing matters so much as to do well, to get ahead, to prosper." He raised his head, looking at them all with sudden fierceness.

"Know this: on the day of judgment you will stand naked before the Lord. Neither wealth nor position will protect you. If there is no love in your heart for something greater than yourself, you will perish."

He drew breath and his voice softened. "Davey Hemper was a good lad at bottom. But he fell into the same trap that is closing around us all. Let us beseech God to show mercy to him, and to us."

In the silence that followed this declaration, Dr. Holbein appeared pale and shaken. It was as though his powerful words had drained him of all vitality. He slumped on his cane, his face grayish and his breathing labored.

Edwards put an arm around him and, murmuring soothingly, led him down the path away from the graveyard. The rest followed. The women had prepared a meal at Missus Hemper's, but Sarah decided not to go. Instead, she slipped away, down a narrow track that led away from the village.

The rain did not trouble her. She was far too caught up in thinking about what Holbein had said. In all the years he had been their curate, she could never remember him speaking so forcefully on any matter. Clearly, this went to his heart.

Was he right? Were the people of Avebury losing some essential part of their character to the demands of the modern age? Were they becoming so steeped in material concerns that their very souls were in danger?

Evil, Dr. Holbein had said, but she was wary of that word. It had been used too often to condemn anyone who was merely different. She thought of Davey in his grave, bright youth suddenly rendered lifeless. Thought, too, of the Gypsies and the blood-stained ground, the standing stones thrown down, builder Tom Robinson and his scorn for all that had gone before, and Sir Isaac tromping amid the ruins, science and mysticism uneasy partners in the vast regions of his mind.

A twig snapped behind her. She did not turn but stood beneath the shelter of an oak tree, gazing out over a sodden field, and felt the quick surge of pleasure that was now as natural a part of her as breathing.

"Are you all right?" Faulkner asked.

She continued looking out over the land. "I will be. Holbein took me by surprise."

"A grim sort."

"He didn't used to be. Perhaps it's the day and the

circumstances." But she knew it wasn't. What Holbein had said ran too deep for any single event to have shaped it.

"You're cold," Faulkner said as he took her hands, touching them through the dark gloves she had dutifully donned. Her garb was somber but her cheeks glowed and nothing could diminish the power glowing within her. "Crispin is taking Sir Isaac back to the inn," he continued.

She nodded against his chest, having no clear recollection of how she had gotten there. "Let's go home," she said and did not let herself question the terrible strangeness of that word where he was concerned.

The house was empty, Missus Damas and the other servants having gone to the funeral supper. Faulkner built up the fire in the drawing room while Sarah heated a pot of soup. They ate together, neither particularly hungry but needing the comfort.

"The Hoddinworths are coming to supper tomorrow," she said.

"Am I invited as well?"

"Only if you're feeling especially forbearing."

He grinned. "I promise to be the soul of discretion."

"You'll have to be. Elizabeth has a rare nose for scandal."

"I'm sure she's had plenty of opportunity to exercise it. Are you afraid of her finding out about us?"

The soup could have used a bit more dill but it was good all the same. She took another sip, set her spoon down, and said, "Some things are best kept private."

"As you wish. Let the Hoddinworths do their worst.

I will play the gentleman and, with a bit of luck, find out what young Justin's made of."

"They've asked to bring a guest. Some friend of the viscount who is staying with them."

"The would-be peacemaker," Faulkner said thoughtfully.

"What's that?"

Briefly, he told her of the scene he had witnessed at the Rose when the coach arrived, bearing the younger Hoddinworth and his companion up from London.

Sarah shook her head. "So Morley won't serve them. Perhaps I'm wrong about Justin's having any money. Besides, if he's been in London, when would he have paid Davey?"

"There's no saying how long he was away, but let's try to find that out tomorrow," Faulkner said. He stood and held out a hand to her. Rupert rose, too, from his place beside the fire. He regarded the man alertly but without concern.

"Rupert likes you," Sarah said on a note of surprise, trying to remember when her dog had mellowed.

"So too, I think, does Rupert's mistress," Faulkner said and drew her to him.

23

"*Why, Sarah,*" *Lady* Elizabeth said, "how sweet you look! I wouldn't have thought you could wear such a girlish dress at your age, but obviously I was wrong."

Faulkner shot a quick look up at the ceiling on the chance that divine intervention might be hovering there, accepted that it was not, and smiled. "Lady Elizabeth, I've been looking forward to meeting you." Much in the same way a man might be anticipating the extraction of a rotted tooth, but there was no point saying that.

Beneath a generous application of powder, the marchioness blushed. "How kind of you to say so," she declared, offering her hand.

Sarah took a breath, closed her eyes for an instant, and followed Faulkner's lead. If he could do it, she damn well had to.

"Lord Harley, may I present Sir William Devereaux Faulkner?"

The marquess bobbed his head. He was a small man with thinning hair and rheumy eyes, rather like an old cock who's long since forgotten his better days. He looked bemused, as though he couldn't quite credit what he was seeing.

"I'd heard you were hereabouts," he said to Faulkner, "but I couldn't imagine why."

"He didn't believe it." Lady Elizabeth chortled as though this was the most amusing thing she'd ever heard. "Even when I told him you'd be here this evening, he said I had to be mistaken."

"Apparently not," the viscount drawled as the introductions continued. He stared at his mother with such open disdain that Sarah had to resist the impulse to slap him. She was no fan of Elizabeth's, but she was appalled that her son should regard her in such a way.

"Shall we," she murmured, gesturing in the direction of the dining room. The sooner they got on with it, the sooner it would be over.

Faulkner offered his arm to Lady Elizabeth, who seized on it with a swiftness that suggested dismemberment was a possibility. Lord Harley offered his escort to Sarah. Justin followed with his friend, who had been introduced as one Bertrand Johnson, son of a baronet and an old school chum.

Bertrand appeared as in awe of Faulkner as Justin was determined not to be. The latter affected to be bored by the proceedings, but Sarah caught him casting glances at Faulkner as though unable to believe he was quite real.

Steeling herself, Sarah took her seat at the far end

of the table. She had placed Faulkner at the head. Lady Elizabeth was to his right, Justin to his left. Lord Harley and the dazzled Bertrand were similarly arranged to either side of her. Fortunately, etiquette provided for some leeway in such a situation. True, she could have seated Lord Harley to Faulkner's left, but it was customary to separate husband and wife by a greater degree, usually because they liked it that way, and as hostess she could rightly claim the senior male as her partner.

That she had sunk to such deliberations proved more than anything else possibly could have how dire her circumstances really were. If Elizabeth hadn't been a second—or was it third?—cousin, and had there been any other prospect of getting the Hoddinworths to remove from Avebury under their own power, Sarah would have said to hell in a hand basket with them all. Instead, she smiled and signaled Missus Damas to begin serving.

The dress she was wearing was not girlish. It was, in fact, quite sophisticated, being made of apricot silk and trimmed with tea-hued lace open in the front to display a graceful stomacher arrayed with ribbon bows and an underskirt of dark blue silk embroidered with tiny golden flowers. The neckline was décolleté, wide but—unlike Elizabeth's—not excessively low. The sleeves were elbow length and ended in several rows of flounces.

She was fortunate to require no corseting but she had bent to the gods of fashion—or, more correctly, to Missus Damas's insistence—enough to accept a modest pannier. Her auburn hair was swept up to the crown of her head and let fall in a long, heavy coil. She wore no powder, nor did she brighten her eyes with belladonna. As it was, they were bright enough observing the antics going-on at the head of the table.

Discretion, had Faulkner said? Seduction was more like it. He had set himself to be charming but appeared to have overdone it. Another few minutes and Elizabeth would require mopping up.

Missus Damas's lobster bisque was renowned in three counties. Sarah barely tasted it. Nor did she pay more than scant attention to whatever it was Lord Harley was saying, something about investments in West Indian sugar, surely of no account.

How old was Elizabeth? She kept herself so well that it was almost impossible to know, but if memory served—and judging by Justin's age—she had to be in her mid-forties. That did not seem to deter her from simpering over a man barely ten years older than her own son, and doing it right in front of her husband to boot.

Not that Lord Harley cared. He gave her not so much as a glance. Justin was a different matter. He clearly loathed his mother, yet he was also torn. Faulkner was the soul of courtesy, including him in the conversation despite Elizabeth's all-too evident preference to exclude him.

"I left London over a week ago," Faulkner was saying. "What has happened since?"

The question came laden with flattery, as though anything the younger man might know could possibly be of interest to this dweller on the high, rarefied cliff called court. Slowly, before Sarah's unwillingly fascinated eyes, Justin too was seduced of sorts. His resentment cracked and, unbending, he began to declaim on events in the capital. It was only what was being said in the coffeehouses and clubs, but Faulkner listened attentively. He nodded several times, asking a further question or two, and even laughed when Justin attempted a bit of wit.

She had thought him a dangerous man, but she had not understood the depth of that danger. He was not merely a slashing force on the battlefield and driving passion in her arms. He was, God help her, intelligent. Deeply, profoundly intelligent. And controlled, so utterly controlled it took her breath away. Until she remembered when he was not, when that control shattered, in her, held close. Then she felt slightly better but still awash in wary fascination, watching this master play out his line.

The fish came and went. The lamb arrived. Wine was poured, candles flickered. The Hoddinworths teetered into ecstasy, spinning on the point of this man's fascination, of his power and his reach, of all he represented. Caught.

Sarah rose. She stood for several moments before Elizabeth noticed. The marchioness looked vaguely surprised to see that she was still there, so utterly forgotten had she been. With a dry smile, Sarah said, "Shall we leave the gentlemen to their port?"

For an instant, she truly believed Elizabeth was going to refuse. Only by the greatest effort of will did the older woman recall the niceties. She rose, but slowly, reluctance evident in every inch. Her gaze fastened on Faulkner.

"You won't be long, will you?" It was said with a smile, as though teasing. But her eyes were utterly serious, filled with a yearning that for just an instant made Sarah feel more sympathetic to her.

"I wouldn't dream of it," Faulkner said easily, the assurance tossed as a bone to a dog.

Sarah turned just in time to conceal the look on her face. She led the way out of the dining room. Barely had they reached the parlor than Elizabeth said, "Is this really necessary? I realize you country mice feel compelled to show off your manners, but we could just as easily have stayed."

"And denied ourselves this rare time together? Why, cousin, you astonish me. Besides, don't you think Lord Harley and Justin are more than capable of making your suit with Faulk . . . Sir William?"

Elizabeth colored. She was on the verge of an acid reply when she suddenly stopped. Her eyes narrowed. "What was that you called him?"

Sarah sat down on the couch and smoothed her skirts. Her hands were steady but only just. "Sir William?"

"No, you started to call him Faulkner." Elizabeth barred her teeth in a feline grin. "What is that, some little pet name?"

There were times when she thought herself the most deceptive of women. But then, long practice concealing madness had made her so. "Why, Elizabeth," she said with a perfectly straight face, "I'm surprised you don't know. Everyone calls him Faulkner, at least at court. If you say Sir William there, no one even knows who you're talking about."

Elizabeth stared, momentarily at a loss for words but still vastly suspicious. She recouped and tried again. "And how would you know what they do at court?"

Sarah managed a small laugh. "Surprising, isn't it, but I thought you of all people would be far better informed than myself. Was I mistaken?"

"No," Elizabeth said slowly. She looked at her cousin

with heightened respect—and caution. "Time together, you say? How nice. Well, then, what shall we chat about?"

Missus Damas had set out a pot of tea for them. Sarah poured. "Davey Hemper was buried yesterday." Although she lacked Faulkner's practiced subtlety, she'd not intended to be so blunt. It was the anger curling around the edges of her soul that drove her.

Elizabeth frowned. "Who?"

"A boy in the village."

"Oh, yes, I did hear something about that." Elizabeth lifted her cup to her lips. "Is there any reason I should care?"

"Only that he was murdered."

"Really? How astonishing. What was it, some rustic tussle over a buxom wrench?"

"No one knows. But as it's the third murder we've had hereabouts—you did know about the Gypsies?"

Elizabeth made a vague gesture of assent, but she was listening more keenly.

"As it's the third, caution does seem called for."

The marchioness lowered her cup. Her eyes glinted. "What exactly are you saying? Are we in some danger?"

"I've no idea," Sarah said. She picked up her own cup and smiled over the rim. "Only that you should be careful." The tea was hot and strong, exactly as she liked it. Her gaze met Elizabeth's. "Very careful."

A board creaked. The first plank in front of the fireplace in the dining room, Sarah guessed. As the fire died and the air cooled, it was prone to crack.

There was a murmur of sound in the hallway outside her room, a whisper really. The wind easing through the sash around the window at the far end of the hall. It needed to be caulked

She sighed impatiently. Every sound was familiar to her. None was the one she awaited. It was night. It was dark. It was late. Where was Faulkner?

There is a murderer about in Avebury, he had said. *I won't let you stay alone,* he had said. *I am not kind.*

That at least was truth.

She lay on her back, hands clenched at her sides, and stared up at the ceiling. Tears stung her eyes but she would not let them fall. Damn him and the horse he rode in on. No, not Rascal. She liked Rascal. It was only his master she wanted to throttle.

"Don't be long," Elizabeth had said.

I wouldn't dream of it.

This then was another kind of madness, more terrifying in its own way that any she had known. Faulkner had no obligation to her. She had made that more than clear. And yet the thought of him with another woman hurt terribly, as though some vital part of her was being twisted apart inside.

He would be gone soon and she would be the better for it. She would retreat back behind her garden walls and never let such pain touch her again. But the memory of it would linger. Without him, she would never be entirely whole again.

Damn him.

A good night's rest, and then tomorrow she'd get out collecting wild herbs. It was too long since she'd done that. There were tenants to visit, repairs to arrange. She had always been very busy in the spring.

Damn him.

She turned over onto her side and looked unseeingly at the wall opposite. Moments passed, time stretching out until she thought it must surely snap.

A shadow moved by the window. A trick of light or of thought? She lay, motionless, hardly breathing. Caution flooded her. What was that she smelled on the cool, night dampness, Elizabeth's perfume, No, not remotely. It was the loamy scent of earth that teased her. Relief flowed and, hard on it, shame.

He thought she was asleep. Not until he reached the side of the bed and saw the flash of her eyes did Faulkner realize otherwise. "You'll never guess where I've been," he said on a whisper, half apologetic for whatever had kept him but excited all the same.

"No," she admitted, her voice husky, "I won't."

"Chasing long-dead monks." He had a boy's eagerness, as though it were all a great adventure.

She sat up in the bed. He sat beside her to pull off his boots. She liked the solidness of him, the reassuring strength. Liked? She liked lemon in her tea and a particular shade of violet. This was sterner stuff.

"Are you all right?" she asked.

He looked surprised. "Of course. Needless to say, I didn't catch them . . . or him. I'm not really sure how many there were."

"What happened exactly?"

"I was slipping out of the inn when I heard moaning and the clank of chains. Morley's haunting again, apparently. It was coming from the graveyard. But when I went there, whoever it was fled."

"You're sure," she said guardedly, "that it was someone?"

"As opposed to a spectral something? Yes, quite sure. I found footprints. It was too dark to tell how many sets there were. I'll have to check again in the morning."

So as she had lain there, damning him, he'd been trying to solve at least one of Avebury's mysteries. Truly, shame was an uncomfortable bedfellow. But at least he didn't know. No inkling of her thoughts shone in his eyes as he slipped into bed beside her. Drawing her to him, he stroked the length of her back with an absent familiarity that had a piercing sweetness to it.

"I wonder who the target really is?" he murmured.

She moved her mouth against his chest, as though by accident. "Morley thinks it's him."

His arm tightened. "Perhaps it's Annalise."

"Or Sir Isaac. The way Morley spoke, the hauntings haven't been going on that long. Indeed," she added, raising herself slightly, "they might even have started since you came."

"Then someone is wasting a great deal of effort." His hand stroked the curve of her cheek. "For I can't be chased away."

Not even, it seemed, by her fears. Night wrapped its veil around them and they forgot all else.

24

The men began to gather in the circle before dawn. They milled about, talking among themselves, while the women offered hot cider to ward off the morning chill. As the sun rose over Avebury, they set off.

This was a solemn task, but there was merriment in their step. A song was raised, voices joined in. The going was easy. They reached the wood quickly and spread out, working in teams to find what was needed.

Nine kinds of wood for the Beltane fire. Nine for the turning of the season. Nine to dance round and rejoice that the winter was passed and the world reborn. Ivy and oak, blackthorn and sycamore, rowan and birch, ash and alder, and plentiful hawthorn to round them out, all for the finding in the forests around Avebury. Nine woods for Beltane.

The hawthorn was already in bloom. Its branches

were carried home to decorate the doorposts. Marigold also flowered, gathered by the girls who followed, twined into garlands for their hair.

The day brightened, the air grew warm. In the pens around the village, the flocks bleated, anxious to be let out. The last of the feed laid away for winter was all but gone. The summer pastures beckoned.

In the ovens of Sarah's house, the May cakes were baking. Missus Damas returned from watching the men go by on the lane, bearing their burdens of wood across their shoulders, and sniffed appreciatively.

"You've still got a light hand, mistress."

Sarah laughed, cheeks warm from the fire and the simple pleasures of the day. Warm, too, from the memory of a night that had left her weary but exultant.

She dropped another ladle of batter on the heated stone and slipped it back into the oven. "There's a great deal still to be done."

It was a day to fling open the windows and drag out the carpets, to sweep and mop, polish and dust. A day for the cobwebs to be blown away and the house filled with the scent of spring.

Sarah was out in the garden, planting seedlings, when Rupert woofed a warning. She rose, brushing the soil from her hands, half expecting—hoping—to see Faulkner.

Had Justin Hoddinworth always had so unpleasant an expression? Tall and slim, overdressed for the place and the day, he had an air of coiled energy that set her nerves on edge. She did not want him in her garden.

"I had no idea you were here," she said by way of pointing out that he had not been announced.

He shrugged dismissively. "I came round the side."

His gaze ran over the garden and settled, lingeringly, on her. "Very bucolic. If you were a painting, you'd be titled 'Country Pleasures,' or some such."

"It's a busy time. Is there a reason you've come?"

He pretended surprise. "Surely you wouldn't deny me an opportunity to thank you for supper. And, of course, the illustrious introduction that went with it?" Without waiting for her reply, he continued. "My mother was much taken with Sir William. She's convinced he's the answer to all our problems."

"You're not?" Sarah asked, more softly. He was so brittle, this distant cousin of hers, and so filled with hurt. For a moment, her fear that he might be a murderer was overtaken by the realization of how very lost he seemed.

"I'd heard about him, of course. Like many, I presumed he'd merely been lucky. Been at the right place at the right time, impressed the right people, that sort of thing. But now I see otherwise. He's formidable. And mother's a fool. He'll never do anything she asks."

"You can't be sure of that."

His eyes flared, filled with the anguish—and the anger—of the very young who feel themselves trapped in circumstances they cannot alter. "But I am. None of us can influence him—not Mother or Father and certainly not myself. Only you, perhaps."

Sarah stiffened. She had tried to be so careful, even deflecting Elizabeth's suspicions with skill that made her proud. Surely it wasn't Justin she needed to worry about? "What makes you think that?"

"I don't know," he said and seemed to her great relief to mean it. "It's merely a feeling I've got, or perhaps no more than a hope."

His voice dropped, false calm cracking to reveal the full extent of his despair. His hands clenched, the nails biting into his palms.

"Whatever you think, I'm not really a bad sort. I'm not afraid of hard work or danger, and I know how to be loyal. Given half a chance, I could make something of myself. But now, when I finally realize that, there is no chance. Unless something changes soon, my life is effectively over."

Sarah wavered. There was a certain contrived quality to all this and yet it was not without truth. His desperation was real enough. So, too, was his yearning for an existence he could call his own. On that score, at least, she couldn't help but be sympathetic.

"I have no reason to believe Faulkner would listen to me," she ventured, the words coming of their own accord for she knew this was foolish, or at least premature. Nothing was proven yet. So ambitious and desperate a man might be driven to kill. But that sense of the trap closing around him and the yearning to be free, she knew it all so well—knew and responded as she could not help but do.

"You would have to prove yourself, you know that? He's a hard man. There'd be no second chance."

"All I need is one." Youthful pride warred with mortal fear. He was teetering on the edge of a precipice, his life a pebble's roll from uselessness.

The seedlings lay pale green on the ground, their white roots curling around them. If she left them too long, they would dry out and blow away.

"I promise nothing," she said, bending to her task. Softly, she added, "Except to try."

He closed his eyes for a moment, opened them again. "Thank you." He turned to go. Laughter sounded in the lane beyond. On an afterthought, he asked, "What is happening here today?"

Sarah should have resisted but could not. "Country pleasures," she said and, smiling, lifted the seedlings tenderly in her hands.

Twilight kisses the land, stars are born. Moonwise, round the circle, dance. Hand in hand, man and woman, laughter gilding, dance. And now the spark, fruit of oaken poles long rubbed to heat, carried high to catch upon the wood.

Beltane comes.

Faulkner stood near the door of the inn, at his ease, and watched it happen. Sir Isaac was beside him.

"Fascinating," the old man said.

"Pagan," Faulkner replied.

Sir Isaac laughed. "Surely you aren't condemning them for that, are you? In such a place, how could they help but keep May?"

Faulkner nodded. He felt no particular surprise, far less shock. Indeed, there was a certain rightness to it all. But he was struck by one thing. "There's no maypole. Why do you suppose that is?"

"I don't know," Sir Isaac admitted. "They're popular enough in other parts. You'd think they'd have one here." He gestured toward the flame, catching fast in the vast pile of wood. "Bright fire, they call it, *Bel tane* in the old tongue. There's no telling how far back it goes."

A fiddle careened wildly, matched by a reed pipe. Feet tapped to the beating drum as the fire crackled, leaping high. Through the swirling smoke, past the whirling forms, Faulkner searched. Where was Sarah? Not at home, surely.

The whole village had turned out, along with everyone from the surrounding farms, babes in arms and elders with their canes, all there before the bright fire. Even old Missus Hemper had come, with her son new in his grave, to honor the day.

But not Sarah? A flicker of concern passed through him. He was straightening from the door, intending to find her, when she appeared suddenly toward the back of the crowd.

She was dressed in white. Her hair, shade of the fire's embers, hung to her waist. There was a garland of marigold on her brow. As he watched, a young girl took the basket she carried from her and began to pass out cakes. Someone spoke and Sarah laughed, but she did not stop. Instead, she continued on her way toward him.

"I thought I'd find you dancing round a maypole," Faulkner said when she stood close enough for him to feel the warmth of her skin and smell the lilac that would ever make him think of her.

She slanted him a look, cheeks flushed, lips full. "That's a Saxon custom."

His heart thudded. "Is it? Next time I meet a Saxon, I'll have to ask him."

Her eyes were sylvan as the dell, lit by the Beltane fires. "Come," she said and drew him, hand in hand, into the circle of stone and flame.

25

Faulkner remembered very little after that. He had a fleeting impression of faces whirling by, of sound and color surging together, of laughter and shouts, and overall the wild music racing ahead, beckoning them on, faster and faster, until there was only a rush of blood through his body and an exaltation of the spirit beyond any he had ever known.

Then silence, sudden and soul deep. His hand in Sarah's. Soft ground beneath his feet and the gurgle of water. Darkness. Marigolds crushed in his hands, a whisper of white cloth dropped like a veil. Velvet-smooth skin, warm, enthralling.

Hunger followed, searing reason, devouring gentleness until there was only a single driving need consuming him. He surged deep, seeking, her strength all around him, fire in his body, in his mind, hotter and hotter until release seized him and he cried out her name to the star-draped sky.

When he was next aware, the stars were gone. He lay on his back in the mossy dell where he had first come upon Sarah—was it only scant days ago? It was morning.

Slowly, Faulkner lifted his head. He was naked. Diamond droplets of dew clung to his body. He stared down the length of himself, bewildered, until memory stirred.

Abruptly, he sat up. His clothes were nearby, scattered over the grass. Judging by the light slanting through the trees, it was very early. A few birds sang but otherwise the dell seemed curiously hushed. He dressed quickly and was pulling on his boots when some instinct made him turn.

Sarah stood looking at him. She had on the white dress he had seen her in the previous evening. Her hair was loose around her shoulders. There were crushed marigold petals in it.

At the sight of her, a hundred questions crashed through his mind. Were the fractured images he recalled of fire and music, passion and release actually true? Had they coupled here in the dell, in the night, in the stirring spring? And if they had, did it signify anything beyond the desire of a man and a woman for each other? Had ancient forces truly been moving over this land, through them, as the season turned and the bright Beltane fire burned?

"Sarah," he said, starting toward her. "Last night—"

Her image wavered before him, the white gown becoming suddenly translucent so that it began to blend with the morning mist. Her features blurred. Before his stunned gaze, she vanished.

Faulkner made a hoarse sound deep in his throat and reached out to where she had stood. His hand grasped air. Coldness went through him. He inhaled sharply and consciously fought to control the primal terror that threatened to engulf him.

"Sarah!" His voice reverberated off the watching trees and the silent stream, mocking him. Only by the greatest effort of will did he force himself to stand still and look around. There was no sign of her, yet he was gripped by the certainty that she was somewhere near.

But in what condition? A murderer was loose in Avebury, a killer who had slain two of his three victims away from the village and near water. The apparition he had witnessed had all the qualities of what people called a ghost. Had he slept, sated and unaware, while Sarah fell into deadly danger?

The thought was unbearable. He called her name again, still to echoing silence, and began swiftly to search the surrounding area. The dell was not large, but the gently rolling ground hid much of it from immediate view. He had gone perhaps a hundred yards, each moment taut with dread, when at last he caught sight of a form lying by the stream.

He reached her in quick strides and gathered her into his arms, heart pounding, breath stopped, terrified of what he would find. Horror at the implacability of death filled him as it never had on any battlefield. He bent, clutching her to him, desperate to impart his own strength into her, to give her life again no matter at what cost.

Her cheeks were ashen, her eyes unmoving. She lay still and silent against him. For a moment, he truly feared her dead and thought he could not survive such cruelty. But then a shaft of sunlight moving through the overarching branches fell on the all but imperceptible rise and fall of her breasts.

Like him when he awoke, she too was naked. But unlike him, she did not stir. He carried her back up the sloping bank to where they had lain and stripped off his shirt, wrapping it around her.

No one moved in the village. The remnants of the Beltane fire still smoldered in the stone circle, but otherwise nothing remained to indicate what had happened there the night before. Faulkner eyed the still curling tendrils of smoke grimly. Later, there would be time to demand explanations, but for the moment he was concerned only with getting Sarah home.

The door to her house was unbarred. There was no sign of Missus Damas or any of the other servants. Upstairs, her bed was turned down and a night robe tossed over the dressing-table chair as though she had expected to retire as usual the previous night.

He laid her on the bed and took a towel from the rack on the wash table, gently drying the dampness from her as best he could. When he had slipped the night robe onto her, he pulled the covers to her chin, then sat beside her and took her hand in his.

Still, she did not move. Her breathing remained so faint that he had to lean closer and listen to assure himself it continued. No color touched her cheeks, and her eyes did not flutter. She seemed in a sleep so deep as to be no more than a step away from eternity.

His throat clenched. He had seen this once before when a fellow officer had taken a terrible wound to the head. He had lain unmoving, hardly breathing, just as Sarah was doing, until some five days later when he finally died.

Yet she showed no sign of any outward injury. Even when he searched the back of her head, dreading that he might find a blow such as Davey had suffered, he discovered nothing. She looked completely unmarred, for all that she appeared close to death.

There was a sound below, followed by another. Slowly, the house was stirring. He held on to Sarah's hand, desperate not to leave her, until he realized that he had no choice. Alone, he could do nothing. She might wake eventually of her own volition, or she might not. Without knowing either way, he had to get help.

Dr. Quack came first, summoned by a frantic Missus Damas, who, when informed of Sarah's condition and having confirmed it for herself, sent the stable boy racing off to fetch the physician. To Faulkner's great relief, Quack seemed to have spent a fairly abstemious night, no sign of the port for which he was said to have a fondness. But when he had listened to Sarah's breathing and held a hand to her pulse, he frowned deeply.

"I don't understand. What could have happened to her that she should be like this?"

A mating in the fire of Beltane? The enactment of an ancient pagan ritual that seems to have all but sapped her of life? The thoughts were in Faulkner but he did not express them. He was half convinced his own sanity was in doubt, affected by the strange mysteries of Avebury and of Sarah herself.

"Is it possible that she could have eaten or drunk anything at the . . . festival last evening that might do this?" he asked.

Quack thought long and hard before shaking his head. "I don't know. There are said to be such things, and perhaps she knows of them, but I can't believe she'd run such a risk with herself, and who would give it to her without her knowledge?"

Faulkner had no answer and Quack was without a solution. The doctor shook his head regretfully. "I can do nothing. We will simply have to wait and see what happens." He lingered a while longer and had a few words with Missus Damas by way of instruction before promising to return.

Missus Hemper came next. She walked slowly, stooped over her cane, aided to the bed by the housekeeper, who had welcomed her hard on Dr. Quack's departure. The death of her son had aged the old woman greatly. She appeared to have little more substance than the sunlight filtering through the windows.

But she gazed at Sarah with great intensity before touching her lightly at brow and throat. "What happened to her?" When Faulkner did not reply at once, she turned her gaze to Missus Damas. "Make an old woman a cup of tea, will you?"

The housekeeper hesitated, clearly reluctant to be excluded. But aged and grieving as she was, Missus Hemper was not without her influence. They were left alone, save for still, silent Sarah in the bed.

"What happened?" the old woman asked again.

"We went to the dell. I woke there this morning with very little memory and found her, like this, by the stream."

Missus Hemper nodded slowly. She looked back at Sarah. "'Tis always been hard for her."

He stiffened. "What has?"

"Being as she is. I've often wondered . . . ." She sighed deeply, burying whatever thought she'd been about to voice. "Never mind, what counts now is getting her better. She chose you, I saw that, and it wasn't the first time, was it?"

Slowly, Faulkner shook his head. There was no point in denial. Besides, Missus Hemper showed no surprise. It merely seemed to confirm what she had suspected all along.

"All right then. This may be a sickness come upon her. If that's the case, there's nothing I can do. Or it may be something else altogether. A part of her seems flown to a far place. Perhaps she simply can't find her way back or perhaps she's hiding, afraid of what's happened. Either way, I cannot reach her. That power's never been mine. But perhaps you can."

She came closer and took his hand, clutching it with gnarled, blue-veined fingers that still held surprising strength. "Understand this. If you venture after her, you may also be lost. There's no guarantee that you won't be. There's things at work here it's probably better not to understand."

The old woman stared at him for a long moment. Slowly, she smiled, a toothless grin filled in equal measure with guile and sympathy. "Mayhap she chose well after all. We'll see. Sit by her, touch her, speak to her, but don't expect any miracles. She's always had one foot in that other place anyway, and now she may have slipped beyond all reach."

Faulkner's mind whirled. If he understood the old woman correctly, he should dismiss her as mad. What other place? What things at work? Pagan mutterings that had no bearing in the real world as he knew it to be.

Yet what was real? Fire burning in a stone circle and love for a woman he could not bear to lose? A scant time ago, he would not have believed any of it possible. But it had happened, and to him. He could not pretend otherwise.

He did not know when Missus Hemper went. Sitting beside the bed, holding Sarah's cold hands in his own, he thought of nothing but the struggle he must wage on a battlefield he did not know against an enemy he still could scarcely believe existed.

Yet wage it he must, and alone. Light faded; people came and went. Faulkner did not move. He sat, almost as still and silent as Sarah herself. Deep within himself, in a place he had not known existed, a gray morning beckoned.

26

She was alone. The ground was hard beneath her body and she felt chilled. Sarah stirred slowly. She was fully awake and aware but bewildered. Where was she?

The air around her, cool though it was, was motionless. She could see nothing, not the shadows of trees or the stars above. Gradually, as her eyes adjusted to the dimness, a few shapes began to take form. She could see several rough wooden branches, the bark still on them, notched together in a simple frame. Stretched across it, forming a wall, was an animal hide or perhaps more than one stitched together.

She was in a hut made of skins, lying on a mattress of rushes with the embers of a small fire in the center and near it a simple clay pot. She was dreaming, obviously. In another moment, she would slip more deeply into sleep, and after a while she would awake. She would be in her world, in her bed or . . .

She hadn't gone to bed. Something had happened to prevent it, something to do with the May fire, the music and the dancing. With Faulkner.

Memory flooded back. They had gone together to the dell, drawn to each other so hungrily that all restraint fell away, and they . . .

Where was he? She sat up suddenly, startled to find herself naked. But this was only a dream, for all that she seemed so strangely awake. None of this was real.

Yet she could feel the rushes against her skin and the cool air raising goose bumps along her arms. Slowly, she stood. Strange dream in which she could reach out and touch the walls of the hut, feeling for herself the smoothness of the tanned hides. Feel, too, the slightly rough texture of the clay pot painted with swirling black emblems she vaguely recognized.

There was a peg on one of the branches. A tunic hung from it. She took the garment without thinking and dropped it over her head. Only when she was garbed did she realize what she had done and how naturally she had done it.

Her legs moved. She walked out of the hut, stooping to clear the low door, and stood upright in the predawn light. She was standing on a hill above the river Kennet, the same hill on which she and Sir Isaac had been measuring a short time before she found the Gypsy's body. The double circle they were examining was a short distance away. Both the small inner circle and the larger outer one were complete, dozens of stones standing upright. From the far side of the hill, connecting with the circles, she could see the stones of Kennet Avenue stretching off into the distance.

There was no one else within sight. But there were others somewhere nearby. The well-tended fields she

saw were testament to that, as were the white puffs of
sheep moving on the hillsides.

The air was growing warmer. She walked down to
the river, where she knelt to bathe and drink. Water
splashed on her skin, sun-browned. She could feel the
swelling of her breasts against the tunic and the slight
abrasion around the nipples where the fabric rubbed.

But that was all experienced at a distance, as though
none of it was really happening to her. As, of course, it
wasn't. It was all a dream, more vivid than the dreams
she'd had all her life but a dream all the same. Soon
she would wake.

But the day brightened and the dream continued.
She walked back up the hill and took from the hut a
basket of berries. Sitting, legs drawn up, she ate. The
berries were sweet. They were a favorite, looked
forward to each summer and still gathered with the
same eagerness she had brought to the task as a child.

But she was a child no longer, nor even the young
girl she had been when the last great stone was
brought and the henge completed. It was a woman
who sat on the ground, eating berries and watching
the newborn day.

A woman, not herself, but known to her all the
same, the priestess. And she was alone. Where was
the young hunter? Where, indeed, was anyone? Why
was she like this, solitary as the sun rose and the land
was bathed in splendor?

The priestess stood. She stared at the circle but did
not approach it. There was an unwillingness in her,
almost a fear. But the day was aging and duty could not
be ignored. Duty that had once been privilege, power
that had once been love, turned now to—what? She
pressed her lips together and stepped into the stones.

*　　*　　*

"Sir William?"

The words, softly uttered, reached Faulkner as though through a fog. He looked up slowly. Sir Isaac stood beside him, the old man's face creased with worry. He looked to the bed and his frown deepened.

"Missus Damas said I might come up. Has there been any change?"

Had there? Faulkner gazed at Sarah, willing color to her cheeks, her eyes to open, willing her back to him. Nothing. He shook his head. "I don't think so."

"There is strange talk in the village."

A harsh sound broke from him. "Yes, I imagine there is."

Sir Isaac sighed. He pulled a stool up beside Faulkner and sat down. Silence drew out between them. Beyond the windows, birds were singing, the sun shone, the spring day unfolded. Inside were shadows and far more questions than either man could answer.

"I should not have come here," Sir Isaac said at length.

Faulkner did not misunderstand. He knew the old scholar was not speaking of Sarah's bedside. "What brought you?"

"Stories I heard, a drawing I'd seen. It's rather hard to explain, but I have a notion that there is what we might call a vitalizing force, a divine spark of sorts that animates all life."

Faulkner was familiar with the idea, although he had thought little if at all about it. It lay behind most of what men called alchemy, a shrouded art in which Sir Isaac was rumored to dabble.

"And you thought to find it here?"

"I felt that the extraordinary effort people expended over what must have been a very long period of time might be explained by the presence of such a force. Perhaps they sensed it and through many generations even learned how to make use of it to a certain degree."

Faulkner shook his head. He was very tired. Little of what Sir Isaac said made sense to him. He had been brought up to believe in a stern but loving God, rather like a father was supposed to be, who had set down certain rules and required them to be obeyed. Later, he had found science and reason, which complicated things but could still be managed.

Now, suddenly, here was this notion of hidden forces, vitalizing sparks, concealed in the earth but reachable—perhaps—by certain people. More disturbing yet, it came from the man who was the giant of his age and whose thoughts had to be respected. Faulkner wanted to dismiss the very idea but he could not. It resonated too deeply in his mind.

"I can't reach her," he murmured.

"What's that?" Sir Isaac asked.

"Missus Hemper said there might be a way, but I have no idea where even to begin. The moment I try, I falter."

Sir Isaac studied him. "When was the last time you slept?"

"Last night . . . I think." He had awakened in the dell but he couldn't honestly say he'd been asleep. Indeed, he wasn't at all sure what had happened to him or why.

"You don't look it. I'll wager you haven't eaten either. Go outside; get some fresh air and something to eat. I'll stay here with her."

Faulkner shook his head. "I can't leave her."

"You can't do her any good like this. I'll be right here at her side. If anything happens, you'll be called at once."

Still, Faulkner hesitated. He knew Sir Isaac was right, he wasn't of any use to Sarah in his present state. But he was loath to leave her even briefly.

"It will be dark soon," the elderly man said. "Go sit in the sun while you can and think things over."

Sunlight warm on his face, soft air and stillness all around. It had a certain attraction. Faulkner rose and touched the back of his fingers to Sarah's cheek, so cool against his warmth. She might have been a marble effigy, so silently did she lie. And indeed, that would be all he had left of her soon unless he could act quickly.

"I won't be long," he said.

He went to her garden. It was very quiet there. A robin darted among the neat rows of herbs poking their heads above the loamy earth and in amid the yew bushes that separated the beds, but otherwise it was still. He sat on a stone bench and tried hard to think of nothing at all. Perhaps if he managed that, something would come to him.

Nothing did. Try though he did, he could not still the clamor of his thoughts. Images filled him: Sarah in the dell, Sarah on Silbury, Sarah smiling, Sarah in his arms, above him, pale in the moonlight.

He saw her prim and proper, even plain as he had once thought, and bathed in sensuality, lost in passion, incandescently alive. She handed him a lemon crisp, laughed at his jest, admired Rascal, drew him out of himself to tell stories of his youth he had told no one. She made him happy, she made him yearn, she shattered the defenses built up so carefully over the years and let in possibilities undreamt.

He could not let her go. And he could not stop her.

There in the garden, poised between night and day, he waited, seeking desperately for an answer.

Missus Damas brought him soup. Beef barley, it was, and good. He drank it down, ate the bread that went with it, and felt a little better. Not much but enough to decide on a course of action.

If he had to find his way in the dark, so be it. When all was said and done, he knew very little about Sarah. He knew she had lived here in this house all her life, that her parents were dead, and that she was well respected in the village. Beyond that, there was nothing. It was time—past time—that he learned more.

He turned and looked at the house. It was a pleasing residence, solid but welcoming. There was nothing particularly distinct about it. But what had Sir Isaac said, something about a far older foundation?

Faulkner stood and went back down a gravel path toward the side door. Behind him, the sun lowered westward, its colors drowned in a cloud bank creeping over the horizon. Inside, it was cool and quiet. There were muted sounds from the kitchen, but he saw none of the servants. That suited him perfectly.

A door at the rear of the main hall gave way to a staircase that led downward. He followed it and found himself standing in a small but well-appointed wine cellar. On a table near the bottom of the stairs were tinder and a candle, which he lit.

In a corner of the wine cellar, half concealed by

staked barrels and crates, was a hole in the ground large enough for a wide-girthed man to pass through. He shone the light down into it and discovered to his surprise narrow stone steps leading into darkness.

Without hesitation, he followed them. The air grew cooler and noticeably damper. The candle sputtered, and for a moment he thought it would go out. But the flame steadied and he was able to look around.

He was in a chamber that appeared to stretch the length of the house. The ceiling was very low so that he had to bend to avoid hitting his head. There were what appeared to be the remnants of stone arches and, here and there, benches. Near the center of the house was a large rectangle cut into the earth and laid on all sides with stone. The Roman bath Sir Isaac had mentioned?

He bent closer, caught now in the excitement of discovery, and found himself staring at a broken pillar on which words could still be clearly seen: *Fata obstant.* The gods will otherwise.

Will what? The destruction of this ancient villa and those who lived in it? It was a gloomy thought but suitable to the surroundings. The Romans had come and gone, as had so many others down through the ages. But the Huxleys had remained, here in this place, always part of Avebury.

What else had Sir Isaac said about the house? That there was an even older well dating from pre-Roman times. It was believable enough. The presence of the baths indicated a stream nearby. He moved farther into the darkness, lit only by the single flame, and felt the ground begin to slope beneath his feet.

He stopped to listen. Yes, there it was, not far away, the faint gurgle of water. He pressed closer and was rewarded when at last he saw the shape of stones marking a well. Not far below the darkness sparkled. He set the candle carefully on the stone and plunged his hands in. The water was cool and sweet. He drank slowly.

When he was done, he sat on the moist ground and let the silence fill him. Only gradually did he realize he was not alone. A face watched from the stone, boldly carved, strong-featured, crowned with antlers. The horned god, consort to the earth herself.

Hardly breathing, Faulkner ran his fingers over the carving. He felt its strength, the confidence with which it had been made, the care. Felt, too, something he could not identify that made the stone warm beneath his touch and sent the blood suddenly rushing through him.

Softly, somewhere between demand and entreaty, he spoke. "Give her back to me."

A whisper of air moved through the darkness. The candle went out.

27

Panic filled him. The darkness was smothering. It pressed in all around, a crushing weight robbing him of breath. Faulkner tried to stand but could not. The ground seemed to hold him captive. He had never before suffered the fear of enclosed places that some experienced, but now it crashed down upon him.

Instinctively, he covered his head with his arms to protect himself from the ceiling that was surely about to fall. His heart raced and his breathing was labored. The control that had always been second nature to him was perilously close to shattering. Only the thought of Sarah steadied him. He had to get out of the cellar, had to return to—

Cellar? There was no cellar. He was crouched on a hillside overlooking a river. Aside from the sharp intake of his breath, it was very quiet. The day was cool, the sky lightly clouded. It appeared to be early morning.

Slowly, Faulkner straightened and looked around.

He felt odd, as though his body didn't quite fit. Several moments passed before he realized that he was somewhat smaller, not quite as tall or as broad as he was used to being.

Moreover, he was dressed not in the riding breeches, shirt, and boots he'd been wearing but in soft doeskin trousers only. The rest of his body was bare, the skin tanned. Around his waist was a woven belt from which a leather scabbard hung. He grasped the hilt protruding from it and pulled.

The blade that emerged glinted dull red in the morning light. Faulkner frowned. It looked like no weapon he'd ever seen. He put a finger to the edge, testing it, and found it sharp enough but was still puzzled as to how steel could have that color. Distantly, it occurred to him that it might not be steel at all.

He replaced the sword and looked around, trying to get his bearings. Shock rippled through him. He could see Avebury, not the village he knew but the henge, as he had never seen it before. As indeed no one could have seen it in a very long time.

The circles were intact, each stone standing straight, none tumbled or missing. Beyond them, not one but two great avenues both lined with standing stones stretched into the distance.

He recognized the nearer as being the route he and Sarah had followed to the river Kennet. But the one going in the opposite direction surprised him. Taken together, they made the henge look as though it stood at the center of a writhing serpent.

Deep within his mind, he marveled at what he was seeing. There had to be some explanation for it, but he could think of none. Reality was the well and the darkness, but they were fast receding down the pathways of memory until he could hardly be sure that he remembered them at all.

He set off down the hill. His body ached, as though it had been worked too hard and allowed too little rest, but that did not slow him. He went quickly with an eager step and was soon following the river. Walking along the bank beside it, he did not slow even where the going became difficult. The path seemed well known to him, almost as though he could have followed it in his sleep.

At length, the ground slanted upward. There was another, smaller hill and, atop it, just visible above the rise, a double circle of stones. Without pause, he started up the hill, taking it in long strides, the sword slapping against his leg.

Belatedly, he became aware of a leather pouch strapped across his back. He had been traveling for some days, living off provisions he took with him and whatever he could find. The journey had been dangerous; he was lucky to have survived it.

Later, he would sit in the circle of elders and tell them the grim news he had brought. But first anticipation filled him. He pulled himself up the last few yards and stopped, muscled legs braced and hands on his lean hips, surveying the scene before him.

A woman stood at the center of the inner circle. Her eyes were closed, her arms upraised. She seemed to shimmer in the morning air, almost as though the light shone not around but through her.

He had not expected to find her at prayer. About to turn away from a sight that was not for his eyes, he hesitated. He had come so far and dared so much that to be denied her even for a few moments seemed more than he could endure.

As he watched, however reluctantly, she crumbled shafts of young wheat and let the pieces fall onto the ground before her. Her lips moved, but soundlessly. He could hear nothing, but he sensed a tension in her he had not felt before. Her brow was furrowed, her shoulders stiff.

That puzzled him. In the great festivals of the changing seasons, when the sacred rites were performed before all the people, she seemed confident and serene. Now she appeared deeply troubled, even afraid.

His instinct was to go to her at once but he held back, mindful of the risk he would be taking if he entered the circle uninvited. Yet the longer he watched her, the harder it became to do nothing. Her color was ashen, her body swayed. Finally, soundless tears trickled down her cheeks.

He could bear it no longer. Heedless of the danger, he stepped into the circle. The ground rippled beneath him. Faulkner lunged, his fingers brushing Sarah. For a wrenching moment, he thought she would slip beyond his grasp. He only just managed to hold on, dragging her hard against him, as the earth opened and darkness swallowed them both.

Sir Isaac stirred in the chair beside Sarah's bed. He glanced toward the window. The day was fading fast. Where was Faulkner? He had not expected the younger man to be gone so long.

His knees ached. He rubbed them absently as he tried to guess how much time had passed. There was no real reason why Faulkner should hurry back, and yet it was surprising that he had not. Had he been called away and Sir Isaac not informed?

He considered going to find a servant to ask, but he did not want to leave Sarah alone. He had promised Faulkner he would not. Instead, he waited, watching the light darken, and tried to decide what to do.

When the bedroom door opened, he was relieved. Faulkner, at last. "There you—" he began, only to break off in some confusion when he realized it wasn't Faulkner at all.

Missus Damas had come to light the lamps. She looked startled to see him. "Still here, milord? I thought you'd gone."

"I'm just sitting with Mistress Huxley while Sir William gets a breath of air."

"Sir William?" The housekeeper frowned. "He was in the garden an hour or so ago, but I haven't seen him since."

"You haven't?"

"No. I thought he'd come back up here."

"Well, I haven't seen him either. You're sure he wasn't called away?"

She shook her head. "Not that I know of, and I would. Seems odd, don't you think?"

Sir Isaac did but he was reluctant to make too much of it. There could be any number of explanations for Faulkner's absence. The problem was that none of them seemed to fit. He was far too decent and resolute a man to simply go off without a second thought. At the very least, he would have said something.

"We should look for him," Sir Isaac said.

"Send to the village, you mean?"

"No, look around here. He's got to be somewhere about."

Missus Damas's face tightened. She looked as though she had a great deal she would have liked to say but thought better of it. Sir Isaac sighed. He didn't pretend to understand such things. The ways of men and women were beyond him. By comparison, he found the universe far simpler.

All the same, it did not escape him that the housekeeper was thinking harshly of Faulkner. Unlike Sir Isaac, she believed her beloved mistress had been ill used by the gentleman from London, even perhaps that he was somehow responsible for her condition. All this in the grim set of her face and the fierceness with which she clenched her hands together as she gazed at—

"Blessed Mary and all the saints!" Missus Damas exclaimed.

Sir Isaac took note that the housekeeper was apparently Catholic, an interesting but hardly significant fact. Far more important was the change that had come over Sarah.

Her color was returning, the warm glow of rose blossoming over her cheeks. As they watched, transfixed, her breathing strengthened, there was movement beneath her eyelids, and her hands fluttered.

Missus Damas hurried to the bed and grasped her mistress's hands in her own. "Her skin is warm," she said joyfully. "Sweet lord, she's coming back to us."

"So it appears," Sir Isaac murmured. He stood off to one side, feeling rather self-conscious about being in a lady's bedchamber now that the lady in question no longer appeared to be in extremis. Medicine was completely outside his field. Like any sensible man, he did his utmost to avoid having any more contact with its practitioners than was absolutely necessary. Yet he couldn't help being fascinated by what was happening.

As he watched, Sarah's eyes opened and she stared up at Missus Damas.

"Mary?" Her voice was weak but clear. There was no mistaking that she recognized the housekeeper.

"Hush, dear," the older woman said huskily. "You've been ill, but that's passing now. Everything's going to be fine."

"Faulkner?"

Missus Damas opened her mouth to reply but Sir Isaac forestalled her. Bluntly, he said, "He's missing."

Sarah closed her eyes for a moment. When she opened them again, they were hard and bright. "We must find him," she said and threw the covers back.

The candle flickered. Faulkner stared into the flame and tried to remember where he was. The cellar . . . the well. The horned god. But there had been something else, hadn't there? A hillside, a circle. Sarah?

He tried harder, but the image dissolved and he was left with nothing but the reality of a damp basement and cramped muscles. Slowly, he rose. His head was brushing the ceiling when he realized that he had been gone much longer than he'd intended. Sir Isaac would be wondering where he was, while Sarah—

He climbed quickly back up through the wine cellar to the main hall. He was crossing it, heading toward the stairs, when he glanced up and saw Sarah standing on the landing above.

Faulkner hesitated. After what had happened in the dell, he no longer fully trusted his own senses. Yet Sarah she was, alive and apparently well, if not precisely flying into his arms.

"Are you all right?" she asked.

He nodded and began to mount the stairs.

She took a breath, steeling herself. Her hands gripped the banister so that the knuckles shone whitely. "I am sorry for the inconvenience to you," she said. "Good day."

Without a further word, she turned and disappeared down the corridor toward her bedroom. He heard the door shut and, a moment later, the key turn in the lock.

28

They were carrying away the last of the Beltane fire, sweeping the ground clear so that not even ashes remained.

Faulkner watched them from his window at the Rose. The women worked companionably, chatting among themselves. They seemed relaxed and at ease, as though there was nothing at all unusual about their chore, as undoubtedly there was not.

Every spring the Beltane fires had been lit and a few days later their remains removed. These same women had undoubtedly seen their mothers at their brooms, performing the same task. The daughters playing around their skirts would do it in their time, as how many daughters had before them?

It was only a fire such as was lit from one end of England to the other in harmless celebration. There was nothing in the least sinister about it, much less mysterious.

He had dreamed, nothing more. As for Sarah? His hands clenched. As for her, he could not say.

The door opened behind him. Crispin cleared his throat. "Breakfast is ready, sir. Would you prefer it up here?"

"I'm not hungry. Has Sir Isaac come back yet?"

"Just now, sir. He's below."

Faulkner nodded. He spared a final glance for the women with their brooms and left the window. Several tables were occupied in the common room, farmers and a couple of peddlers at their morning tea. Sir Isaac was seated alone near the fire. He looked up when Faulkner entered.

"Lovely scones. Care for some?"

"You have them," Faulkner said. He sat down, stretching his long legs in front of him, and stared into the fire. It was cold, the ashes swept, just like outside. They were a tidy people, these residents of Avebury. "Did you see her?"

Sir Isaac sighed. He put down his mug. His powdered wig was slightly askew. He straightened it. "Briefly. She says she is fine but is not receiving callers."

"Callers," Faulkner said. His lips curled. "I have difficulty thinking of myself as such."

"I don't pretend to understand. My experience—"

"No man would understand this, I assure you. It's beyond anything. The woman is . . ."—he paused, seeking the precise word—"maddening."

"As to that, what exactly did happen, if you don't mind my asking?"

Faulkner's eyebrows rose. "Really, Sir Isaac, I thought you were a man of discretion."

"Oh, no, you misunderstand me." The old scholar was flustered. "Believe me, I would never—that is, whatever—oh, never mind. What I meant was, what happened when you were in the cellar? Were you there the whole time? Is there any truth to Missus Damas's tale of Roman baths and ancient wells?"

"Considerable truth, and no, I wasn't there all the time. I sat in the garden for a while, had a bowl of soup as I recall. Then I got the idea to explore the older part of the house." Faulkner was silent for a moment. "I'm not sure exactly why."

"You really did see what she said was down there?"

"Oh, yes, the house is ancient, there's no doubt about that."

"Extraordinary. I must ask Mistress Huxley if I can take a look for myself, although I fear in her present frame of mind she won't be inclined to agree."

"It's just what you'd expect, nothing more." Faulkner glanced around, seeking Annalise. It was early, but a bit of ale would help him swallow the lie better. That and his frustrating, infuriating standoff with Sarah. Callers? She dismissed him as lightly as she would some fan-fluttering society matron come to bore her ear off or some overdressed fop making a lunge at her fortune.

His jaw tightened. No woman had ever treated him like this. None had ever dared. He'd kept his emotions safely stowed, concentrated on the future he was determined would be his, and made sure women stayed in their proper place.

Or at least he had until now.

"What are you going to do?" Sir Isaac asked. Most other men, indeed all that Faulkner knew save the duke, would never have asked. They would have had too much sense or not enough courage to risk so sore a subject. But Sir Isaac was something of an innocent for all his brilliance. He ventured where others would not dare.

Annalise caught Faulkner's glance. She paled slightly but nodded and quickly pulled an ale, bringing it to him. He took a long swallow and said, "I came to find a killer. I don't intend to leave until I've done so."

"That was my fault, of course, the letter I sent. I do feel quite bad about it. I'm sure, if you want to go, I can explain to the duke that you've done everything anyone could possibly—"

"I'm staying."

"Well, yes, if you wish, but it only seems to me that—"

"Staying," Faulkner repeated and put the tankard down with a thump. "And Mistress Sarah Huxley be damned." He stood, hitched up his breeches, and glanced again at Annalise. "She's a pretty thing."

"What? The girl? Oh, yes, I suppose she is."

"And scared to death of the likes of me. See if you can't get her to talk to you. I'd like to know what she thought of Davey Hemper."

"Her father keeps her busy. It's difficult."

"I have every confidence in you."

Sir Isaac smiled nervously. "Do you really? Well, then, I suppose I shall do my best. By the way, young Edwards wanted to have a word with you when you had the time."

Faulkner nodded. He took his leave from the elderly scholar and ventured out into the sun. The women had finished and the lane was empty except for a few children scampering about. As he started out the door, Crispin hurried after him.

"Your jerkin, sir, if you please."

"I don't need one. It's warm enough."

"I realize that, sir, but there are certain standards even in the country." In Crispin's mouth, the last word had a dark, vaguely smelly sound. "One must keep up appearances. To be frank, you were better about such things on the battlefield than you've been here."

"Just one more of Avebury's odd effects." Faulkner shrugged into the jerkin. It was easier than arguing. He started walking again, Crispin trotting after him in a futile effort to smooth the fabric over his master's shoulders.

"What did you learn in Bath?" Faulkner asked. The valet had returned after several days' absence, but they'd not yet had a chance to talk. Or, more correctly, Faulkner hadn't wanted to. He'd been too busy fuming over Sarah.

"That coach drivers have prodigious thirsts and that the pubs they frequent make the Rose look a close cousin to Hampton Court."

Faulkner laughed. Things were never so bleak that Crispin couldn't point out how they were actually worse. "Is that how the drivers speak of this place, a hob-nob pub full of fine ladies and gents?"

"They say Morley pours an honest measure."

"And?"

"They don't like him, and I'm not sure why. In fact, I'm not sure they know."

"Interesting, what is there to dislike?"

"He never smiles."

Faulkner paused and looked at the other man. "The drivers said that?"

"No," Crispin admitted, "it is my own observation. He rubs his tankards, serves his customers, and watches his daughter. But he never smiles or, for that matter, passes the time of day with anyone. Have you heard him tell a story or a joke, indulge in a bit of gossip, or exchange a piece of news? He's a close-mouthed man and a dour one."

"Perhaps it's the haunting."

Crispin's face lightened. "Ah, now, as to that there are all sorts of theories, most concerning the long dead monks but a few touching on other matters."

"What other?" Faulkner demanded. He kept walking in the direction of the church, Crispin following.

"Having to do with the general reputation of Avebury, a pleasant enough place, good folk, and good fields but not quite right somehow. Not like other places. One of the drivers even said that if he was offered a house and land here, he wouldn't take it. When I asked him why, he went on about ancient spirits and the stones moving."

"Exactly how much ale had you bought him?"

"A fair amount," Crispin admitted. "Most likely, that's what was talking."

"Most likely?"

The valet hesitated. Softly, he said, "Well, sir, you will admit it's a bit strange here, living amid all these stones. People say there used to be a good many more of them, but if you ask me there's more than enough right now. And then there's the shape of the land, very odd if you ask me, nothing quite as it ought to be." He shook his head. "Perhaps it's only my imagination. I'm not a country man."

"You complain if you're dragged five miles out of London. All right, Avebury has a mixed reputation and Morley isn't liked. Anything else?"

"Mistress Huxley is very well respected."

"We do not need to discuss her."

"As you will, sir," the valet said. He inclined his head. "If you have no further need of me, I will see what I can do about that shirt with all the grass stains."

"They must have laundresses here, Crispin. Find one and let her deal with it."

"Thank you, sir, but I like to think I know my duty. If there's nothing else?"

Faulkner dismissed him with a wave. He hated it when Crispin sulked but it wasn't to be helped, at least not right now. The church lay ahead, down a narrow gravel path.

29

Sarah went out to the garden after Sir Isaac left. There were beds to be weeded, seedlings to be planted, the yew to trim back, and a dozen other chores. That was the good thing about a garden; one never lacked for things to do.

The sun warmed her. She was plainly dressed in a loose day robe, the kind she'd favored before Faulkner came. That was how she thought of it, before he came and afterward.

For a lifetime, she had lived with the mystery of Avebury, learning to accommodate to it. She had even managed to strike a balance of sorts. Most importantly, no one else had been hurt. Until now.

He had been there in the circle of stones on the hillside, there with the priestess and the hunter. There with her.

"Dreadfully worried about you, he was," Sir Isaac had said. "Didn't want to leave you for a moment. I finally convinced him to get a bit of air and then, strange thing, he ended up down in the cellar. It makes no sense, does it?"

None at all, at least not in the real world of budding seeds and gentle spring breezes. The world of the stones was another matter entirely, but she would not speak of that.

He had brought her back, or she had brought him, or they had brought each other. She had no idea which was true, but she did know with absolute certainty that they had come very close to not getting back at all.

If that happened to her one day, she could accept it. But not Faulkner. He belonged in this time and this world. Eventually he would go back to London, where he would be safe. Until that happened, she could not risk drawing him further into her private madness.

Pain twisted through her. She ignored it and dropped another seedling gently into the earth, carefully shaping the soil around it. She had only to stay here in her house, behind her walls, and wait for him to go. Only . . .

Tears blinded her. She blinked them away and went on planting. It would require the strictest exercise of her will to keep that resolve, but she was determined to do so. It was all she could give to him now.

She stood finally and dusted her hands off, staring at the yew hedges and the walls beyond that they could not fully conceal. Odd how she had never before noticed that the garden and the house together were surrounded by stone, encircling her, holding her captive.

He would go. She clung to the thought as she left the garden and went back up to her room, where she sat by the window, looking out at the trees, and tried very hard to think of nothing at all.

"A terrible business," Curate Edwards said. "I don't mind admitting that it's shaken me deeply."

"As it has everyone," Faulkner said, striving for patience. He had arrived at the parsonage half an hour before, had turned down an offer of tea, refused something stronger, and listened to the young minister talk at some length about the events of the past few weeks. All without ever getting to any particular point. Perhaps there was none.

"This isn't that sort of place," Edwards went on. "One simply doesn't think . . . murder . . . well, it doesn't really fit, does it?"

"You find Avebury ordinary, then?" Faulkner asked.

"No, not precisely, but these are good people, a bit set in their ways to be sure—" Edwards broke off, startled. "I said something amusing?"

"I'm sorry," Faulkner said, struggling not to burst out laughing.

The notion that the residents of Avebury were "a bit set in their ways" struck him as almost painfully funny. Clearly, he should have had the "something stronger."

"It only seems to me that a great deal has survived here that vanished elsewhere."

Edwards looked at him cautiously. "Do you mean the monks?"

An imp of mischief settled on Faulkner's shoulder.

He was normally a direct man, but this time he was willing to make an exception, if only to see where it might lead. "Is that what you think?"

The curate hesitated. He shifted in his chair, reached for his tea, and set the cup back down, all actions of a man venturing into territory that made him uncomfortable.

"Not entirely. I've thought sometimes that this place isn't quite what it seems. But I've never really dwelled on that. It makes me feel rather . . . odd." He went on. "At any rate, what I really wanted to discuss are the murders. Sadly, I've come to the conclusion that you may be right about the killer being one of our own. Or at least being resident in Avebury."

It was an interesting distinction. Faulkner remained silent, waiting for more. "I am troubled by what it is proper for me to say or not say," Edwards continued. "Clearly, I would not discuss anything confided to me in a pastoral sense."

"You are not bound by the seal of the confessional, as a priest would be."

"That is true. If ordered by a court of law, I could speak about such matters. But that isn't of concern here, fortunately. My worry is that I not cast suspicion where it does not belong."

"Given what we know so far," Faulkner pointed out, "it's all but impossible to determine who could actually be a suspect and who couldn't."

"I was hoping you would say otherwise. It would relieve me greatly if you already had a strong sense of who might be responsible."

"Regretfully, I do not."

Edwards sighed. He appeared to be a man wrestling with an unpleasant duty. Finally, he said, "Very well, then, I feel I must tell you that shortly before Davey Hemper's body was found, I saw someone coming from the direction of the alley behind the inn. This person's presence there may be completely coincidental, but I believe myself obligated to—"

"Who was it?" Faulkner demanded. He had tolerated the curate's finickiness long enough. Now he wanted facts.

Edwards swallowed hard. "Justin Hoddinworth. He's the one I saw."

Faulkner frowned. "You're sure?"

"Yes, it was Justin."

"Where were you at the time?"

"In the garden thinking about my Sunday sermon. I happened to look in that direction and saw him."

"I see. And this was only a short time before Annalise found the body?"

"Yes."

"Then it may indeed be significant."

"Or it may be a coincidence," Edwards insisted. "After all, we must ask ourselves what could possibly drive a man to murder."

"That isn't really so puzzling. Most crimes are the result of either lust or greed. I don't think this is any different."

Edwards looked away. His hands shook slightly.

"In this case, greed wouldn't seem to apply," Faulkner went on, watching him. "Unless it's Davey Hemper's greed. He had money from somewhere."

"He worked—"

"Not enough for what he had. I think someone bought his silence."

Edwards looked up sharply. "Hoddinworth?"

"It's possible, but why would he bother? Was he

engaged in some activity that Davey—and the Gypsies—tumbled to and that he wanted to keep concealed?"

"I suppose we may never know. When—that is, if—he learns that you suspect him, isn't he likely to flee to the continent or the colonies?"

Faulkner smiled. He leaned forward, holding the curate's gaze with his own. "Is that what you think? If Justin Hoddinworth is responsible for three murders, the only place he'll be is at the end of a hangman's noose. I promise you that."

Edwards paled. "You can't arrest a man without evidence, much less execute him."

Faulkner rose. His smile deepened. "It is true that we are governed by laws, not passion. However, exceptions have been made." He turned toward the door.

"Wait," Edwards said, hurrying after him. "I don't want you to think . . . that is, I only meant—"

"Don't concern yourself," Faulkner said. "You've simply done what you had to. No one will think badly of you."

"But, I—"

"Good day, curate," Faulkner said. He could still hear Edwards sputtering behind him as he walked briskly down the path and away.

30

"*If I might* just have a bit more tea," Sir Isaac said encouragingly. He smiled up at Annalise and was rewarded when she smiled shyly in turn. They were alone in the common room, Morley having gone downstairs to count beer casks. He seemed to think that the elderly scholar was no risk.

Sir Isaac tended to agree, but he was determined to make the best possible use of the opportunity. "You've been most kind," he said. "Why don't you sit down for a moment and have a cup yourself?" He gestured to the teapot.

"Oh, no, I couldn't, sir," Annalise said softly.

"Nonsense, of course you can. Chalk it up to being courteous to a guest. That's what your father would want, isn't it?"

"Yes, I suppose." She hesitated, glancing over her shoulder toward the basement door.

"It's quite excellent tea. I must say, I'm pleasantly surprised by the quality to be found here. That's your doing, I'm sure."

"Not really," Annalise demurred. "My father—"

"Sit down, my dear, really I insist. These old legs don't hold me as well as they once did, and I feel quite uncomfortable that you must always stand." Warming to his subject, Sir Isaac went on. "Besides, if you want the truth, I'm a bit lonely at the moment. Mistress Huxley isn't up to measuring, Sir William's gone off somewhere, and there's nothing for me to do. I'd welcome company."

Annalise flushed. She looked at once uncertain and flattered. Slowly, she slipped into the chair opposite Sir Isaac. "You're very kind, sir, but I hardly think any conversation I can offer would divert you."

"Now that simply isn't so. Do you know, I have a dear friend in London little older than yourself who is assembling a book of recipes and other useful things having to do with household management. She contends that we look far too much to France for the last word in fashion, while we would be better to look to ourselves."

"Does she really?" Annalise asked, her attention caught. "It is true that Paris sets the standard in all things, but sometimes I have wondered—"

"Precisely, we have much of worth right here. For example, that excellent ham you served last night. If you could possibly find your way clear to provide the recipe, I'm sure my friend would include it in her book."

Annalise's eyes widened. "In a book? Really?"

"Most certainly. It's the best ham I've ever had."

"Surely, there's much better to be had elsewhere."

"Your modesty does you credit. Tell me, have you always lived in Avebury?"

And so it went, Sir Isaac drawing the young woman out until the conversation turned from recipes for ham to more meaningful matters. Annalise remained reticent. It seemed to him that she wanted to talk but had little experience doing so, especially when the subject was herself. She cast several more glances toward the basement door. Sir Isaac had to hope that Morley would stay busy with the beer casks for some time yet.

He was just bringing Annalise around to talk of the people in the village, the objective being to get her to say what she knew about Davey Hemper, when there was a noise outside. She stiffened and quickly pushed the chair back.

"Someone's arriving."

Sir Isaac suppressed an exclamation of pure annoyance. Why must they be interrupted right now? "The coach isn't due for several hours yet."

Annalise didn't reply but hurried toward the door. As she did, Morley emerged from the basement, drawn by the possibility of new customers. He took a quick look around the common room, saw nothing amiss, and hurried outside.

Sir Isaac subsided into his chair. He had tried, really he had, and he'd been rather better at it than he'd hoped. Having a young female housekeeper, who also happened to be his beloved niece, had helped. But he still hadn't gotten what Faulkner wanted.

Resolved to try again, he was freshening his tea when Morley returned accompanied by a young, hard-looking man Sir Isaac vaguely recognized. The man had a black cape draped over his shoulders. Emblazoned on it was the royal seal.

A messenger, then, come in haste to Avebury, and not, Sir Isaac guessed, for himself.

"Would you happen to know where Sir William's at, milord?" Morley asked.

"He went to see the parson," Sir Isaac replied, looking at the messenger. "You're from—"

"The duke, sir. He sends his greetings but informs you that Sir William's presence is required in London."

"Ah, I see. Do you know why?"

The messenger hesitated. Like all of his chosen kind, he was circumspect in the extreme. But this was Sir Isaac. "The Scots are acting up, sir, making trouble at the last minute about the unification. His lordship wants Sir William to help smooth it out."

"Very sensible of him, and certainly far more important than what he's doing here. Very well, then, you should find him at the parsonage or nearby. He goes with my blessings."

The messenger nodded. He spared a last glance for Morley, who had retreated to his tankards and was endeavoring to look as though he had heard nothing at all, then went on his way.

Faulkner entered the common room a few minutes later, trailing the messenger. "Get a drink and something to eat," he instructed the man. "I'll be ready to leave shortly."

The man nodded gratefully and went to do as he was bid. Faulkner joined Sir Isaac, who thought he looked very grim. "You've heard?"

"Indeed: the Scots causing problems, you needed. I quite understand."

"I don't. They should be able to handle this without me."

Sir Isaac looked at him in surprise. He had thought Faulkner would welcome an iron-clad excuse to be gone, but clearly that was not the case. A thought of Mistress Huxley flitted through his mind. It was all so strange to him, this business of a man with a woman, he would never grasp it. But seemingly Faulkner was more serious in his regard than would have been expected.

"Your duty . . . " Sir Isaac ventured.

"I am sick to death of duty," Faulkner said.

Silence reigned round the table. Sir Isaac was too deeply shocked for anything else. He had come to know the younger man well enough to realize what a startling change this was for him.

Faulkner's face was hard. "I had no intention of leaving until I found the killer."

"I know that, we all do. But Constable Duggin will carry on. Now that he knows the importance placed on events here, I'm sure he'll do a decent job."

Faulkner looked unconvinced. His eyes were shadowed and he appeared deep within his own thoughts. "It isn't clear how long I will be needed in London."

"I quite understand," Sir Isaac said, brushing that aside. He thought it merely courtesy.

"Do you intend to remain awhile?"

"Awhile," Sir Isaac agreed. "My return is not so urgent, and besides, this place draws me, as you know."

Faulkner nodded. He looked away, staring at the rough-planked wall. "Sarah isn't likely to see me, is she?"

Sir Isaac was struck by the anguish in his tone and the hard acceptance. "I'm afraid she was quite adamant—"

"Give her this for me, will you?" He slid a heavy gold insignia ring from his finger and handed it to the older man.

Sir Isaac nodded slowly. He stared down at the coiled metal. "I am sorry for what has happened."

Faulkner nodded once, curtly, and stood. Quietly, so that Sir Isaac had to lean forward slightly to hear him, he said, "If Mistress Huxley should need for anything, send word to me."

"I will," the scholar said and felt the weight of the promise like the ring resting in his palm.

Faulkner kept his mind deliberately blank as he went to inform Crispin that they were leaving. The valet did not hide his joy.

"Oh, blessed day," he exclaimed, "to shake the dust of Avebury from our boots!"

"Contain yourself. I will ride on ahead with the messenger. You follow with the coach and luggage."

"Most certainly. I can hardly wait. If you don't mind my saying, milord, this has been a most difficult sojourn."

"Yes," Faulkner murmured, "difficult." He lifted his saddlebag from beside the bed where it was always kept ready, a legacy of his soldiering days, and took a final glance around. Had there been any way to deny the duke's summons, he would have seized it in an instant. But there was not, and for that he was strangely torn. A part of him wanted desperately to remain. Another was as relieved as Crispin to go.

Rascal was waiting, already saddled by the messenger. The stallion tossed his head with pleasure and pawed the ground in his eagerness.

Faulkner mounted. He allowed himself a single glance down the lane in the direction of Sarah's house. The shutters were drawn against the midday light. Birds rested on the high garden walls. It looked peaceful, silent, untouched by all the world and preferring it that way.

So be it. He turned his face toward the sun, put his heels to Rascal, and did not look back again.

31

"*Gone?*" *Sarah repeated.* She stared at Sir Isaac blankly. "Did you say gone?"

"Not an hour ago. He received an urgent summons from the duke and had to return to London." Pointedly, Sir Isaac added, "I'm sure he would have called to say his farewells, however pressed for time he was. But you had said you were not receiving."

Sarah flushed. They were in the drawing room. Sir Isaac had been admitted by Missus Damas, but Sarah herself would never have considered turning him away. They all knew whom she meant when she said no callers.

"I see. . . . Well, I hope he has a pleasant journey." Gone, not here, departed. Even as she spoke, she struggled to accept his absence. It hurt deeply. That was the first reality she had to get used to. The second was that she was angry—deeply, coldly angry—

at him, at herself, at the whole bloody circumstance.

"He left this," Sir Isaac said and dropped the ring into her hand.

Sarah turned it over slowly. The ring was heavy. It felt cold to her touch. Twin bands of gold coiled around each other, almost like serpents tangling. The inside was smooth, except for the words etched there. She read them slowly. "*Finem respice.*"

"Look to the end," Sir Isaac murmured. "A good motto for a man who has always seemed to know what it is he wants. I remembered after he asked me to give it to you that it was a gift from the duke. Marlborough had it made for him as a remembrance of the victory at Blenheim and, of course, of his own esteem for Sir William."

Sarah's throat was tight. She did not trust herself to do more than nod.

Sir Isaac smiled and patted her hand. "I was wondering if you might be available to do a bit of measuring tomorrow?"

He had to repeat the question before she really heard him. There was nothing to keep her in the house now. She could go back out into the village, back to her ordinary life, do all the things she had been used to doing before Faulkner came. They would not lie together again on the hillside or stand together within the circle. Time would not slip its boundaries for them, and the forces of the earth would not threaten to sweep them away. He was safe.

And she was alone.

"Yes," she said quietly, "of course," and closed her fingers tight around his ring.

*   *   *

Faulkner rode hard. He knew Rascal was up to it and he was anxious to reach London. Besides, the more he pressed himself, the less he dwelled on Sarah. Even so, he had covered only a part of the distance before nightfall. The messenger had gone on ahead, taking fresh mounts at the posts scattered along the route and riding without cease to let the duke know that Faulkner was on his way.

Alone, he drew rein in a small copse just off the London road. The night was clear and pleasantly warm. He found water for Rascal and himself, then set the horse to graze. From his saddlebag, he took a bedroll and spread it out under the stars. Supper was a portion of bread and cheese washed down by spring water. He wanted nothing more.

Weary but not inclined to sleep, he stretched out and lay with his head pillowed on his folded arms, looking up at the night sky. It was the first night he had spent alone for a while, and he did not like it. Try though he did, he could think of nothing but Sarah.

No callers.

Maddening. It was the only possible word for her. But why? What strange assortment of events had created a woman at once so whimsical and so infuriating?

He wanted to think it out, to come to some conclusion that would soothe his temper and his pride. But the day had been long and wearying. He slept. No dreams troubled him. No whisper of the past surfaced in his mind. He slept the sleep of the innocent and untroubled and woke startled to discover how well he had rested.

Rascal, too, appeared renewed and eager to be on his way. The stallion pawed the ground as Faulkner saddled him. "Don't worry, boy," he said, "we'll be home soon."

He could hardly wait to shake the dust of the country from his feet and be in London again. To walk once more the teeming streets, to listen to the shouts of the peddlers, to feel the full, unbridled vigor of what was surely the center of the world, or deserved to be.

Ahead lay London, coming ever closer, majestic, sublime, incomparable. Closer now and closer still until at last country gave way to proper streets crowded with all the vigor and excitement of the great city. Nothing could ever be as fine, as welcoming, as fit for him. He—

Splat! A clump of offal flew past his ear. He dodged just in time and found himself engulfed in a pushing, shoving mob of riders and pedestrians all trying to force their way through Aldgate simultaneously. Rascal shied nervously. Faulkner tightened his hold on the reins and cursed under his breath.

Sweet lord, what was the matter with them? If they'd just take turns, let the person in front of them go first, they'd all get through much faster. But oh, no, it was push and shove as best you could until the whole teeming mass threatened to burst the old city walls.

Faulkner got through, but only just, and pulled up on the other side to calm Rascal. They were on the Whitechapel Road not far from Tower Hill and close to Lombard Street, where the merchants held sway. He had always liked this part of the city and felt at home here. But he had been away often enough before. How was it he hadn't noticed how extraordinarily dirty and noisy it was?

His house stood near the river in a pleasant enclave not far from Westminster and within easy reach of Whitehall. Ordinarily, the location suited him very well. But on this day, he chafed at having to traverse most of the length of London in order to reach it. In hindsight, he should have taken a more circuitous route but in his haste he hadn't thought of it. Instead, he managed as best he could but was greatly relieved when at last he stopped in front of the imposing brick house he occupied, set back from the road and surrounded by a pleasant garden.

A servant, alerted by the messenger to expect him, ran out and led Rascal away with strict instructions to care for him well. Faulkner went inside. Without Crispin to fuss over him, he bathed quickly—in cold water for there was no time to heat any—and dressed in haste. Barely half an hour after his return, he was off again, headed for Westminster and an audience with the duke.

His stride was quick and sure. This was where he belonged. Yet he grimaced at the smells and found himself surprised at noticing how even in the palace, the air was stale with the scents of food and unwashed bodies. He had always been rather more fastidious than most of the people around him, but he had never been particularly bothered by the realities of city life. Until now.

By the time he reached the duke's inner sanctum, he was in as sore a mood as he had ever been. Only genuine respect for Marlborough and long schooling in discipline kept him from revealing it.

The duke looked up when he entered. He was seated at a desk littered with papers, his wig left off as usual and his shirtsleeves rolled up. He looked surprised to see Faulkner, but pleased.

"Ah, there you are. I didn't expect you for another day."

"Rascal's a good soul. He didn't mind being pressed."

The duke nodded. Like Faulkner, he had a vast love of horses and considered them in certain respects worth more than people. "Sit down. I'll call for tea."

A servant came and went. They were left alone. Marlborough leaned back in his chair and regarded Faulkner benignly. "Well, then, how is Sir Isaac faring?"

"Well, enough. I think he's tired himself. About the Scots?"

"Oh, yes, my message. They appear to be having last-minute doubts, demanding that all sorts of points be reopened that were settled months ago. Parliament's up in arms, several of the ministers have actually mentioned war, and Her Majesty is most displeased. I thought it best that you be here."

So, a full-blown crisis, exactly what he handled best. Faulkner nodded. "I'll do what I can. Where do you suggest we start?"

They spoke an hour longer, together devising a strategy for dealing with both the recalcitrant Scots and the royal government, which on a good day both men thought prone to hysteria. The queen was, of course, another matter entirely. They regarded her with the highest possible respect. But she was a woman, after all, and it was only right that she be spared the hue and cry of battle—including the political variety—as much as possible.

Faulkner caught himself thinking of another female who would have resisted being so protected. He frowned.

"Something wrong?" the duke asked.

"No, not at all, merely that I left the business in Avebury undone."

"The business . . . oh, yes, the murders. That can't be helped. You're needed here."

"As you say."

"Besides, the important thing is that Sir Isaac

knows we tried. How did the two of you hit it off?"

"Very well. He is a fascinating man, if given to some odd preoccupations."

Marlborough laughed. "Odd indeed. But if he's happy crawling around old mounds and the like, so be it. Now, as to the Scots."

And so it went as the afternoon waned and the lamps were lit. Faulkner was in his element. This was who he was and what he did. By nightfall, a strategy had been worked out for dealing with most of the objections the Scots had raised—and doing so peacefully.

"I've had enough of war," Marlborough said, a private admission he would not have made to anyone else, even his beloved wife. Queen and country wished to see him as a conqueror. He was willing enough to oblige them so long as that did not oblige him to take up his sword again.

Faulkner murmured his agreement as he continued to bend over the list of responses they had worked out, penning in a word here, scratching out another there. He, too, wanted to be done with war. In particular, he had no wish to march north to Scotland at the behest of an irate Parliament and a hand-wringing queen and lay waste to the Highlands, presuming an English army would even have been able to do such a thing.

They would bring the Scots round with words, surround them with promises that might even be kept, so determined were Faulkner and the duke to put an end to war. Determined in the way only battle-scarred warriors can be when the adventure has lost its glory and there is nothing left but regret.

Faulkner left Westminster shortly after dark. He declined an invitation to sup with the duke in his apartments. The volatile Lady Sarah would be present and, much as he enjoyed the duchess, he didn't feel quite up to dealing with her that evening. Besides, thoughts of another woman continued to haunt him.

He went home instead. At his command, a hot supper was provided, hot water fetched, clean clothes laid out, and the whole house sent into a bustle from which it did not recover until the watchman was calling near to midnight. When, at last, silence descended, Faulkner sat up alone in his study, planning what would be done the next day. It was an elaborate game they were embarked upon, he and the duke—one in which the moves had to be precisely correct. Too much rested on failure: peace and war and the fate of a kingdom.

That should have been enough for any man and yet, when Faulkner at last put his head to pillow, it was Avebury he thought of, strange, mysterious, and deadly. And Sarah, floating over all, gazing off into the distance as though she could neither see nor hear him no matter how he struggled to reach her.

Faulkner spent the following day going between Westminster, the Scots housed at St. James's, and Parliament. Ordinarily, he tried to stay as far away from the last as he could manage, but the circumstances called for desperate measures.

By afternoon, he was tired, out of sorts, and fed up with the whole business. But he was also making progress. Now if he could only get the Scots to talk to the duke, and the duke to talk to the Commons, and the Lords just to stop talking, they all might be able to make some progress.

Hospitable people, the Scots, really, to a fault. Every time he trotted over with a new proposal or suggestion, they insisted he join them in a toast to everyone's continued goodwill. Much more of that and he'd be dead in the gutter. Also, he had to let it be known that he absolutely would not eat haggis. A man had to draw the line somewhere, and he did at stuffed sheep stomach.

And so, to evening and the faint stench of the river floating over Londontown. Rascal knew the way home. Faulkner let him take it and prayed the fetid air might somehow clear his senses. The things he did for England!

"Sir," Crispin said as he opened the front door, looking none the worse for his journey. The single word carried a wealth of meaning, mostly having to do with the deplorable state of his master's boots, the smell of whisky hanging about his clothes, and the fact that he needed a bath.

"I'm just going to lie down for a few minutes," Faulkner muttered. He hadn't slept well at all the previous night. Weariness dogged him but he'd rebound quickly; he always did. All he needed was a short rest.

Crispin pursed his mouth most effectively and waited until Faulkner was halfway up the stairs. "I wouldn't advise it," he said.

"What's that?"

"Nothing, sir. I'll send the bath water up in half an hour."

Fine, he'd sleep in the tub. Anything to stop the spinning of his head and the twinge in his shoulders that told more eloquently than anything else that he was no longer a high-blooded nineteen-year-old riding into battle without a thought for anything save victory.

He opened the door to his chamber, entered, and flopped down in the nearest chair. Intent on pulling off his boots, it was several moments before he realized he was not alone.

The woman on the bed—his bed—smiled. No powder dimmed the golden radiance of her hair, piled in ringlets atop her head. No artifice was needed to enhance the alabaster glow of her skin, liberally revealed above the daring gown she wore. She was exquisitely made, sheer perfection. And why not? It was her job.

"Hello, Chantra," Faulkner said and dropped the boots.

32

"*How many?*" *Sarah* asked.

"Twelve," Sir Isaac repeated. He looked at her gently. "Are you all right, my dear?"

She glanced up, startled. "Yes, of course. Why do you ask?"

"It's only that you've asked to repeat measurements four times so far. I wonder if you aren't perhaps distracted."

She took a breath, seeking a believable denial, and found only truth instead. "I fear you are right, Sir Isaac. My mind has not been on the work. I will try to do better."

"There, now," he said in an almost fatherly way. "There is nothing so urgent that it cannot be postponed. You are only just recovering from your indisposition." So was her prolonged period of unconsciousness delicately called. "We must caution against tiring you."

"I'm fine," she murmured, grateful for his concern but afraid she would be undone by it. "If you don't mind, I would prefer to continue."

They did for another hour or so. Through studious concentration, she managed to note down the numbers without having to have them repeated. But her heart was clearly not in it, and at length Sir Isaac called a halt.

He did it in the most gentlemanly way possible. "I fear these old bones are not as strong as they used to be. What do you say to tea?"

She allowed as to how that would be very welcome and accepted his proffered arm. Together, they made their way down the hill above the Kennet and along the avenue back to the village.

Constable Duggin was at his forge. He nodded at them as they passed but kept working. Jobs had piled up in the last two days as he made a concerted effort to be seen doing something—anything—about the three murders. In Faulkner's absence, he was clearly determined not to be called lax. But the effort had been without success, so far as Sarah knew. They were no closer than ever to finding the killer among them.

Indeed, the more time passed, the more people murmured that it must have been a stranger after all, someone long gone from these parts. They were well content with that explanation and inclined to promote it strongly.

She remained unconvinced, but she would also have been hard pressed to explain why. All she could have said was that something seemed not quite right in Avebury. A faint smile twisted the corners of her mouth. All things considered, the explanation was almost ludicrous.

Annalise normally set a good tea for the Rose, but this day she seemed wearier than usual. She went about with her head down and a heaviness to her step. Sarah presumed she was still sorrowing over Davey and took special pains to be kind to her.

Sir Isaac noticed. When the girl had come and gone, leaving the tea behind, he sat back in his chair and regarded Sarah gently.

"You know," he said as though having come to a significant decision, "you are a good woman."

Sarah laughed weakly. "There are many who would not agree with you."

"Narrow minds seek fault in everyone but where it rightly belongs, in themselves. No, I stand by what I said. However, you also appear to be a sad one."

"I am worried about events here."

"And about your own ability to affect them."

"Yes," she admitted, "that too."

"It is not your responsibility," Sir Isaac said quietly.

She looked up, meeting his eyes. "In some ways it is."

He did not dispute her; indeed, he seemed to understand in an odd sort of way. They sipped the tea. Sarah ate half a tiny sandwich. Sir Isaac ate rather more.

"I have never eaten better than I do here. The air gives me an appetite."

"You are too much in the city," she suggested.

"Too true. I spend my days going between London and the observatory at Greenwich. Fascinating places, both. Have you ever visited them?"

"London, yes, but years ago. I have never been to Greenwich."

"Ah, well, we must remedy that." He thought for a moment, then appeared seized by inspiration. "As you have been so very kind to me in my stay here, what say you to coming with me back to London? I would be delighted to have you visit, and it would give me great pleasure to show you the sights."

Before he finished, Sarah was shaking her head. "Oh, no, I thank you but I couldn't possibly—"

"Afraid?" he asked, the voice soft, the eyes suddenly shrewd.

"No, certainly not. It's only that—"

"Why should you hesitate, I wonder? A woman of your abilities surely wouldn't feel intimidated by London."

"Surely not."

"Or by any of the people she might meet there."

"Hardly."

He nodded, pleased with himself—and her. "I tell you honestly, Mistress Sarah, I fear you are too much restricted here. This is a fascinating place, but it can take one over if proper care isn't exercised. Come to London, if only for a spell. It will do you a world of good."

"I would not care to impose." Was she actually considering this? Absurd even to give it a thought. London was the last place she should be. Faulkner was—

"Not at all," Sir Isaac said. "I have a ridiculously large house, and my niece who looks after me will be delighted for the company. What say you?"

"I . . ." Can't, shouldn't mustn't. Thank you so very much but really—

Not afraid.

London was a vast place. There was nothing to say her path would ever cross Faulkner's. But if it did—

"I'll go," she said and reached quickly for the tea, thinking that it ought to be something stronger.

Sir Isaac being an elderly man, Sarah expected the journey to take a week or more and packed accordingly. She was surprised to discover that he liked to travel and was perfectly willing to stay on the road all the daylight hours, rising in gray dawn and not resting until evening came.

They reached London in four days, weary and dusty but more pleased with each other's company than ever. Had she been able to spend another few days in the coach with him, Sarah thought she might even begin to understand something of what he meant when he talked of the workings of the universe.

Sir Isaac's house was blessedly outside of London proper on the road that wound near the river not far from Westminster. His niece was a delightful young woman in her twenties who lived in the house with her husband and young children. They all welcomed Sarah warmly.

Sarah was pleased to discover that Sir Isaac lived in the bosom of such a loving family, the best possible influence to stave off the loneliness that undoubtedly would otherwise have been the lot of so brilliant a man. Without comparing herself to him in any way, she was herself all too well acquainted with what loneliness could do. It was the food of madness.

Here in London, she wondered why she had not realized that before. But then she had always told herself that she wasn't lonely. She had Missus Damas and the other servants, all the villagers, even cousins such as the Hoddinworths—heaven help her.

Yet lonely she had been and too much given to her own thoughts. Perhaps that explained the strange visions she had experienced.

It was a soothing thought. She nurtured it through supper at Sir Isaac's house, when the whole family sat down together and he regaled them with tales of Avebury, and to bed in the high four-poster under the eaves. Lying there, she listened to the muted sounds of the neighborhood and, beyond, the city.

There was a good deal to hear, certainly far more than she was accustomed to. For a time, she thought she would be unable to sleep. But that proved untrue. Between the flicker of one sound and the next, night fled on stolen feet.

She woke to her first full day in London.

33

"Westminster," Sir Isaac said, "was constructed in the eleventh century but underwent extensive renovation three centuries later. The hall is particularly noteworthy for its hammer-beam roof, an innovation requiring very little support. It is still possible to see—"

Sarah smiled attentively, or what she hoped would be taken for such. Sir Isaac was proving a more than adequate tour guide. Much more. So far they had seen St. Paul's Cathedral, for moral uplifting; the Royal Exchange, for shopping; the Tower, for history; and Locket's Tavern, for luncheon.

And all this in a few short morning hours. Her feet throbbed and her head whirled. Westminster was marvelous, very impressive, all those serious-looking people to-ing and fro-ing, but she was beginning to long for a bath and a nice cup of tea.

"Horse Guards," Sir Isaac was saying.

"What's that?"

"The Horse Guards are about to parade. You really must see this. It's quite possible Her Majesty will be present."

It was on the tip of Sarah's tongue to admit that she was too tired to view England's sovereign. But she couldn't bring herself to dampen Sir Isaac's enthusiasm. They went along to the palace yard—the new one by Westminster Hall, not, as Sir Isaac was at pains to point out, the old one farther down and on the other side. One could get hackney coaches at the old yard—Hackney Hell Carts they were called because of their extraordinary discomfort—but one could not see the Horse Guards on parade.

Drums were beating even as they arrived. There was a good crowd assembled, mostly gentry from the look of them, for the lower orders weren't permitted within the confines of the palace. But here and there—

"Watch your pockets," Sir Isaac advised as he took her arm and guided her over to a good spot from which to watch. "We have the best dressed thieves in the world here in London. You'd swear you had your purse lifted by an earl."

Alerted, Sarah glanced around nervously. So far, she'd been having a perfectly pleasant—if footsore—visit. But now, for the first time, she was conscious of being among people of her own class. She was startled by the elaborateness of their dress and the extravagance of their gestures. Everything seemed rehearsed, artificial, overdone. And fascinating.

She watched, bemused, as a young dandy arrayed in a brocade frock coat and extraordinary snug breeches waved a lace-edged handkerchief languidly beneath the nose of a beauty in a tightly corseted gown with a neckline so daring as to preserve her modesty by no more than a hair's breadth.

Sir Isaac followed the direction of her gaze. He looked away hastily. "I fear morals here aren't quite what you're used to, my dear."

Sarah shot him a hasty look. Was he jesting—and rather cruelly, at that? His entire manner said otherwise. A gentle and innately courtly man, Sir Isaac appeared genuinely to believe her to be a woman of high moral standards. Never mind that he must know full well—or at least strongly suspect—that her dealings with Faulkner were quite irregular.

The courtesan fluttered her lashes and rewarded the dandy with a coquettish smile, all the while making a shrewd appraisal of his appearance and the wealth it might indicate. Beside such goings-on, a mere parade of the royal guardsmen could hardly compare. Yet when the drumbeat grew louder and the whinnying of horses was heard, the crowd pressed forward, Sarah with it.

Scarlet-clad officers paraded into the palace yard, each superbly mounted, staring straight ahead, seemingly unaware of their appreciative audience. They whirled in place, perfectly formed into a long line four abreast, and came to a stop before the raised entrance of the hall. The double doors opened. A small, plump woman emerged to the sudden cheers of the crowd and the enthusiastic waving of hats.

Sarah raised herself on tiptoe to get a better look at her sovereign. She had never seen Queen Anne but had heard a great deal about her, most particularly her sad and not very successful struggles to produce an heir through interminable pregnancies. Yet the woman she saw did not appear weighed down by failure. She seemed solemn but self-possessed, a sturdy-breasted woman very plain of face and ridiculously gotten up in a gown of such ornateness that it put the dandy and all the others to shame.

Anne was encased in pearls, sewn onto every inch of her silk and lace gown, wound round her neck, even suspended from her earlobes. Surely all the oysters in all the seas had contributed to create such a display. Courtiers were ranged behind her, but it was the little dogs that held pride of place. They scampered all around her, barking at the riders and generally making a nuisance of themselves.

So busy was she staring at the queen, who looked like a living statue, that Sarah momentarily forgot all else. The Horse Guards were passing, swords extended, drums beating, the crowd applauding. It was all very stirring, her first real look at royal pageantry. Although she tended to take a dry view of such things, even her heart beat a touch more rapidly.

Until she happened to glance off to the side and saw a tall, lithe body, far more somberly dressed than all the rest, with ebony hair tied in a neat queue, a flashing smile and . . . a blonde fastened to his arm so firmly it appeared wild horses could not have dragged her off.

Sarah made a choking sound and turned away.

"My dear," Sir Isaac said, alarmed. "Are you all right?" When he got no answer, he looked in the same direction she had. "Oh."

Sarah hardly heard him. She plunged through the crowd, pushing past the dandies and their ladies, the grand and the pretend, the true and the false, shoving them all away, heedless of her direction, knowing only that she had to escape or the pain would devour her.

She reached the edge of the palace yard out of breath, heart thudding, and with a sick knot in her stomach. Sir

Isaac was far behind, lost somewhere in the mass. She was alone.

That suited her perfectly. She picked up her skirts and forced herself to walk, not run. Pride was an issue here. She absolutely would not break down. Nor could she stop walking. She had to put as much distance between herself and what she had seen as was possible.

At length, she came to the river. From a distance, it looked ordinary enough and quite pleasing. Close up, it had an unpleasant brown tinge and an appalling odor. Wrinkling her nose, she looked around for somewhere she might safely go. Before long, she would find her way back to Sir Isaac's house—she was far too considerate a guest to worry her host. But for the moment she desperately needed to be by herself.

That was impossible in a city so teeming with people, but there had to be someplace she could go, as an unaccompanied woman, and be left alone. The coffeehouses were out of the question. She was not so naive as to think otherwise. Similarly, she would not venture into any public house. But what had Sir Isaac mentioned—the bookstores near St. Paul's? He'd suggested they might return later to the neighborhood so that she could browse.

Fine, she would seek sanctuary among the books and perhaps—only perhaps—find some way to soothe a shattered heart. Grimacing at her own foolish vulnerability, she set off on foot, retracing the same path she and Sir Isaac had taken earlier to reach Westminster.

But her thoughts were disordered, her attention lapsed. In the twisting warrens of London's streets, she took a wrong turn and continued on, all unknowingly, lost.

34

As soon as he saw Sarah, Faulkner plunged into the crowd after her. Chantra gasped and tried to hold him back, but he shrugged her off without a second thought.

Having sent her packing several nights ago with a heavy purse but nothing else, he had not expected to encounter her again. When she appeared, seemingly by accident, in the middle of the palace yard, he had felt just a bit contrite about treating her so cavalierly and had tried to be courteous.

But Sarah's sudden appearance changed everything. He could hardly believe she was here, in London. The mere possibility delighted him, unlike the expression on her face when she saw him with Chantra. That he was determined to put right at once.

The crowd could not have stopped him, but the Horse Guards did. Just as he was closing the distance between himself and the fleeting glimpse of azure silk up ahead, the entire body of horsemen whirled in front of him, blocking his path. He cursed but could do nothing until the last of the riders was past. The moment they rode by, while the dust was still swirling, he went on. It was too late. Sarah, if that really was who it had been, was gone.

Faulkner stood, looking in one direction and the other, trying to convince himself he hadn't been mistaken. It was so improbable, as though he had willed a wish into reality, that he feared his eyes had tricked him.

He had almost convinced himself of that when a gentle hand laid on his arm drew him up short.

"Sarah," he began, his voice rough with gladness and relief, only to break off when he found himself staring into the bright, far-seeing eyes of Sir Isaac.

"Faulkner, dear boy, so nice to see you."

"Yes, you too. Very nice. I was just—"

"I fear Mistress Huxley may have been taken ill. We were here together, you see. She left quite suddenly. Unaccustomed as she is to London, I am rather concerned."

"She *is* here? Really?"

"Why, yes, we came together. I thought some time away from Avebury would do her good."

He said it in all innocence, but Faulkner had his doubts. He had seen Sir Isaac play the master mechanic before, arranging things as he thought they ought to be.

"How fare the Scots?" his elderly friend asked.

"They're coming round. I must go after her."

"By all means. She is staying at my house, but she may not go there. We talked about the bookstores."

Faulkner thought quickly. There were few other places she could safely go. He only hoped that would occur to her.

"Which bookstores?"

"By St. Paul's. I will go home to await her. May I suggest that you—"

He was talking to the air. Faulkner had already gone.

Quickly enough, Sarah realized she had erred, but by that time it was too late to do anything about it. She was hopelessly twisted around with no idea of how to get back to where she had started.

A street urchin darted by. She stepped out quickly in front of him. "Your pardon, but would you direct me to St. Paul's?"

The boy—or was it a girl?—gave her a long speculative glance, taking in her clothing—of good quality if not the height of fashion—and her genteel manner. Sharp eyes gleamed. "By swear, milady, I'll do better than that. I'll take you there meself."

There now, the perfect solution. She gave a small sign of relief and nodded. "I'll pay you, of course."

The urchin said nothing more but set off through the narrow streets with Sarah following. Struggling to keep up with him, she quickly became even more disoriented. It seemed to her that they were going deeper and deeper into a warren of lanes, but she was surely wrong.

Wasn't she?

A corner turned, another, faster and faster, until she was calling on the child to slow. Instead, he darted up ahead and vanished through an alley. She was alone, far within the depths of an area even country Sarah knew to fear.

A prank then, nothing more, curiously played by a child who seemed to savor its naughtiness more than the money she would have paid for safe passage. No harm done, really. It was daylight still. She would find her way out.

She turned to find a man, roughly garbed, filthy dirty, closing in behind her. Another to the front. Two more to either side. And from every window in the stinking hovels all around her, heads peering, toothless mouths grinning, the audience assembled to watch this particular baiting not of bears or rats but of far more exotic fare, a genteel lady ripe—oh, so very ripe—for the plucking.

Terror gripped her. She opened her mouth as though to scream but her throat clamped shut so that no sound came out. This was not Avebury, where she might reasonably expect help. If they would only just take her purse—

"Smooth skin for the selling, what?" the leader said. "We'll get rich on this one."

Her stomach churned. She gripped her purse—absurd weapon but the only one she had—in both hands and swung it widely, striking the leader in the face. He grunted and kept coming, not at all deterred.

Not by her at any rate, but the blood-curdling yell that suddenly echoed up and down the lane was another matter entirely. As was the slashing sword that split the filth-encrusted doublet and sent the leader's blood pouring out onto the street.

"Damned scum," a cold, arrogant voice said, sword slashing for the other assailants, "run for your lives before I kill the lot of you."

Cursing, the attackers vanished into the shadows. Sarah was left, breathless but unharmed, shaking like a spring leaf in a thunderstorm.

"T-thank you," she began, only to break off in astonishment. This was not some anonymous rescuer who had come to her aide. Instead . . .

"Justin?" she asked, hardly believing. "Is it really you?" Surely, he was a conjuring of her imagination, a reminder of the suspicions and the worry that dogged her no matter how far she might remove herself from Avebury. The mystery lingered—murders and magic— whispering always in the dark corners of her mind.

The viscount, showing no sign of his exertions, wiped his sword off as best he could on the unconscious assailant's doublet, then resheathed it. He regarded her calmly. "Mistress Huxley, might I ask what you are doing here?"

"I was lost," she explained, still grappling with the astonishing coincidence of his appearance.

Justin smiled tightly. He took her arm and began walking swiftly in the direction from which she had come. Every few seconds, he glanced over his shoulder to make sure they weren't being followed.

"I meant what are you doing in London," he said, as the houses began to grow less grim around them and the street widened. "When I left, you were still in Avebury."

"I came with Sir Isaac. He thought I might enjoy the trip." They had come out on Fleet Street at almost the exact spot where Sarah had gone wrong. Sunlight shone on the prosperous men and women passing by. Fine carriages rolled along. A door opened in an elegant brick house directly across from where Sarah stood and a neatly dressed servant emerged to walk gravely down the steps probably on an errand.

It was as though the dark, twisting evil she had just confronted was part of an unreal world. And yet it existed, as the still rapid beating of her heart confirmed, side by side with this other London.

"I was going to St. Paul's, to the bookstores." She could hardly explain about seeing Faulkner with a woman at the Horse Guards parade and running off in distress. In hindsight, it would sound extraordinarily foolish, as indeed it had been.

"This way then," Justin said and guided her expertly until they were within sight of the domed church, nearing the end of its rebuilding following the great fire of the previous century.

"I am most grateful to you," Sarah said quietly. She regarded her distant cousin with some bewilderment. He was strangely cast in the role of a Sir Galahad. "But I still admit to being astounded that you appeared when you did. Should I credit it to a benign deity?"

"Credit it to my own bad habits," he said shortly.

When she looked unconvinced, he sighed deeply. "You are determined to know the worst of me."

"No, not at all. I simply don't believe in guardian angels."

Justin gave a hard laugh. "You are wise not to, as they are notoriously unreliable. Very well, then, much as it goes against my nature, I will tell you the truth. Mother—dear Mother—wrote to say you were coming to London with your elderly friend. I decided to see if I couldn't make myself useful in some way in the hope that you might be more willing to champion my cause. So I followed you."

"You followed?"

"You and Sir Isaac. Shouldn't a man his age be dead after such a morning? I've seen more of London in one day that I would have been content to see in a lifetime. And then, just when I think you must certainly have had enough, you go racing off as though all the hounds of hell are at your heels and end up in Newgate, of all places. Really, Sarah, it doesn't become you."

"What doesn't?" she asked dazedly, still trying to come to terms with his confession. Justin had been following them and she'd never even seen him. Sir Isaac's oblivion she could justify; he was an elderly man, increasingly short-sighted though he denied it and inclined to be carried away on his own enthusiasms to the exclusion of all else. But she . . . she should most certainly have noticed.

And would have had not thoughts of Faulkner—curse him!—been swirling through her mind.

"I saw them too," Justin said quietly. "Do you know who she is?"

The pain was really more than she could bear. It was going to choke her if she let it. "No, and I don't want to."

"As you wish."

She waited a dozen heartbeats, perhaps a few more. "You're not going to tell me?"

He shook his head in mock exasperation. "You just said you didn't want to know."

"Yes, but I didn't expect you to believe me."

"Sweet lord, are you sure you were country raised? You're as fickle as the best-schooled belle."

"No," Sarah said softly, "the problem is I'm not."

Justin's look was sharp. "Is that the way of it then? Pity, you'd be better off if you could manage a bit of armor. Still, they say knowledge is a shield—if not a sword. She is Chantra Deschamps, although I don't imagine she was born to the name."

"I see," Sarah murmured. "She is very beautiful."

"Well, of course she is. If she weren't, she wouldn't be anyone at all."

At Sarah's startled look, the viscount rolled his eyes. "What an odd combination you are, a country gentlewoman who sees far too much yet can still be startlingly naive. Dear thing, what do you imagine the Deschamps *does*?"

"What do you mean, does?"

"How she earns a living. Her attraction for men like . . . well, men like Sir William?"

At Sarah's sudden flush, he sighed exaggeratedly and went on in the tone of a kindly teacher attempting to instruct a pupil who, while not precisely dense, has shown an amazing gap in education.

"London has many sorts of women but only a very few of them are courtesans of the Deschamps's standing. So exalted is she that when she seemingly conceived a tendresse for Sir William and dismissed her other admirers—apparently at his insistence; he's not inclined to share—there was a vast gnashing of teeth to be heard in all the better clubs. Recently, rumor had it that she wished to marry. Now ordinarily that would have been out of the question for a lady so generous with her favors, but in the rarefied world of the Deschamps it isn't actually impossible."

He leaned forward confidingly.

"One or two others of her standing have married into the aristocracy. It isn't generally talked about, but it has happened. In fact, Lady—" He stopped himself and took a breath. "Never mind. As I was saying, there were rumors. And then suddenly she appeared to have been dismissed and Sir William departed for parts unknown, which turned out, absurdly enough, to be Avebury. So there you have it."

"And now he has returned and they are together again."

"So it seems. Am I forgiven?"

"For what?" She was completely at sea, swamped

by thoughts of Faulkner with the golden woman and hardly aware of what she said.

"For following you."

"If you hadn't I would have been killed. Of course you're forgiven."

"Most kind. Now the question is, what do we do next?"

"Do?"

"I realize you're upset, but try to pay attention. Do about the Deschamps, of course."

Sarah drew herself up. She had to get a grip on herself. "I don't see why you should be interested in doing anything at all about her."

"That's because you're not me. My preference is for you and Sir William to be on the best possible terms so that you can ask him very nicely to find a suitable position at court for your very dear, very talented, and very deserving cousin. Naturally, I don't want him to have any hesitation at all about granting your request. To that end, the Deschamps must go. It would be easier if you'd help." He smiled kindly.

Sarah stared at him. She didn't know whether to laugh or cry or merely to hit him. He had saved her life, she must remember that. Yet now he wanted to use her bruised and battered heart as a tool to achieve his own ends.

Truly, she was learning more in London than she had ever wanted to.

"I fear that, grateful as I am for your assistance, I can be of little use to you," she said. "Now if you would excuse—"

"You give up far too easily."

"No, I don't. I simply know when a cause is futile." Far better than he ever could, for she alone knew how impossible it was for her to have any sort of future with Faulkner. Safe within her walls, she had resolved not to see him again. Tempted out, she had faltered and come close to being destroyed. It was a reminder she would not need again.

"Is it really so bad?" Justin murmured. For just a moment, the pose of artifice and sophistication dropped. She caught a glimpse of a young man no stranger to pain himself and capable of genuine kindness.

"Thank you again," she said by way of answer. "I don't think I'm really in the mood to shop for books after all. Would you mind helping me get a carriage—"

"That won't be necessary."

The voice—deeper, smoother, but with an edge of harshness—sent a tremor of shock through Sarah. In a day heaped with surprise, here was the greatest yet.

She stared into Faulkner's pewter eyes and saw there a light that made her tremble far more than the dangers of Newgate ever could.

35

Justin was delighted. He couldn't have been more pleased to see Faulkner than if he had personally conjured him up. Grinning widely, he took a quick step back. "Don't mind me, I was just leaving."

Faulkner looked at him hard. "You're right, you were."

"Take due note of how quickly I leap to obey, milord." He sketched a swift bow to Sarah, tipped his hat with a bold smile, and vanished into the crowd.

Faulkner scowled. "Popinjay."

"No such thing. He just saved my life."

Was it her imagination or did he truly pale? "What are you talking about."

Belatedly, it occurred to Sarah that it really wasn't wise to tell him about the Newgate episode. "Nothing. My, but this is a day for coincidences! First I encounter the viscount, and now you."

"Don't be an idiot. I followed you."

"Apparently I've become a parade. Why would you have done that?"

"Because I saw the look on your face—oh, never mind. We can't talk here. Let's go." Without another word, he took hold of her by the arm and began marching off.

Sarah dug her heels in. It wasn't easy, considering that this part of London was paved in cobblestone, but she did the best she could. "I was going book shopping. It was so nice to see you again. Good day."

As hints went, she thought that was perfectly clear. Faulkner seemed to feel otherwise. He did not so much as slow his pace. Before she could catch her breath, she was being lifted into a familiar carriage, the same one he'd brought to Avebury. He stepped in beside her, slammed the door, and knocked hard on the roof.

"You are being outrageous," Sarah said as the wheels turned. She was thrown back against the seat, and slightly winded, but did not allow that to deter her. If he thought he could—

"Chantra Deschamps was my mistress. We parted amicably but permanently before I came to Avebury. Under no circumstances will I resume that liaison."

Sarah raised her eyebrows. "Did I ask?"

"No, of course not, you wouldn't give me the satisfaction. You're the most infuriating woman I've ever encountered. Why did you come to London?"

"To see the queen."

"You've done that. Now perhaps I could suggest more interesting pastimes."

"I really don't think—"

"Shut up, Sarah," he said, and very rude of him it was, but how was she supposed to mind when he had that rough-gravel timbre in his voice, the one that never failed to send shivers through her and he was moving so very close?

His mouth covered hers, hard, possessive, coaxing. Wonderful.

The carriage rattled on.

There were two problems, the Scots and Sir Isaac. Lying in bed that afternoon, Faulkner suggested that the solution might be to put them in a room together and let the elderly scholar and the high-spirited Highlanders slug it out. His money was on Sir Isaac.

Snuggled against him, Sarah laughed. She was devastatingly content. They had sent a message to her host, assuring him of her well-being, but were now attempting to devise a way for her to move from beneath his roof without undue upset.

She could not bear the thought of offending Sir Isaac. Neither could she endure being separated from Faulkner. That would come soon enough in any case. Each moment they had together was to be cherished.

She stirred, naked in his arms but for his ring, fastened by a golden cord around her throat, where she had worn it since the day Sir Isaac placed it in her hand. Faulkner had been particularly pleased to discover it, expressed some envy for its position, and proceeded to show her exactly how delighted he really was.

Truly, it was frightening how he made her feel: how beautiful, how desirable, how loved.

She must not think of that. Live for the moment, those were her watchwords. She would refuse to consider either past or future. Only the present counted here in smelly, crowded, furious, fascinating Londontown.

"About the Scots," she said. "How stubborn are they being?"

"About the same as usual. It's only the timing that's bad."

She sat up, propping herself on her elbow so that her hair fell as a veil on either side of him. Gazing down into his eyes, she smiled. "Why am I so confident that you will make short work of them?"

"Because I have an excellent incentive?"

"Flatterer," she murmured and lowered herself to him.

Sarah slept. The sun lowered westward; a cooling breeze swept over the city. She woke in the morning to buttered scones, apple tarts, strong tea, and a sense of well-being so intense it bordered on sin. But then what was one more?

Crispin appeared resigned to her presence. He was the soul of aloof cordiality, providing in succession hot bathwater, belated breakfast, freshly brushed and pressed clothes, and books with which to amuse herself pending Faulkner's return.

"He said he didn't believe he would be long, madam," Crispin informed her when she had settled in the drawing room overlooking the garden at the back of the house and the river beyond.

"Has he gone to see the Scots?" Her surroundings absorbed her. The room—like the rest of the house—was large, elegant, expensively furnished, yet with the emphasis on comfort rather than fashion. She liked it immensely.

"I believe so."

"But not for long?"

"So he said."

She nodded, but doubtfully, cautioning herself not

to expect too much. Faulkner was involved with issues of great importance. They naturally had to take priority over her. And yet—

Left alone, she tried to read but with no great success despite a vast number and variety of books that would ordinarily have delighted her. Finally, she stood and drifted around the room, pausing to examine a painting here, a statue there.

Her conscience stirred, inconvenient beast but not unamusing. She felt guilty not for having lain naked in the arms of a man not her husband nor for having engaged in intimacies that would have shocked her a scant time before. No, her guilt was the tug of Avebury, pulling her back, reminding her of unfinished business and a murderer as yet uncaught.

Like it or not, wish or yearn otherwise, she could not linger here long. Duty would always call. But for just a short time, a few scant days, surely that much she could claim for her own?

Running her fingers over a carving of a horse and rider, she tried not to count the passing minutes. He could be gone the entire rest of the day and well into the night. He might not return before morning, if then. She had to reconcile herself to that, had to—

There was a flurry of sound in the hall outside, doors opening, servants bustling. She went to look and saw Faulkner, smile flashing, black cape swirling as he handed it to Crispin.

"Mistress Huxley?" he asked.

"In the drawing room, milord," the valet replied.

Faulkner turned, saw her. The smile vanished, replaced by a look of such fierce desire that her breath was stolen away. Heedless of the servants, who had to be pardoned for stealing a glance in their direction, he strode toward her, put an arm around her waist, and drew her firmly back into the room, his intention nothing short of blatant.

Sarah blushed but did not demur. She clung to him, arms twined round his neck, body pressed to his, and gave herself up to the hunger neither of them could deny.

When at last he raised his head, his eyes were molten silver. Huskily, he said, "I missed you."

She smiled despite the traitor tears that suddenly threatened. "I thought you would be gone longer."

"Our Highland friends had already decided what they wanted—and what they would give. We settled quickly."

"Isn't that unusual?" She knew little of such things, but it seemed to her that men were generally inclined to make a greater fuss.

"Very," he said, grinning.

"How ever did you convince them?"

"I explained that I had a hot, sweet woman waiting in my bed."

Her cheeks burned. "You didn't!"

He regarded her guilelessly. "I most certainly did. Being Scots, they understood at once. And," he added, nuzzling her throat, "after that I went to see Sir Isaac."

"You didn't tell *him*—"

"Of course not. I merely reassured him again that you were well and suggested that, after being absent from the city for several weeks, his duties as president of the Royal Society must have mounted up, making it difficult for him to show you as much of London as he would have liked. I suggested myself as a substitute."

"Was he overwhelmed by your gracious offer?"

"Actually, he seemed to find it amusing. I fear it is impossible to get anything past Sir Isaac, for all that he claims to be unworldly. At any rate, he was very understanding."

Her eyes lit. In the overall scheme of eternity it was such a small thing, this tiny morsel of time they could have together. But it was more than she had ever thought would be hers.

She was swept by sudden, tremulous joy, so much so that she did not realize she was crying until he bent his dark head and began, one by one, to kiss her tears away.

36

Diamond droplets of water fell from Sarah's fingertips. She leaned her head back and gazed up at the sky through the web of straw that was the brim of her hat. Not just any hat, mind. A confection, a fantasy, a delight of silken flowers and ribbons purchased on a whim that morning as she and Faulkner strolled along St. James's Street, and then worn—sweet foolishness of it all—to go punting on the Thames.

She'd heard of punting, of course, but had never expected to experience it. It was a pastime for languid young ladies of the upper class seeking amusement with their earnest swains, quite beyond anything she had ever known in her life of daily routine and eternal mystery.

Until now, on this sun-speckled London day with the city far behind them and only the river to wind through placid countryside. She turned her head and gazed out across the neat fields with a sense of wonderment. They were perfectly ordinary fields in a perfectly ordinary land. Not the slightest flicker of the unusual hovered over them.

So it was true, then, what she had always suspected. Avebury was a special place, set apart from almost everywhere else. It had set her apart, as well, without the chance for a normal life.

Later, she could mourn that. But the day was too bright and the moment too precious. She let the water run through her fingers again and laughed.

At the back of the boat, standing up with the pole in his hands, Faulkner gave a very loud sigh. "Just like a woman, lie there at your ease while the poor man does all the work."

With boldness she would never have believed herself capable of a few short weeks before, Sarah ran her eyes over him. He had taken his doublet off and laid it aside, leaving him in a white shirt unlaced at the neck and tucked into black breeches. Beneath the finely woven linen, the muscles of his shoulders and chest flexed with each push of the pole. It was a thoroughly distracting sight.

She smiled languidly. "I wouldn't call you poor. Indeed, you're what Missus Damas always terms a fine specimen."

"I'm touched beyond words. Still, I don't think I should have all the fun. Come back here and help me."

Sarah looked doubtful. She knew nothing whatsoever about punting, but the boat was slim and shallow. She wasn't sure that—

If only he hadn't looked so enticing, standing there, with the light of challenge in his eyes and a grin to tempt the angels lifting the corners of a mouth chiseled to perfection.

"Oh, all right." She stood, carefully, and made her

way slowly toward the stern. She was almost there when the boat wobbled suddenly. Arms flailing, she struggled to keep her balance, only to teeter precariously.

Faulkner laughed and took hold of her, drawing her the few remaining feet. She fell against him, gasping. The heat and power of his body made her forget everything else, at least for the moment. Distantly, she noticed that the prow of the boat was rising in the water but thought no more of it.

"Here," he said and put the pole in her hands.

"What do I do?"

"Lift, then push down hard."

It sounded simple enough. He'd been doing it for half an hour or so, and it hadn't seemed to require any great concentration or effort.

She lifted. The pole was heavier than she'd thought but not unmanageable. A push and the boat picked up speed again, skimming the water.

Surprised by her own success, she tried again. Their speed increased slightly.

"I knew you could do it," Faulkner said. He let go of her and made to move away.

"Don't go," she cautioned. "I'm not sure I can—"

Distracted, she pushed down again but forgot to lift the pole. The river bottom was soft with mud. The pole settled, she clung, the boat moved on, and quite suddenly Sarah found herself trying to be in two places at the same time.

Faulkner realized, almost too late, what was happening and grabbed hold of her. "Let go," he ordered.

Instinctively, she obeyed. The boat moved on, with them in it, leaving the pole stuck in the mud.

"We have to go back," Sarah said.

"How?"

"What do—"

"Sweet Sarah, we're traveling downstream. Without the pole, there's no way to get back to get the pole. Follow?"

She did, all too well. They were continuing along the river, carried by the current, but with no ability to control their speed or direction. But perhaps that wasn't so bad. They'd just go along until eventually they nudged up gently against the bank, where they would get out and make their way on foot back to the boathouse. Everything would be fine. . . .

"We'll have to jump," Faulkner said.

"What?"

"See that bend up ahead? Just beyond it are rocks and rough water. When the boat arrives there, it will capsize and us with it. Better to jump now."

"I can't—"

He looked alarmed. "Can't swim?"

"No, can't jump." She fingered her gown. Dry, it wasn't especially heavy, but she had no illusions. There were layers of petticoats underneath, Weighed down with water, they would feel like lead.

Faulkner spared another glance downriver. The bend was fast approaching. "Like hell," he said, wrapped a steely arm around her waist, and leaped.

They came up several yards away from the boat, in time to see it topple over. Faulkner kept a firm hold on Sarah as together they swam for shore. It wasn't far, the river not being very wide at that point, but by the time they reached it, both were soaked through. Clambering up the bank with Faulkner's help, Sarah surveyed her waterlogged clothes. She thought she must look like the second cousin of a cat she'd had once who, having slipped on a rock while hunting frogs, had to be fetched out of the pond a sodden mass of fur.

"Strange customs, you Londoners have," she muttered as she began wringing the water from her skirts. "In the country, when we get into a boat the usual idea is to stay in it."

"When you go punting, the usual idea is to lift the bloody pole," Faulkner retorted.

"I wouldn't know since I'd never been punting before, *and* I wouldn't have found out if a certain person hadn't absolutely insisted on it. Not that I wasn't fine where I was, doing what a lady is supposed to do, which is to say being picturesquely useless. Oh, no, just when I was actually making some progress learning how to do that, you decide I should do the poling. Well, let me tell you—"

"I'd never been punting before either." He was standing there, hands on his hips, soaking wet, and grinning at her. But there was a look about him, a wary hopefulness that this sudden admission of truth wouldn't be regretted.

Sarah caught her breath. "I thought you were at sea for a while."

"For God's sake, we didn't punt there. And besides, I hated it. Didn't I tell you I'd steered clear of boats ever since?"

"You did mention that."

"Well, then, how could you possibly have imagined that I knew what I was doing?"

She started to answer, stopped, and started again. "Foolish me." She took a breath, stared at him, and laughed. It started as a small giggle but didn't stay that way. Half a moment later, she was in full-fledged guffaw.

"Never went punting before . . . hated the navy . . . so, of course, we have to go and I have to take the pole . . . oh, God, my ribs hurt!"

"They deserve to," Faulkner said stiffly, but a smile was working its way around his mouth. He fought it, unsuccessfully. Quickly enough, he too was laughing. "I guess it was rather silly."

"No," Sarah murmured, catching her breath. She met his eyes. "Rather wonderful, actually." That he should be so powerful a man, so indomitable in the opinion of the world, but unafraid with her to risk revealing a secret wish. Punting on the Thames on a golden day, so very ordinary and so beyond anything either of them had ever done.

And so wet.

"Well, then," she said, recovering, "I suppose we have to do something."

Clothes really did dry more quickly when they were hung over a bush. The spot beside the river was quiet and secluded. Passion grew, so quickly that they were both caught unawares and tumbled backward onto soft ground only waiting to receive them.

By the time they got back to the boathouse, evening was falling. Sarah skulked around outside, doing her best to hide her disheveled state, while Faulkner made amends for the lost punt. He emerged to find her peeping round a corner, which made him laugh, and her, and then both so that laughter followed them all the way back in the carriage to the house by the river in Westminster.

Crispin had the most marvelous expression of forbearance. The longer Sarah knew him, the better it became. But then he was also getting a great deal more practice, courtesy of her.

"Will you be having supper in, sir?" he inquired

without quite looking at either of them as they stood, wrinkled and smelling of the Thames, in the center of the marble entry hall.

"No," Faulkner said, "we will be going out."

"We will?" Sarah asked as they went upstairs, hand in hand. "To where?"

"Paradise," he replied and refused to say anything more no matter how diligently she tried to make him.

Much later—far later than they would have been had she not tried so very hard and he been so receptive— they returned downstairs freshly clothed. The carriage awaited. Faulkner handed her in and had a quick word with his coachman before following.

"Now," she said when they were under way, "you really must tell me."

"Vauxhall," he said and watched her eyes widen with delight.

37

Sarah had heard of Vauxhall, of course. What person with the slightest claim to refinement hadn't? But she had never actually imagined herself going there.

The pleasure garden outside of London was a place of fantasy.

Gravel paths wound through carefully tended lawns and flower gardens, all strung with colored lanterns that were so plentiful as to turn night into day. Gloriously dressed men and women strolled the paths—or availed themselves of the concealment of strategically placed trees. Some were of the highest nobility, others masters—and mistresses—of pretense. At Vauxhall, none of that seemed to matter.

Alighting from the carriage on Faulkner's arm, she looked around with frank delight. A band played jaunty tunes from a gazebo. Peddlers circulated, offering all manner of confections and fripperies. Jugglers juggled, magicians awed; there were singers and clowns, mimes

and puppeteers. Everywhere she glanced, something
new sprang up to amuse and surprise.

"Like it?" Faulkner asked.

"Oh, it's all right," she said airily, then laughed at his
chagrin. "It's the most wonderful place I've ever seen."

"There are other places," he said as they strolled
along a path. "For instance, there's a certain quality to
the light in Paris that makes it unforgettable. Venice,
on the other hand, can be murky, but it has a sense of
excitement that sweeps everything else along. Then
there's Rome, where it seems impossible to get anything done yet people manage extraordinarily well."

"You've traveled quite a lot," she said. Try though
she did, she couldn't quite keep a note of longing
from her voice. The world was so wide and her own
part of it so small.

"You could too," he replied quietly. "We could
together."

Her throat tightened. She was suddenly incapable
of saying anything at all. It was all a dream—beautiful,
precious. Fleeting. She loved him so desperately. And
she was so determined to keep him safe. How to
explain any of it?

The music saved her. It climbed above them, urging
them on, promising that, for the moment at least, the
rest of the world need not exist. Grabbing his hand,
she pulled him into the swirling light and sound.

At midnight in the country, people were sensibly asleep
in their beds. Owls stirred, and field mice, but most
everything else was lost in dreams of one sort or
another. Except on cloudless moonswept nights, the
darkness was so impenetrable that a hand held in front

of the face could escape unseen. There, very little had changed through all the march of centuries.

Not so at Vauxhall. Here, surely, was a glimpse of the future made stunningly real. Sarah's breath caught as a rocket soared into the air, exploding in a shower of scarlet diamonds flung out across the sky and reflected in the pool below. People cheered, laughing and talking among themselves as the music played on and the fireworks exploded, turning night to shimmering day.

Faulkner leaned back against a tree, his arms around Sarah's waist as together they watched the display. She could feel the reassuring ebb and flow of his breath and the steady beat of his heart. For just an instant, she closed her eyes and let the full force of her yearning for this man sweep over her. If she could, she would gladly pay any price to stay exactly as she was, safe in his arms forever.

But she could not, and nothing she did or said would change that.

The fireworks ended at last and they moved on, strolling along the shadowed paths. The crowds thinned as people began heading toward home.

"Are you hungry?" Faulkner asked.

To her surprise, she was.

"I know just the place," he said, with the secret pleasure of a boy about to share a rare treat, and led her back to where the carriage waited.

London possessed several elegant eating establishments that were open at all hours to serve a discerning clientele. But it was not to such genteel surroundings that Faulkner turned. Instead, they made their way to the streets and lanes around Cheapside that housed the food sellers of London. Where Newgate loomed dark and threatening even by day, Cheapside shone with the light of pitch torches and the bustle of butchers and poulterers, fishmongers and bakers, all setting up for the day's business.

A dizzying whirl of noises, smells, and movement sent Sarah's senses spinning. She was glad for the firm support of Faulkner's arm as he led her down a crooked flight of steps into a room whose sloping flagstone floor and soot-darkened beams testified to its great age.

A dozen tables were ranged in front of a fireplace. Several men and a few women were seated at them, eating. They looked up when Faulkner and Sarah entered but after a brief glance returned to their meals.

A plump, gray-haired woman bustled out from the back, wiping her hands on her apron. When she saw Faulkner, her face split in a grin.

"Where you been keeping yourself, lad? It's been an age."

"Duke's business," he said and let it go at that. "This is Mistress Sarah Huxley, a friend of mine. Sarah, this is Gertie Blakiston. She's the mayor of Cheapside, knows everything and everybody."

The woman laughed, hands on her hips, cheeks like polished apples. Her sharp gaze swept over Sarah. She nodded in satisfaction. "Gaining a bit of sense in your old age, are you? Well then, sit down. I'll warrant you're hungry."

"I wouldn't dare come here if I wasn't," Faulkner confided as they took a table in the corner. "Gertie sets the best table in London."

Sarah looked at him bemusedly, watching the firelight flicker over his strong face. Once again, she was seeing a side of his nature sharply at odds with his public image. Countrywoman that she was, she was certain that the upper classes did not customarily venture into such places. Yet he was as much at home here as he was in the highest reaches of the court. Moreover, as far as he had risen, he had not forgotten his origins. That told her much about the quality of this man she loved.

And made the sorrow growing in her all the harder to bear.

Gertie returned, bearing tankards of strong amber ale and a basket of bread so fresh the steam still rose from it. She followed quickly with large bowls of fish stew, the mere smell of which was enough to make Sarah's mouth water.

At the first taste, she closed her eyes in delight. A variety of tastes exploded on her tongue—sweet fresh cream, succulent oysters, potatoes, and several herbs she was determined to identify.

"Dill," she murmured, almost to herself. "Basil . . . a touch of thyme."

She opened her eyes to find Gertie nodding. She looked at Sarah with respect. "Not bad. There's damn few gentlewomen who could do that. You must cook."

"Every chance I get. But I missed something . . . wait." She took another spoonful. "Parsley—that's what it is, but the broad-leafed one the Italians grow, not the curly kind."

Gertie shook her head in amazement. "Now I'm really impressed. How would you like the recipe?"

"I'd treasure it."

"Fair enough."

To Faulkner's ears, what followed was too quick and complex to catch. But Sarah was nodding eagerly. She repeated several points, then said, "That's ingenious, what you do with the oysters."

"Brings out their flavor better if you steep 'em in milk instead of water. Now then, how about a nice sweet?"

When she'd bustled off to get it, Sarah said, "What a nice woman!"

Faulkner leaned back in his chair, smiling. "Actually, most people think she's a terror. You seem to have charmed her."

Sarah's cheeks warmed. They were staring at each other when their hostess returned, bearing plates laden with warm apple tart. She looked at them both and laughed. "Enough of that, now. You've got to eat to keep up your strength."

They did, for the tart was too good to resist. Gertie kindly provided the recipe for her pastry as well, the secret there being a touch of vinegar and keep the lard very cold. She sent them on their way a short time later with warm wishes and smiles of approval.

Emerging into the street, they found night swiftly fading. The day spanned by sun-sparkling water and star-strewn sky was over. Sarah felt the shift and shuddered. This new day dawning in grayness and a dank breeze off the river would be far different.

The pitch torches were sputtering, the last of their smoke curling away. A boy splashed a bucket of water across the cobblestones. The blood of a slaughtered beast foamed pink into the gutter.

The wind picked up. Riding on it came the scents of the world beyond the city, fertile earth and eternal stone. Deep within Sarah, in a place of silence, Avebury called.

38

"What did you say?" Faulkner asked. He stared at her in disbelief. Around them, people pressed past, hurrying about their business. At the curb, the carriage waited. Crispin, resigned, was already aboard. In another moment, they would be going. She had left it to the very last.

"I'm going to return with Sir Isaac," Sarah said. Her voice was faint. Try though she might, she could not manage this very well. "He says his business in Avebury isn't finished yet, although I'm not sure what else he intends to do. At any rate, he is going back and kindly invited me to accompany him."

"So am I, too, returning," Faulkner said, gesturing to the carriage without his eyes ever leaving her. "I presumed—"

"It is better this way," she interrupted. On a whisper, she added, "Please believe me."

"Believe what?" he demanded. She sensed no anger, for he was a deeply controlled man except for those times when passion shattered all bonds. But he was also genuinely bewildered.

And for that, she ached. "I am sorry."

His hands closed around her shoulders. The sudden touch took her by surprise, but she should have expected it. He was a man bred to action. "For what?" he asked.

She took a deep breath, fighting regret so profound it threatened to swallow her whole. For a sickening instant, she hated herself. Down that road led destruction. There might be nothing else for her in the end, but she wouldn't accept it lightly. She was, would always be, Sarah of Avebury. That was both good and bad.

It was only now that the bad threatened to wipe out all else.

"When we return," she said, refusing to meet his eyes, "we cannot . . . that is, our dealings with one another—"

"Go on," he insisted, refusing to help her.

She raised her head and met his gaze unflinchingly. For what she did, he might well despise her. But she did it for his sake alone, and that gave her courage. "We must not be together again," she said.

"What are you saying?" he demanded, incredulously but with something more, a sharp edge of what felt very much like fear that she might truly slip beyond his grasp.

As, indeed, she must.

"You know why," Sarah said.

He was shaking his head before the words were barely out. "No, I do not. Explain it to me. Have you suddenly been struck by a belated flash of false morality?" His hands tightened on her. "My God, Sarah, I never thought you a hypocrite."

"Nor am I," she shot back. Strength flowed between them, touch to touch, and truth with it. She lowered her eyes slightly. "It is for your sake."

His laugh was harsh. "Mine? Forgive me, mistress, I don't see how."

He was going to insist, drag it all out of her, leave her not even the pretense of a lie or any place safe to hide.

So be it.

"You know what happened between us at Beltane."

He paled. For a moment, she thought he would let her go. But his hands remained firm. "What are you talking about?"

Her gaze flashed, hot and sharp as the fire that night. "Did you tell yourself it was all a dream, Faulkner? Or some sort of misunderstanding? Which of the many excuses people use to dismiss the unknown did you resort to?"

"Nothing happened. I had a dream."

"We dreamt together, then, and I was very nearly lost in it. If you hadn't come after me, I doubt I would have been able to get back. As it was, you could have been lost as well."

The muscles of his throat worked. He stared at her in disbelief. "It wasn't real. It couldn't have been."

She shrugged, knowing this argument too well. It had absorbed her all her life. "What is real? What you can see, touch, hear? When you came after me, did it feel like a dream? Or did it seem as though you were simply living another life, as another person, with no idea of how that could have happened?"

The look on his face told her everything. She smiled in grim satisfaction. "I know that feeling well, Faulkner. It has happened to me over and over, although I admit never with the force that it happened at Beltane. The experience terrified me. I realized how very easy it could be to become lost forever."

She raised her hands and covered his.

"I am Sarah of Avebury. If the stones claim me, it will be because that is my fate. But you are different. You have no part in it." Fiercely, she said, "I will do anything to keep you safe."

"I cannot accept this."

Gently, finger by finger, she loosened his hold on her. "You have no choice," she said and stepped away.

Sir Isaac was the soul of understanding. He seemed to realize that she was little inclined to conversation and contented himself through much of their journey with jotting various notations down on scraps of paper, reading, and gazing out the carriage window.

In the evenings, when they stopped at inns along the way, he urged her gently to eat and spoke to her of simple things—the stars, gravity, the way matter was constructed. Things far less bewildering than the workings of the human heart.

At length, they came to Avebury. All was exactly as she had left it, the neat row of houses along the lane, the church, the Rose. The stones. All of it.

"There now, poor lamb," Missus Damas cooed as Sarah's bags were brought into the house, "it's a good hot soak you need and a decent meal. Nothing else can make the body ache and the soul weary as quickly as a journey. Come along and let me care for you."

Sarah went. It was simply too easy. Later, washed and wrapped in her favorite robe, she sat at the small table in her room and sipped tea as Missus Damas unpacked her bags and gave her all the news.

"Very quiet it's been, more like old times than of late. Reverend Edwards preached a very good sermon on Sunday. Shame you missed it. Oh, wait now, there was one bit of excitement." Her eyes glowed. "Morley's had the haunting again."

"The same as before?" Sarah asked, her interest caught, if only slightly. She petted Rupert's shaggy head. He had followed at her heels since her return and refused to leave. She didn't have the heart to try to make him go.

"Seems to be. A great clanking of chains and a moaning was heard. Woke him from a sound sleep, he claimed." She shook her head gravely. "Looks terrible, he does. If it doesn't stop soon, I don't know what will become of him."

"What does Constable Duggin say?"

"Nothing at all. He's been far too busy trudging up and down the lanes of a night, hardly a wink of sleep." She leaned forward confidingly. "Been terrified something might happen and then Sir William be on him like the avenging angel, saying he wasn't taking proper care."

"I can't imagine Faulkner ever saying anything like that."

The words—in all their familiarity—were out before she could stop them. Missus Damas cast her a gentle look. "Ah, well, there's the way of it. Now eat your soup like a good girl. London looks to have worn you to the bone."

Perhaps it had. She slept deeply and without dreams. By the time she woke, she seemed to have slipped back completely into the rhythms of Avebury, as though she had never left.

Woke to morning and the knowledge, without

anyone having to tell her, that Faulkner was somewhere very close.

And that she would have to face him here in the
place that would most sorely test her resolve.

Slowly she rose and slowly she dressed. When she
came downstairs, the sun was shining, fresh scones
were on the table, and in a chair beside the window
Annalise was weeping.

39

"I couldn't turn her away, mistress," Missus Damas said. Her brow was creased. She stared at the young woman. "Said it couldn't wait, she did."

"That's all right," Sarah murmured. She nodded to the housekeeper. "You did as you should."

Missus Damas hesitated, but it was clear that Sarah would not hear what the girl had to say until they were alone. With a last look at the publican's beautiful daughter, she disappeared out the door.

"Well, now," Sarah began. She patted Annalise's shoulder awkwardly. Used as she was to being consulted about all manner of problems concerning the village, she wasn't accustomed to weeping young women turning up in her morning room. It left her feeling at a loss. "Suppose you tell me what's wrong," she suggested.

That didn't sound very persuasive to her, but Annalise needed no encouraging. She blew her nose on a lace-edged scrap of cloth and said, "I can't stand it any longer, mistress. I must get away from here."

Sarah took a deep breath. This accorded very well with what Madame Charlotte had told them, if indeed Annalise was the young woman for whom Davey Hemper had tried to find work.

"I see," she said slowly, as she slipped into the chair facing her guest. The girl had been weeping for some time. Her normally limpid eyes were red and swollen. So, too, her lips appeared bitten as though in agitation. She twisted the lacy cloth in her hands hard enough to rip it.

"Why must you get away?" Sarah asked softly.

"It's the work, mistress," Annalise replied, very quickly. "Ever since Mother died, I've been taking care of all the little ones as well as working night and day in the pub. I just can't do it anymore. Davey said I might—"

"Davey? Was he trying to help you?"

The young woman gulped, as though she hadn't meant to reveal that. But having gone this far, there was no going back. "He was sure I could do better," she said with a touch of pride. "He said I knew clothes as well as any lady he'd ever seen and I could get a job sewing any time I wished."

Sarah didn't dispute this, even though she suspected that Davey Hemper had seen very few ladies in his time. Annalise did dress surprisingly well. She had a flair for putting together a few items in a way that was memorable. And it was well known that she loved to sew.

"He spoke to Madame Charlotte about you."

Annalise's eyes widened. "Did he really? He said he would, but I didn't know. It all happened so quickly." Tears slipped down her cheeks. She wiped them away with the back of her hand, but they continued to flow. "I can't stay here," she said again.

Sarah was silent for a moment. She wanted to help the girl; indeed, she was determined to do so. But far in the back of her mind she had the sense that something was not quite right.

It was true enough that Annalise worked hard, but so did virtually everyone else in the village. And in her case, the work was surely more congenial than for most. If her appearance was any guide, her father saw to it that she had ample rest, healthy food, and even luxuries.

"Have you spoken with your father about this?" she asked.

Annalise's head shot up. She looked suddenly terrified. "Oh, no, I couldn't. That's why I had to come and see you. I thought if I could just go away and then you tell him; he'd have to understand, if you were the one. After all, you're the mistress. If you say it's all right, he'd have no choice but to accept it."

The words came out in such a rush that Sarah had trouble following them. But she got the gist.

"You want to leave Avebury and then have me tell your father?"

"It sounds dreadful, I know." More hand wringing. "But I just don't see any other way."

"You could tell him yourself," Sarah suggested gently. "I would go along with you, if you liked."

Annalise shook her head so hard it looked in danger of falling off. "I couldn't possibly. He'll think me a traitor, I know he will. It's such a bad time right now with the haunting and all—"

"Is that why you really want to leave? Because of the ghosts?"

Annalise hesitated. Her eyes, as she looked up at Sarah, were not without a certain desperate shrewdness. "It *is* passing awful, mistress."

"But there has to be an explanation for it. Sir William thought he saw someone one night when it was going on. We could set a watch, catch whoever is doing it."

"If you say so." Annalise was doubtful. "I don't rightly see how anyone can catch a ghost, but you'd know best. Still, it's how I said, the work and all." She broke off and took a deep, shuddering breath. More quietly, she said, "I'm twenty years old, mistress, and do you know how many suitors my father's allowed to come calling? None. Not that there haven't been those who have tried, but he won't have any of it. I'm to stay where I am, looking after the family and the pub, until I'm old and worn."

Was that it then? Sarah wondered. The perfectly natural desire of a young woman to marry and have a family of her own? Now that she thought of it, it was strange that Annalise had no suitors. She was a beautiful girl, and her father was prosperous enough to dower her well.

"If you leave," she said gently, "without your father's permission, he may withhold your dowry."

To her surprise, Annalise seemed to have thought of that and not be discouraged by it. "I'm not afraid to work and earn my own way. There's nothing says a woman has to be married." She shot a quick look at Sarah. "You do very well on your own, don't you? Better than many a married woman. No one tells you where to go or what to do. You can decide for yourself. That's how I want to be."

Not marriage then, or children. Something else made Annalise so determined to leave.

"That's it then?" Sarah asked. "You want your independence and you're willing to work hard for it?"

The younger woman nodded. "I want a place of my own, even if it's a tiny little room in an attic somewhere.

I want to be able to go into it at night and shut the door and not have to worry about anything."

"What do you worry about now?" Sarah asked gently.

Annalise looked surprised by the question. This was something she hadn't rehearsed.

"The little ones," she said tentatively, "if they have everything they need. We have to talk about that. They're too much for Father. If I'm gone, they couldn't stay."

Sarah's breath caught. What was this the girl was saying? Not merely that she wanted to leave but that she expected her brothers and sisters to do the same?

"You mean someone else will have to take care of them?"

"That's right." Annalise raised her eyes defiantly as though she knew full well the magnitude of what she was saying and refused to apologize for it. "Father couldn't manage," she repeated. "There'd be no point expecting him to. Missus Goody would take the girls. Father can pay her well enough to care for them, so long as it's clear to him that he has to. And Constable Duggin would apprentice the boys. But again, Father has to pay."

"And I'm to tell him this as well?"

Small white teeth worried Annalise's lower lip. It looked ready to bleed. "You're the mistress," she said again and stared down into the lacy cloth sodden with her tears.

"I don't know what to make of it," Sarah said a short while later. She was sitting in the garden, watching a flock of sparrows peck at bread crumbs she had put out. Sir Isaac sat beside her.

"I have never had children of my own," he said, "but if I did, I have to admit I would find it odd for a daughter to want to go off into the world without the protection of either a husband or a private income. It seems very peculiar."

"She is absolutely determined, even to the extent of having already planned what should be done with the younger children."

"Surely Morley would bring in a woman to look after them. He's prosperous enough. I can't imagine him farming them all out."

"Have you seen him since we returned?" Sarah asked.

Sir Isaac frowned. "He's looking very poorly. I gather the haunting has continued. Peculiar business. Do you think it has anything to do with her wanting to leave?"

"She says not. If she's to be believed, she's simply tired of all the work and wants a life of her own. It's not an unheard-of desire."

"Not at all," Sir Isaac agreed. "In fact, I'm most sympathetic to it, as I suspect you are too. She picked her champion well."

"I haven't agreed to be that," Sarah said quickly. "If she wants to go off, I believe she should have the right. But to do it without a word to her father—I can't accept that."

"You told her?"

Sarah nodded. "She tried to convince me otherwise, and I suspect she will try again. But for the moment, I think she will stay where she is."

"Are you sure?"

"No, but I promised that if she would do so, I would try to find a better alternative for her and for the other children. All she asked was that I do so quickly. She says she is eager to go."

"Eager to go," Sir Isaac repeated slowly. He bent down and scratched Rupert behind the ear. The big dog thumped his tail. "She doesn't sound afraid at all."

"No," Sarah agreed, "she doesn't."

"Yet surely she must know that it takes money to survive. She will have to find lodging, food, and so on at least until she secures employment. If she is so certain she can do that, she must have some means set aside."

They looked at one another. "Money," Sarah said thoughtfully.

"A girl in her position wouldn't have much opportunity to set funds aside, would she?"

"I don't really see how. Morley is always watching her."

"Then how could she—"

Sarah listened but from a distance. Staring off into space, she remembered what Madame Charlotte had said about Davey having a sackful of coins. It had never been found.

"I wonder if Faulkner realizes," she murmured.

"What?" Sir Isaac asked.

"That Davey's money is missing. Annalise discovered the body. It's possible that she took it."

The elderly man nodded. "It is indeed."

"Finding that money might help determine where he got it from."

"Possibly."

"Please," Sarah said, "would you tell him? He must be back by now. If you could just—"

"He's been at the Rose since the day before yesterday. Apparently, traveling doesn't agree with him. He seems in a dark mood."

Sarah's throat tightened with remembered grief. If

he could only find the killer and be gone. If she did not have to keep seeing him. If—

"You'll tell him?" she asked.

Sir Isaac hesitated. He was a kind man but he could in his own way be quite determined. "I have a rather full day planned, my dear." His smile was gentle. "I'm afraid you're going to have to tell him yourself."

40

"*I have no* idea, mistress," Crispin said. "Sir William did not inform me where he was going."

"You must have some clue," Sarah urged. It was several hours after her talk with Sir Isaac. She had needed that long to get up her courage. Having mustered it at last, she could hardly believe her quest was in vain.

"I regret," Crispin said, inclined his head, and returned to polishing what appeared to be his own boots.

Back outside in front of the Rose, Sarah looked up and down the lane. There was no sign of Faulkner. And yet there was activity: specifically, Bertrand Johnson out for a stroll. Upon catching sight of her, Justin's friend quickened his pace so that his path intercepted hers.

"Mistress Huxley," he said, "what a delight to see you again. I heard you were in London. I am devastated that we didn't meet there."

Her brow furrowed. "You were in the city?"

The young man nodded. He had a pleasant countenance, more open and relaxed than Justin's. She wondered how the two of them had become friends. "The viscount and I went down together. He stayed but I"—he hesitated as though unsure of what to say—"I find I've become quite attached to this place, so I returned ahead of him."

"I see. How nice. Well, it was lovely to talk with you again. If you would excuse me—"

"Have you plans for today?"

"Yes, actually I do."

He looked so forlorn and so determined to conceal it that Sarah wished she could relent, but it was imperative that she find Faulkner. "Have you see Sir William, by any chance?"

"He rode out about an hour ago in that direction." He gestured toward Silbury, looming in the distance.

Sarah paled. What possible reason would he have for going to one of the most ancient and potent spots in all the area? A chill ran through her. Surely, he would not think to test the warning she had given him.

"I must go," she said and turned quickly to the stables. Faulkner's lively little mare was still there. Sarah saddled her in record time. Moments later, as she road out through the stable yard, she glimpsed young Johnson entering the Rose.

When they had visited Silbury before, taking the carriage to accommodate Sir Isaac, the trip had been lengthy. But alone on a fleet mount, Sarah covered the distance far faster. She drew rein in the shadow of the hill and looked around urgently for Faulkner.

At first, she could see no sign of him. Just as she was beginning to wonder if Bertrand could have been mistaken, the mare whinnied softly and moved ahead of her own accord. They rounded the curve of the hill and found Rascal grazing contentedly.

"Where's your master, boy?" Sarah murmured to him when she had dismounted and set the mare to graze as well. Patting his mane, she waited as though for some sign.

The horse tossed his head, eyes rolling in the direction of the hill. She looked. A man was there, standing on the crest, silhouetted against the sun. Faulkner.

Her skirts impeded her. She tucked them up so that she could climb more swiftly. When she reached the top, she paused to catch her breath. Her skin was flushed and her heart beat far too rapidly for the climb alone. Damn man.

"Nice day," Faulkner drawled.

He was lying down, arms crossed behind his head, looking for all the world as though he was perfectly at ease. Tired, hot, and not at ease about anything at all, Sarah glared at him.

"What are you doing here?" she demanded.

He looked surprised. "I? You're the one who likes to hide behind her garden walls. To what do we owe this great honor, Mistress Huxley?"

"Oh, for heaven's sake."

"Heaven's? I thought this was the earth's place."

"What do you mean?"

He sat up and looked at her. His eyes were shuttered and his gaze unreadable, but she could feel the tension coiling in him. Despite all that had passed between them—and because of it—she took a small step back.

"Coward," he said, and smiled almost pleasantly.

"I am not."

"All that talk about Beltane and the stones. Didn't

you think I'd be curious? I did a little research before I left London. Who's place is this supposed to be, Sarah? The undefiled maiden? The fertile mother? Or is it the crone's, the hag of death? Was it for her that Silbury was built?"

"Who told you all this?" Sarah asked. Hearing him speak of such things, so long hidden, affected her greatly. She felt as though the ground were slipping beneath her feet.

"I made inquiries at the Royal Society, explaining that I had met Sir Isaac here and been impressed by his work. They couldn't do enough to help me."

"How nice."

"There are records, you know. Caesar actually wrote some of them when he visited here almost eighteen centuries ago. But there are many others, ancient legends, even country songs. The music, it seems, is a particularly good source of clues about what people in these parts used to believe."

He rose suddenly without warning, coming lithely to his feet, and strode toward her. There was nowhere for her to go save for a tumble down the side of the hill. She chose to stand her ground instead.

"*Used to,* Sarah. What people *used to* believe. It was all over and done with long ago, so why do you persist in trying to keep it alive? You're part of this time, this Avebury. Can't you be content with that?"

That was the way of it then? He had convinced himself that she was deluded, lost in a dream of the past that no longer existed? How much better for him to believe that.

And how terribly it hurt.

"I came to tell you Annalise may have the money Davey Hemper got from whoever he was blackmailing."

Faulkner stopped and stared at her. He was not prepared for so swift a change of subject. "What?"

"She is quite desperate to leave here, and she seems to have no immediate concern about how she will survive. I think it's possible she has Davey's money. If we—that is, if you—could find it, it might help to determine what happened to him."

"Sarah." Again, he stepped toward her, concern now in his eyes.

"No," she said quickly, "don't touch me. I only wanted you to know about Annalise. She may not have the money at all and she is very unhappy, so I hope you will go gently with her. But I thought you had to know."

"Yes, of course. Wait, where are you going?"

"Back to the village. I must find a way to help her, and there is much else to do."

"We need to talk."

"We *have* talked. I am most impressed by your knowledge. Please do not be unkind to Annalise."

"You've asked me that already. I'm not some ogre to—" He was coming after her even as she began walking down the hill. The slope was too steep to take quickly and keep her balance. But she had to get away.

"I borrowed your mare. I'll return her to the stable. By the way—"

"What?" he stopped. She kept going. Yet even now, knowing the conclusion he had reached, she could not deny the past that was still and always would be present.

"Silbury is sacred to the fertility of summer and fall. It is the long barrows that are the winter crone's."

"And the maiden?" he called after her. Strange

question for a man who thought he knew it all.

She smiled, faint and wistful, born of memory she would always treasure. "Seek her in the springtime circle. And now you know far more than you should. Find your killer, Faulkner. Neither one of us can stand this much longer."

Whatever he said was lost to her. She sprang up on the mare's back like the colt of a girl she had been, before womanhood overtook her and with it all the pain of longing. The horse responded at once. Together, woman and mare raced away across fields of fertile earth turning green and gold beneath the eternal sun.

41

It was Rupert's barking that woke her. Sarah turned over in the bed reluctantly. She had fallen asleep very late and was in desperate need of rest. But the barking continued. She could not ignore it.

Rising, she went to the window and looked out. The moon had set and the lane was very dark. She could see little. Opening a pane, she called out, "Rupert, stop it, there's a boy. Quiet now."

Instead of obeying, he barked all the louder. Sarah groaned. There was nothing to be done for it. She couldn't have him disturbing the whole neighborhood.

Taking a wrap from the clothespress, she slid it on and left her room. The stairs creaked as she went down them. Other than that—and Rupert—the house was quiet. She opened the door and peered outside. Even after her eyes had a chance to become accustomed to the dark, she could see almost nothing. Quickly, she lit a candle and ventured out.

There was just enough breeze to make the flame flicker. Shielding it with her hand, she went down the flagstone path. Rupert sensed her coming and came to join her. With the dog leading the way, she reached the gate—and stopped there, looking around cautiously.

Had he treed one of the village cats? That had happened before but not recently. The cats had all grown too canny and Rupert, no longer a pup, seemed to have lost his taste for the sport.

A badger then? Or, worse, a skunk? But there was nothing in any of the nearby trees, at least so far as she could tell, and Rupert's interest seemed to lie elsewhere. He danced about at her heels, a big gray shadow against the blackness, and whined sharply.

She whispered to him to be quiet and lifted the candle. In the back of her mind, she knew she was being foolish. She should go back inside, summon help.

But Rupert didn't seem to be warning her off. Indeed, he appeared to be trying to get her attention.

That was odd. Since when had the stone wall that ran in front of her house had that bulge in it? Were the stones coming loose? Had something knocked into them?

She went closer, straining to see through the nearly absolute darkness. The candle cast a very small circle of light. She was almost at the wall before she saw—

Blood on the stones, dark and shining in the light. And the man, face down, sprawled over the wall like a broken doll carelessly discarded.

Like Davey Hemper. Like the Gypsies.

It was all happening again.

This time, she did not scream. There was no point. Instead, she stepped up closer to the man and angled the candle so that she could see his face. Her breath caught.

Bertrand Johnson's face was contorted in terror, but his eyes were empty. They had turned inward upon eternity.

Pity and grief welled up in her. She reached out a hand and touched his shoulder gently. Through his doublet, she could feel the lingering warmth of his body.

Fresh kill, dumped almost at her very door. Anger surged, washing out for the moment even her profound regret for the life so viciously extinguished. She turned and walked swiftly back toward the house.

She had said they could not be as they were in London. She had told him bluntly that she was a danger to him. She had spelled it all out as clearly as she could, and she had meant every word of it.

But Bertrand Johnson's body was lying slung over her garden wall, and there was only one man she could turn to for help.

She delayed just long enough to put on a pair of shoes and light a lantern instead of the candle. Still in her wrap and with Rupert beside her, she hurried down the lane.

The Rose was dark and still. As expected, she found the door barred. Morley was a cautious man by nature but never more so than when a murderer was loose. Fortunately, he was also firm in his country ways. The back door was unlocked.

She slipped inside and made her way through the common room to the stairs. At the bottom of the steps, she told Rupert to wait. For a change, he obeyed. It occurred to her that she had no idea which room Faulkner occupied. To go through an inn at night, room by room, seeking a particular man was to invite a certain amount of talk, but she would have to risk it.

Ear to the first door, she listened. No, not him. In the time they had been together, sharing her bed here and his bed in London, she had never heard him snore. Particularly not like a beached whale.

The next room was empty, which all things considered was just as well, since no one in it would have been able to sleep. She paused before the third. It was on a rear corner overlooking the garden in the back and at least from the hall, looked to be somewhat larger than the others. The best room in the house would naturally be reserved for the noblest guest.

Hardly breathing, she cracked the door open and peered inside. There was a figure in the bed. She stepped closer and lifted the lantern.

Light fell on a finely formed face, handsome features, a noble bearing—

Crispin opened his eyes, beheld a woman in white apparently drifting above him, and let out a blood-curdling scream.

Sarah took a quick step back. "I'm so terribly sorry. I was just—"

"Just what?" an iron-edged voice demanded from the direction of the door. Faulkner stood, naked as God had made him, save for the very lethal-looking sword he gripped in his right hand. He stared at Sarah in astonishment. "What in the name of hell are you doing in my valet's bedroom?"

"I was about to ask her that myself, milord," Crispin said stiffly. He sat up in the bed, clutching the covers to his chest, and did his utmost to look at neither of them.

Not so Morley, who came roaring down from the third floor, a vast figure in a flapping nightshirt, with a club waving above his head and the light of desperation in his eyes. "Damn ghosts, it's them again, isn't it?

I swear this time I'll—" He broke off as he caught sight of the tableau before him: mortified Crispin, thoroughly embarrassed Sarah, and naked, fully armed and completely unapologetic Faulkner.

"Milord," Morley sputtered, "for the love of God, garb yourself. Mistress Huxley is—"

"Very sorry to have disturbed you, Mister Morley. Actually, I was looking for Sir William." She turned to Faulkner. But then, how could she not? He was far and away the most compelling sight, especially after the horror left at her garden wall. Bertrand's death was in danger of becoming a farce. She could not let that happen. "If I might have a word with you?"

"By all means," he replied, the soul of nonchalance, and lowered his sword.

"After you've dressed, of course," she added, far too belatedly to preserve even the pretense of her modesty. "I'll wait below." With an apologetic nod to Crispin, she fled.

Rupert thumped his tail. Seeing it, Sarah sighed and straightened from the table she'd been leaning against. Faulkner came down the stairs. He had dressed quickly in breeches and a shirt. The sword was buckled around his lean waist.

"Changed your mind?" he asked, pain lingering behind disdain.

She did not flinch. "Bertrand Johnson is dead. His body is hanging over my garden wall."

He stared at her for a long moment. A pulse leaped in his jaw. Abruptly, he turned away. "Let's go."

*   *   *

"Much the same," Quack said. He rose from beside the body slowly, rubbing the small of his back. Night was fading. By the soft gray light before dawn, it was possible to see details that had eluded Sarah earlier: for instance, the scuff marks along the lane that indicated the body had been dragged some distance before being left in front of her house.

"He was carried at least partway," Faulkner said. He had seen the drag first and followed it as far as he could. "It was only the last few yards that he was pulled."

"The killer grew weary under his weight?" Sarah ventured.

Faulkner nodded. "So it seems." He stared down at the young man. Death had frozen the expression on his face. He had not died easily.

"I suspect that though he was struck a blow to the back of the head," Quack said, "in the same manner as Davey and the Gypsies, it did not render him fully unconscious. He appears to have seen his killer before his throat was cut."

"Too late to be able to save himself," Sarah murmured. She had gone inside the house just long enough to throw on a dress and warn Missus Damas not to come outside. It was bad enough that she herself would never be able to forget what she saw. Sarah didn't want anyone else to confront it unnecessarily.

"Bloody hell," Constable Duggin interjected. He had arrived late, awakened by Morley ranting and raving about ghosts, the utter lack of morals among the gentry, and the fact that he was going to sell out and buy a place in Bath. Now, gazing down at the body, he shook his head in disgust. "We can't keep this up. It'll get so no one will want even to come through here."

"By all means, let's not let the killing go on if it will interfere with trade," Quack muttered.

"I didn't mean it that way," Duggin sputtered. He passed a hand wearily over his face. "Fact is, I don't know what I mean. I've never seen anything like this in all my days." He turned to Faulkner. "It's different for you, milord. You've been in battle, and Quack here's tended the dead. As for mistress . . ." He paused, eyeing Sarah cautiously. "No offense, milady, but you seem to be taking this very calmly."

"I did my screaming with the first one," Sarah said. She was sorry to shock him, as she clearly did, but she was too angry to care about courtesies. "Somebody killed this man and brought him to my front door. I want that person found—now. There will be no further delays."

Faulkner stood a little aside, watching her with a thoughtful expression on his face. She ignored it and went on.

"Every house in the village is to be searched—thoroughly. Look for bloodstained clothes, a knife with blood on it, anything that looks at all suspicious. There is no coach due today, which is just as well. No one is to enter or leave Avebury until the killer is caught. Is that clear?"

Duggin nodded, head bobbing up and down in his anxiousness to keep up with her. Quack look worried but offered no objection. Together, the two men went off, carrying Bertrand's body.

They did not so much as glance as Faulkner, far less ask him for his own instructions.

"Very impressive," he said when he and Sarah were alone again on the lane.

She did not pretend to misunderstand him. "They will do as I say. This will end."

"Provided no one here objects to the privacy of his home being violated without a royal warrant."

"No one will."

He accepted that, for the moment at least. "And provided the killer has been careless."

"It's not a question of carelessness. This killer is mad. He wants to be caught."

"That's a leap, isn't it? He's gotten away with murder three times. What makes you think he wants to change now?"

"Because he brought the body here, to me."

She turned to go. It was simply too painful to stand there in his presence, so close, and be unable to touch him.

Her back to him, she said, "It's a challenge and a plea, both at the same time. I can't ignore either."

"Sarah," he called.

She stopped and slowly faced him.

"There's something else it could be."

"What?" she asked.

His hand flexed on the sword hilt gleaming darkly in the morning light. Quietly, he said, "Whoever is doing this may be after you. He may be trying to goad you into something foolish."

"Then he's made a bad mistake," she said and went back up the path into the house.

A short time later she came out again and, finding the lane empty, walked quickly in the direction away from the village.

42

The marchioness was not receiving. Indeed, according to her startled maid, she wasn't even awake.

"Nonetheless," Sarah said firmly, "I must see her." She brushed past the girl, went through the small entry hall, and mounted the steps to the second floor. Elizabeth's room was at the near end, as far from her dear husband's as she could contrive to be.

Sarah knocked once, sharply, and entered. The room was very dark. Thick draperies pulled across the windows shut out the day. The air was stale.

She went over to the windows, pulled the drapes aside, and forced several panes open. Her efforts were rewarded by startled groans from the bed.

Elizabeth sat up, rubbing her eyes. "Stupid girl, what do you think you're . . . ? Oh, my God, it's you." She yanked the covers up in front of her but not before Sarah glimpsed her in all her glory, face covered by a thick layer of cream, hair hidden beneath a turban, and a strap fastened around her chin.

"Sarah, what a surprise. It's customary to be announced, you know."

"Bertrand is dead." There was no gentle way to put it, and Sarah didn't try. She waited a moment, letting the news sink in, then added more softly, "I'll be in the drawing room. Please don't take long."

To give her credit, Elizabeth was down before the maid could bring a pot of tea. She flung open the door, paused for effect, and put a hand to her heart. "You can't possibly be serious."

Sarah felt a tiny surge of admiration. She had left Elizabeth barely five minutes before but the cream was gone, the turban banished, and the chin strap tucked away. Attired in a flowered silk robe with her golden hair hanging in artful curls around her shoulders, the marchioness looked lovely. And not remotely grief-stricken.

"It's hardly the sort of thing I'd joke about. His body was left draped over my wall."

"Dear God, what a horrible thing. Who did it?"

"I don't know. That's what I came to talk with you about. I saw Bertrand for a few minutes yesterday. He mentioned that Justin was still in London and that he'd returned here on his own. Wasn't that unusual?"

Elizabeth glanced away. She sat, back straight, hands folded gracefully in her lap. "Not really."

"I don't understand."

"Of course you don't. It would be an absolute miracle if you did." When Sarah still looked at her blankly, the marchioness sighed. "Oh, for heaven's sake, Bernie came back because he had a bit of a tendresse for me. Not that I encouraged it, absolutely not. He was far too poor."

Sarah smiled wryly. Not "too young," or "my son's

friend." Simply "too poor." Elizabeth was nothing if not practical.

"I see. He came back to be with you."

"Please don't put it that way. He returned to press his suit—unsuccessfully."

"My apologies. I'm not up on all the nuances."

"Dear girl, if that's the case, whatever were you doing in London?"

Score one for the marchioness. Sarah rallied quickly. She wasn't about to be distracted. "Who else was aware of his feelings?"

Elizabeth shrugged her graceful shoulders. "How would I know?"

"You must have some idea. He didn't strike me as particularly discreet."

"He wasn't, but if you're suggesting that my dear husband . . . " At the very thought, Elizabeth laughed merrily. "It's too absurd. Neither one of us has cared about who the other slept with since Justin was born. Thank God he was a boy. I couldn't possibly have gone through that again."

"Speaking of Justin—"

He had saved her life in London. And all he had ever asked her for was a small chance to begin his own life again. She didn't doubt for a moment that he was a rogue, but she had a very hard time seeing him as a killer. Still, she had to know.

"Are you sure he's in London?"

Elizabeth's eyes widened. She stared at her incredulously. "What are you saying?"

"Nothing, merely that I would like to be sure Justin isn't here."

"Why would I lie about that?"

"You are his mother."

Elizabeth shook her head in frank amazement. "Dear girl, you really ought to try to get out of the country more often. That means nothing to me."

"It has to mean something," Sarah insisted. She could not imagine a mother who didn't have at least some feeling for her child. Were she to ever be blessed with a child of her own, she would love it unconditionally and forever.

But the marchioness was adamant. "Justin's sole significance was that he provided an heir for my dear husband so that I no longer had to endure his attentions. Of course," she added with a touch of bitterness, "now that there's nothing left to inherit, the whole exercise seems particularly pointless."

"Four people have been killed. Either their deaths were random murders with no motive beyond madness, or they had a purpose. Davey Hemper's killing suggests that it may have been to conceal a secret."

"You're suggesting Justin could have something he wanted to hide?" Elizabeth laughed again. She seemed genuinely to enjoy the notion. "Sweet child, he's completely shameless. Whatever he's done, far from trying to hide it, he'd be more likely to proclaim it to the skies. No, I'm afraid you're looking in the wrong direction if you suspect him. Besides, he really isn't here. He's in London, chasing some heiress."

Sarah was inclined to believe her but she had to be sure. She rose slowly. "I'm sorry to have disturbed you. Would you be so kind as to give Constable Duggin an address for Bertrand's family? He has to get in touch with them."

"I'll send the girl round with it."

Sarah waited, thinking she might ask something more about the death, but Elizabeth said nothing. She merely fingered the fine silk of her robe and smiled vacantly.

Out on the lane a short time later, Sarah struggled to contain her anger. She could not bear such callousness, yet neither could she dwell on it. Justin seemed effectively removed as a suspect. That left—

"What took you so long?" Faulkner asked. He was leaning against a tree on the opposite side of the lane. When she saw him, Sarah almost jumped. She only just managed to control herself.

"What are you doing here?"

"Waiting for you."

"I told no one where I was going."

"Yes, I know, that's a bad habit of yours, particularly under the present circumstances. However, it wasn't difficult to guess."

Maybe not for him, but she doubted anyone else could have done it. A wave of longing swept over her. He understood her so well, this proud, indomitable man who was capable of such incandescent passion. In his arms, she felt more complete than she had ever done.

For the first time in her life, she deeply resented what had always seemed her fate. Indeed, she could feel herself pressing against it, as though trying to break out of a confinement that had suddenly become unbearable.

"Justin's not the killer," she said.

"I suspect you're right." There in the bright day, he reached out his hand for hers. "But don't go off after Edwards alone."

She accepted his gentle reprimand as far less than she deserved. Absurdly close to tears—thinking of Davey and Bertrand, of the Gypsies and Annalise—she curled her fingers around his and let his strength console her.

43

"*I am most* terribly sorry," Reverend Edwards said. "Ordinarily, the place is a good deal tidier, but it's been a difficult few days."

"It's fine," Sarah reassured him. She glanced around the drawing room of the parsonage, noting that the fire was not laid, there was dust in evidence, and several pillows lay squashed flat on the settee as though someone had lain there restlessly.

"Is something wrong?" she asked.

Edwards hesitated. He looked exhausted, his face pale and strained, but it was clear he was reluctant to say anything. "Dr. Holbein has been ill."

"I'm sorry to hear that," Faulkner said. "I hope it isn't serious?"

"An ague of the chest. He . . . he is a very sincere man."

An nonsequitur, Sarah thought, doubting that ague and sincerity somehow went together. "You've heard about Mr. Johnson?"

"I have, yes." The curate ran a hand through his rumpled hair. As the light fell on his face, she saw that he was unshaven and his eyes were bloodshot. "What can I say? We live in terrible times."

She had expected more—greater shock and horror, perhaps, or a hint of guilt. Not this weary acceptance and despair in a man who, if anything, had always struck her as overly optimistic.

"You have exhausted yourself," she said gently.

Edwards frowned, as though he was having difficulty following what was said. "I must do what I can to help Dr. Holbein. I have a responsibility—"

"Surely, one of the ladies from the village could come in to help? I'm sure quite a few would be willing."

"No, no, that's all right. I can manage. I think he would prefer that."

"As you wish," Faulkner said. "We won't keep you, but we do have to speak with you about the killings."

"Yes, all right. I could fix some tea—"

"That isn't necessary," Sarah assured him. She was reluctant to press him any further but accepted that it had to be done. Still, she could not bring herself to begin.

Faulkner caught her beseeching glance. He cleared his throat. "Reverend, kindly tell us where you were last night."

The color drained from Edwards's face. He stared at Faulkner as though he were an apparition. "Last night?"

"If you don't mind."

"I was—that is, I don't quite see . . . why would you . . . ?"

"That's when Johnson was killed," Faulkner explained quietly.

Edwards stared at him. "You can't mean . . . you think I—"

"We think nothing at all," Sarah interjected. "It is simply that every possibility has to be eliminated." Deliberately, she added, "I have told Constable Duggin to search all the houses in the village. He will come here before long."

"Surely not," Edwards protested. "This is a parsonage. You can't expect—"

"I do. There have been four killings already. We cannot allow there to be any more."

"I realize that, but the parsonage—"

"Dr. Holbein need not be disturbed," Faulkner promised, "if that is what you fear."

If. The word echoed in the silence that descended. Edwards looked from one to the other. Sarah's hands clenched. She wished desperately for something she could say that would soothe his anguish, but there was nothing.

He sighed heavily and stood. Instinctively, Faulkner also rose. Edwards looked at him bemusedly, then turned to Sarah. "I must tell you," he began. He spread his hands, as though beseeching understanding, and walked toward her.

Faulkner stepped between them. Quietly, he said, "Tell us, old man. Get it over with."

"Dr. Holbein—"

Sarah frowned. What had the old curate to do with it? He had talked about an evil loose in Avebury. Had he somehow known what lay behind the murders? A sudden horrible thought went through her. It wasn't possible. He couldn't be—

"Dr. Holbein is disordered in his mind," Edwards said. He sighed deeply, as though the mere admission lifted a great weight from him.

Faulkner and Sarah exchanged a troubled glance.

"I'm not sure I follow you," Faulkner said.

Edwards straightened his shoulders. With the air of a man confronting a terrible truth, he said, "Our beloved former curate has become a . . . Catholic."

"A what?" Sarah blurted. She couldn't help herself. It was absurd, all that buildup for the news that the old minister had converted? But upon a moment's reflection, she realized that Edwards would see it quite differently. He was such a serious young man, so deeply imbued with his faith.

That had irritated the villagers to be sure, herself included, but it was nothing to mock. To him, the notion of a respected leader who had given his life to the Church of England suddenly embracing papacy would be almost too much to bear.

"A Catholic," Edwards repeated. It came more easily the second time. Urgently, he added, "So you see, you must not allow the parsonage to be searched."

"Reverend," Faulkner began, "I hardly think the discovery of a few Catholic tracts and Bibles here would truly shock the villagers. They have more pressing concerns."

"Good lord, it isn't that. You see, Holbein's the one who—"

The drawing room door opened. Edwards broke off. Abruptly, his face softened. All the weariness seemed to vanish out of him. Sarah turned, following the direction of his gaze. Annalise stood there, a very pale and self-possessed Annalise to be sure, lacking her usual fripperies. She took in the scene in a glance.

Head high, she went to Edwards and touched his arm in reassurance. It was a small gesture but one of telling familiarity.

"Reverend Holbein's been behind the haunting," she

said softly. "He's had some notion that he could drive my father from the Rose and restore it as the Catholic monastery it used to be."

"He used some old chains we had here to make the noises," Edwards said. Freed of the burden of disclosure, he was more forthcoming. "If we're searched, they'll be found. Disturbed as he is, he doesn't deserve such humiliation."

Sarah shook her head dazedly. She would never have expected this. "Are you sure?"

"Sadly, I am," Edwards said. "I had suspected it for some time. Last night, I was up later than usual. I had"—he glanced at Annalise—"I had an engagement. At any rate, Dr. Holbein couldn't have known that. I heard him leave the house. Given his age and the fact that he has not seemed well, I was concerned. It seemed best to follow him."

"To where?" Faulkner demanded.

"The graveyard behind the Rose," Edwards said promptly. "When I realized what he was up to, I intervened and convinced him to return here with me."

"Were you able after that to keep your engagement?" Sarah asked. She gave the last word no special inflection but Edwards flushed all the same.

"No, regrettably I wasn't. I had to stay with him."

"But someone else came into the stable yard last night, didn't he, Annalise?" Faulkner spoke with as much gentleness as Sarah had ever heard him use. Yet the young woman flinched all the same. She turned shadowed eyes on Faulkner. "Another young man of idealistic nature, who, in the darkness, could well have been mistaken for Reverend Edwards."

"I don't know what you mean," she said, her voice faint.

"Yes, you do." Quietly, he said, "You asked Davey Hemper for help, and Mistress Huxley. You asked Reverend Edwards, and my guess is that you also asked Bertrand Johnson. In short, you were desperate enough to ask anyone you thought might possibly be willing to help you. That's so, isn't it?"

The girl had turned a ghastly shade of gray. Tears flooded her eyes. She looked like an animal trapped in the glow of a hunter's moon.

"I never meant . . . I swear, I didn't even realize until after Davey, and then—"

"And then you still didn't feel able to turn your father in to the authorities. Is that it?"

Miserably, she nodded. Her face crumbled. Instinctively, Edwards put an arm around her shoulders. At his touch, she started violently and pulled away.

"Don't," Faulkner warned him. He himself made no attempt to touch Annalise, but only stood looking at her with an expression of such mingled anger and compassion that Sarah knew she would never forget it. A horrible fear was growing in the pit of her stomach. Please God, let it be wrong.

"He killed the Gypsies as well?" Faulkner asked.

Annalise nodded.

"Why?"

Haltingly, head bent, she told them.

44

The women gathered outside the inn as the day waned. They stood silently, hugging their shawls around themselves, and waited.

Faulkner had gone inside. He found Morley at his tankards.

"What will you have?" the publican asked. His voice was rough with fatigue, but his eyes darted nervously.

"Truth," Faulkner said. "I think I've got it all now, but I want to know for sure."

"I don't know what you're talking about. If you want a drink, fine; otherwise I've work to do. Annalise is off somewhere. Can't depend—"

"She's at the parsonage, and that's where she'll stay until this is over."

"What the hell—?"

"The Gypsies caught you, didn't they?" Faulkner asked, almost pleasantly. "They tend to wander at night; it's their wont. They saw something they shouldn't have. That's why you killed them."

He leaned closer across the bar. Morley stared at him, caught in horrified fascination and unable to turn away. "Then Davey tried a bit of blackmail, and he had to go too. The only one I had trouble figuring was the last. But Bertrand had a tender heart. He sensed Annalise was desperate and wanted to help her."

Faulkner straightened. He wanted this done. "So you decided to finish him as well. Or did you think he was Edwards? When did you actually know who you'd attacked? When he turned and saw you?"

The publican's face contorted. He slammed the tankard down on the bar, denting it, and lunged at Faulkner. "By God, I'll—"

"You'll what?" Faulkner asked calmly. It was the work of a moment to get an arm around Morley's throat and render him helpless. As the other man gasped, his back bent over the bar and his feet dangling, Faulkner said, "I'm not like the others. Killing's my trade. You should have thought of that."

The only response was a gurgle. Deliberately, Faulkner tightened his hold, cutting off the other man's air.

"How does this feel? Like it? No, I didn't think so. This is what hanging will be like, presuming that's what they decide to do to you. It might not be, you know. For what you've done—for the whole of it—the sentence could be drawing and quartering. From what I hear, that's even worse."

Morley was turning purple. His eyes were beginning to bulge from his head. Faulkner released his grip and shoved him away. He landed hard against the opposite wall, gasping for air.

"There's another choice," Faulkner said. "To protect

Annalise, to give her some chance at a normal life, you can go quietly. Count your blessings for that, Morley." He turned to leave, unable to look at the creature before him any longer. At the door, he said, "Don't make the wrong choice."

The women watched silently as he walked away. When he passed onto the lane, they began to move in, slowly but inexorably, toward the door of the pub.

Faulkner went back to Sarah's house. Sir Isaac and Crispin were already there. Together, they settled in the morning room to wait. Sir Isaac had only one question. "When did you first suspect him?"

"When Sarah came to the inn," Faulkner said. The anger and disgust had gone out of him. He was left only with deep sorrow. "Morley rushed downstairs when he heard the noise. He was wearing his night-shirt, as was natural since he'd supposedly been in bed, but he also had his boots on. When it turned out that Justin Hoddinworth was in London and Edwards was effectively eliminated as a suspect, I remembered that."

Sir Isaac nodded. He fell silent again. After a time, he looked at Faulkner. "Is it possible, do you think, that some things are truly fated to be? Part of some grand design, as it were?"

Faulkner raised an eyebrow, evocative of doubt but a certain willingness to be persuaded. How much could change in so short a time. A fortnight before he would have denounced the notion as superstition. Now he was not so sure.

"It would mean," Sir Isaac went on slowly, "that what we commonly think of as reality—past, present, and future all occurring neatly in sequence—isn't necessarily like that at all. Time might be able to bend, as it were, to twist back upon itself. But then that would mean—"

His voice faded, slipping away into his vast, searching musings where stars whirled and the great engine of time chugged endlessly. He settled more comfortably into the chair, supremely content upon the sea of his own mind. Slowly, wonderingly, he smiled.

Faulkner was left to his thoughts. They were not nearly as pleasant. He did not want to know the details of what would happen to Morley, how exactly it would be done or by whom. But he presumed it would be poison and he knew Sarah would play a central role.

After they returned from the parsonage he had watched her go into the still room and emerge a short time later with something in a covered basket. Sitting now in her morning room, the canary chirping contentedly and late sunlight streaming through her garden, he was surprised at how readily he accepted that.

It seemed right that the mistress of Avebury should expunge the horror that had come upon it. More just, really, in its own way, than what any court of the land could have done. And ultimately more merciful for all concerned, even Morley himself.

Time passed. The light began to fade. A door opened, then closed. Sir Isaac and Crispin exchanged a glance. Faulkner stood and went out into the hall. Missus Damas had returned. She gave him a quick nod and went down to the kitchen.

Outside on the lane, singly and in pairs, the women of Avebury were returning to their homes. It was done.

Morley was buried at twilight, a Christian burial in a far corner of the graveyard that Edwards insisted on— as the young curate said—for the sake of the children.

They were with Missus Goody while the service was performed, but Annalise was there.

When it was over, Edwards walked away with her, not touching, but his step matching hers and their heads bent close together. It would take a very long time, yet, watching them, Faulkner hoped that the day would come when Annalise would at last be able to put aside the twisted memories of a father who had violated the innocence of his daughter in the most terrible way possible.

Four deaths had resulted, all murders committed to hide perversion. All here in ancient Avebury where the natural order had been respected and nurtured through time beyond memory.

It would have been a terrible violation, anywhere but in this particular place he thought it could have had powerful reverberations. He had a sudden flashing image of a sail, sturdy against the wind, but in a few places where the fabric thins, tiny holes appear, pin-pricks, really, and hard to see unless one knows exactly where to look for them to spy the wind flowing wild and unhindered.

So, too was Avebury, a place where past and present seemed to coexist in a way they did almost nowhere else. But Sarah had said that she never dreamed as intensely as she had at this Beltane. Something then had changed. Was it Faulkner himself? Could the passion between them have caused the rent in time?

Or was it Morley and the evil he brought?

There was only one way to know. One chance at a future together. But to take it meant risking all.

45

"Come with me," Faulkner said. It was very late. Exhaustion weighed her down. She thought of her bed, the quiet of her room, wrapping round her and soothing her, keeping her safe. Forever.

"All right," she said and smiled gently when she saw his surprise. "Did you think I'd say no?"

"I had an argument all prepared," he admitted. Taking her hand, he led her down the lane and beyond the village, out onto the broad avenue where the stone sentinels had stood and where a few still remained.

"I intended to be very persuasive," Faulkner added.

"As I'm sure you would have been. Where are we going?"

"I think you know." He pointed up ahead to where the hill rose above the river. The night was clear. Beneath the rising moon, the stone circle shone.

She sighed deeply but did not protest. They continued walking. Quietly, she said, "You know why I said we must not do this?"

"And I know you believe it. But what's the alternative, Sarah? A life without each other?" He paused and looked at her there on the darkening road, beneath a sea of stars. "Is that what you want?"

She was silent for a long moment, enough for him to anguish over what her answer would be. He could not bear to lose her, this woman who was everything he had ever sought in every dream and every prayer all unknowingly through the long years. Rather than be without her, he would gladly lose even himself.

Sarah looked into his eyes, into his heart, into the very essence of the man he was. She thought of Annalise and Morley, the sorrow and the evil, of old Dr. Holbein trying to restore the past, Sir Isaac seeking truth among the stars, all the tumult and tragedy, despair and glory, the crazy, careering struggle of life pouring down through the ages. All to what purpose?

To turn aside, dare nothing, stay safe?

"No," she said, "that isn't what I want." And touched her mouth to his.

They lay within the circle, pillowed on the new grass. There was passion enough to rekindle the fires of Beltane, but also great tenderness, for this was a love that did not depend on the tautness of body and the perfection of form but would endure forever, beyond life itself.

A man and a woman, loving and being loved. And finally, inevitably, falling asleep in each other's arms, there in the stone circle, against the breast of the eternal earth.

The ground slanted upward. There was another, smaller hill, and atop it, just visible above the rise, a double circle of stones. Without pause, he started up the hill, taking it in long strides, the sword slapping against his leg.

Belatedly, he became aware of a leather pouch strapped across his back. He had been traveling for some days, living off provisions he took with him and whatever he could find. The journey had been dangerous; he was lucky to have survived it.

Later, he would sit in the circle of elders and tell them the grim news he had brought. But first anticipation filled him. He pulled himself up the last few yards and stopped, muscled legs braced and hands on his lean hips, surveying the scene before him.

A woman stood at the center of the inner circle. Her eyes were closed, her arms upraised. She seemed to shimmer in the morning air, almost as though the light shone not around but through her.

He had not expected to find her at prayer. About to turn away from a sight that was not for his eyes, he hesitated. He had come so far and dared so much that to be denied her even for a few moments seemed more than he could endure.

As he watched, however reluctantly, she crumbled shafts of young wheat and let the pieces fall onto the ground before her. Her lips moved, but soundlessly. He could hear nothing, but he sensed a tension in her he had not felt before. Her brow was furrowed, her shoulders stiff.

That puzzled him. In the great festivals of the changing seasons, when the sacred rites were performed before all the people, she seemed confident and serene. Now she appeared deeply troubled, even afraid.

His instinct was to go to her at once but he held back, mindful of the risk he would be taking if he entered the circle uninvited. Yet the longer he watched her, the harder it became to do nothing. Her color was ashen, her body swayed. Finally, soundless tears trickled down her cheeks.

He could bear it no longer. Heedless of the danger, he stepped into the circle. The ground rippled beneath him.

She turned and, seeing him, reached out her arms. He went into them, grasping her close. Her tears fell against his bare skin, searing him. "You found them," she said, not a question but a statement, as though she had been there with him on the journey, seen what he saw.

He nodded. The strangers she had felt as a change coming upon the land were few, but more were coming every day. They were a taller race, bold and proud, and they were very powerful. Their swords were made of a stronger metal than his. He had seen how they could cut and slash. The warrior in him knew what that would mean. The lover wanted to reject it but could not.

"I have tried," she said, her voice breaking. "I have sacrificed and prayed, pleaded, done everything I can think of. But there is no answer, only silence." She looked up into his eyes. "Our time is passing as surely as the season. I can no more stop that than I can prevent this."

He stared down at her, this woman he loved as much as life itself. For her, he would have done anything. But he was powerless to prevent the change that was coming over the earth. And so, it seemed, was she.

He drew her closer, his hand stroking her back. The stiffness eased from her. She calmed, the fury and the fear draining out of her. The ground had steadied; it no longer seemed to ripple but instead accepted them with gentleness.

They lay within the circle, pillowed on the new

grass. There was passion enough to rekindle the fires of Beltane, but also great tenderness, for this was a love that did not depend on the tautness of body and the perfection of form but would endure forever, beyond life itself.

A man and a woman, loving and being loved. And finally, inevitably, falling asleep in each other's arms, there in the circle, against the breast of the eternal earth.

Dawn came as they were walking home. Sarah looked over her shoulder at the circle, empty now, the stones standing white against the morning sky, unchanged and ever-changing like the world itself.

Faulkner's hand tightened on hers. She felt the strength in him, the power and the certainty that made him all he was, Marlborough's man and his own, bound for greatness in an England moving rapidly toward empire. For him, the bustle of city streets, the feint and parry of the court, the tumult of high politics were all as mother's milk.

While she was Avebury, the deep, endless silence of the earth, the rhythmic cycle of life and death, eternity bound in fecund soil beneath the star-specked sky.

Irreconcilable? She was astonished that she had ever thought so. They were sensible people for all that they were in love. And this was, after all, the eighteenth century. Good English roads spanned the country, and carriages rattled over them every day.

Not all change was to be regretted.

For them another cycle from the gaudy present to the glory of eternity, back and forth, human and more, always reaching for what has been and will be, hard by the stone circles of memory and hope where past and future wait.

"Faulkner," Sarah said, "I am looking forward to meeting the duke."

"And I," he said, "can hardly wait for you to meet his Sarah."

"Formidable, is she?"

"No match for you," he assured her.

She smiled. Together they walked down the road and out of sight.

Author's Note

Go sixteen miles north of Stonehenge across the Salisbury Plain, down into the Vale of Pewsey, and up again onto the chalk downs surrounding the river Kennet. Go carefully. You are on sacred ground.

For more than a millennium, this was the major religious center of Britain, the heart and soul—and womb—of a people who though they have vanished from conscious memory linger in dream and desire. Of everything these people left behind them, the stone circle at Stonehenge is best known. Yet compared to Avebury, Stonehenge is—as one of England's premier archaeologists put it—a parish church dwarfed by a cathedral.

The Avebury complex is about the size of midtown Manhattan from the Hudson to the East River and from 30th to 50th Street. To reconstruct it today would be a daunting task. Yet Avebury was begun almost five thousand years ago at the dawn of the Neolithic era in Britain.

Interest in Avebury is not new; for hundreds of years it has attracted the curious. It has been hailed as the achievement of a race of giants and reviled as the work of the devil. Much debate continues over its precise significance.

Recent scholarship contends that Avebury represents a series of religious stations in which the different seasons were ritually honored. For example, Silbury mound just north of Swallowhead (which rises only in the spring) was constructed in the shape of the pregnant Goddess ready to give birth to the new world. The long barrow south of Swallowhead represents the hag, the Goddess as death, to which all life must eventually return.

Avebury henge itself was used for astrological and religious observances. It is linked by two great avenues to ancient sanctuaries, one close to the Ridgeway, a Neolithic hunting track that connected northeast and southwest England over several hundred miles. North of the henge is the river Winterborn, named because it rises at winter's end, and to the west is Windermere camp, the original settlement at Avebury.

It has been suggested that Avebury was deliberately selected to become a major religious center because of its peculiar features: namely, springs that rise or fall with the changing of the seasons, closeness to what was then a major highway, and ready accessibility of materials. What we see is the physical manifestation of belief in earth as Goddess, dyng and being reborn each year while endlessly nurturing her children.

Five thousand years ago, people gathered there to rejoice in life, find comfort in death, and renew their covenant with the earth. In memory, they do so still.

AVAILABLE NOW

FOREVERMORE by Maura Seger
As the only surviving member of a family that had lived in the English village of Avebury for generations, Sarah Huxley was fated to protect the magical sanctuary of the tumbled stone circles and earthen mounds. But when a series of bizarre deaths at Avebury began to occur, Sarah met her match in William Devereux Faulkner, a level-headed Londoner, who had come to investigate. "Ms. Seger has a special magic touch with her lovers that makes her an enduring favorite with readers everywhere."—*Romantic Times*

PROMISES by Jeane Renick
From the award-winning author of *Trust Me* and *Always* comes a sizzling novel set in a small Ohio town, featuring a beautiful blind heroine, her greedy fiancé, two sisters in love with the same man, a mysterious undercover police officer, and a holographic will.

KISSING COUSINS by Carol Jerina
Texas rancher meets English beauty in this witty follow-up to *The Bridegroom*. When Prescott Trefarrow learned that it was he who was the true Earl of St. Keverne, and not his twin brother, he went to Cornwall to claim his title, his castle, and a multitude of responsibilities. Reluctantly, he became immersed in life at Ravens Lair Castle—and the lovely Lucinda Trefarrow.

HUNTER'S HEART by Christina Hamlett
A romantic suspense novel featuring a mysterious millionaire and a woman determined to figure him out. Many things about wealthy industrialist Hunter O'Hare intrigue Victoria Cameron. First of all, why did O'Hare have his ancestral castle moved to Virginia from Ireland, stone by stone? Secondly, why does everyone else in the castle act as if they have something to hide? And last, but not least, what does Hunter want from Victoria?

THE LAW AND MISS PENNY by Sharon Ihle
When U.S. Marshal Morgan Slater suffered a head injury and woke up with no memory, Mariah Penny conveniently supplied him with a fabricated story so that he wouldn't run her family's medicine show out of town. As he traveled through Colorado Territory with the Pennys, he and Mariah fell in love. Everything seemed idyllic until the day the lawman's memory returned.

PRIMROSE by Clara Wimberly
A passionate historical tale of forbidden romance between a wealthy city girl and a fiercely independent local man in the wilds of the Tennessee mountains. Rosalyn Hunte's heart was torn between loyalty to her family and the love of a man who wanted to claim her for himself.

COMING NEXT MONTH

FLAME LILY by Candace Camp

Continuing the saga of the Tyrells begun in *Rain Lily*, another heart-tugging, passionate tale of love from bestselling author Candace Camp. Returning home after years at war, Confederate officer Hunter Tyrell dreamed only of marrying his sweetheart, Linette Sanders, and settling down. But when he discovered that Linette had wed another, he vowed never to love again—until he found out her heartbreaking secret.

ALL THAT GLITTERS by Ruth Ryan Langan

From a humble singing job in a Los Angeles bar, Alexandra Corday is discovered and propelled into stardom. Along the way her path crosses that of rising young photographer Adam Montrose. Just when it seems that Alex will finally have it all—a man she loves, a home for herself and her brother, and the family she has always yearned for—buried secrets threaten to destroy her.

THE WIND CASTS NO SHADOW by Roslynn Griffith

With an incredibly deft hand, Roslynn Griffith has combined Indian mythology and historical flavor in this compelling tale of love, betrayal, and murder deep in the heart of New Mexico territory.

UNQUIET HEARTS by Kathy Lynn Emerson

Tudor England comes back to life in this richly detailed historical romance. With the death of her mother, Thomasine Strangeways had no choice but to return to Catsholme Manor, the home where her mother was once employed as governess. There she was reunited with Nick Carrier, her childhood hero who had become the manor's steward. Meeting now as adults, they found the attraction between them instant and undeniable, but they were both guarding dangerous secrets.

STOLEN TREASURE by Catriona Flynt

A madcap romantic adventure set in 19th-century Arizona gold country. Neel Blade was rich, handsome, lucky, and thoroughly bored, until he met Cate Stewart, a feisty chemist who was trying to hold her world together while her father was in prison. He instantly fell in love with her, but if only he could remember who he was . . .

WILD CARD by Nancy Hutchinson

It is a dream come true for writer Sarah MacDonald when movie idol Ian Wild miraculously appears on her doorstep. This just doesn't happen to a typical widow who lives a quiet, unexciting life in a small college town. But when Ian convinces Sarah to go with him to his remote Montana ranch, she comes face to face with not only a life and a love more exciting than anything in the pages of her novels, but a shocking murder.

*M*onogram Harper · **The Mark of Distinctive Women's Fiction**